Judy Astley became the author of witty, contemporary novels after several years as a dressmaker, illustrator, painter and parent. She has two daughters and lives in London and Cornwall.

For more information on Judy Astley and her books, visit her website at www.judyastley.com

Also by Judy Astley

JUST FOR THE SUMMER
PLEASANT VICES
SEVEN FOR A SECRET
MUDDY WATERS
EVERY GOOD GIRL
THE RIGHT THING
EXCESS BAGGAGE
NO PLACE FOR A MAN
UNCHAINED MELANIE
AWAY FROM IT ALL
SIZE MATTERS
ALL INCLUSIVE
BLOWING IT
LAYING THE GHOST
OTHER PEOPLE'S HUSBANDS
THE LOOK OF LOVE
I SHOULD BE SO LUCKY

and published by Black Swan

IN THE SUMMERTIME

Judy Astley

BLACK SWAN

TRANSWORLD PUBLISHERS
61–63 Uxbridge Road, London W5 5SA
A Random House Group Company
www.transworldbooks.co.uk

IN THE SUMMERTIME
A BLACK SWAN BOOK: 9780552777490

First published in Great Britain
in 2013 by Bantam Press
an imprint of Transworld Publishers
Black Swan edition published 2014

A CIP catalogue record for this book
is available from the British Library.

Addresses for Random House Group Ltd companies outside the UK
can be found at: www.randomhouse.co.uk
The Random House Group Ltd Reg. No. 954009

The Random House Group Limited supports the Forest Stewardship
Council® (FSC®), the leading international forest-certification organisation.
Our books carrying the FSC label are printed on FSC®-certified paper.
FSC is the only forest-certification scheme supported by the leading
environmental organisations, including Greenpeace. Our paper procurement
policy can be found at www.randomhouse.co.uk/environment

Typeset in 11/15 pt Giovanni by Falcon Oast Graphic Art Ltd.
Printed and bound by CPI Group (UK) Ltd, Croydon, CR0 4YY.

2 4 6 8 10 9 7 5 3 1

ACKNOWLEDGEMENTS

Thanks are due to all the usual suspects.

To editor Linda Evans for eternal patience yet support when I need it.

To my agent Caroline Sheldon who is a supreme non-nagger yet always wonderfully positive.

To writer friends for knowing just how it is, especially fellow members of the Romantic Novelists' Association. And to Janie and Mickey at Chez Castillon (www.chez-castillon.com), who have the most wonderful writers' retreat with gorgeous accommodation, glorious setting and amazing hospitality. If you need time out just to work you can do no better than to book in here, especially if you have such fab retreat-mates as I did: Katie Fforde, Kate Lace, Jane Wenham-Jones and Jo Thomas.

And to my family and closest friends who tolerate the inevitable and unpredictable highs and lows of the writing process and know when *not* to ask that question all writers dread: 'How is the book going?'

ONE

Jack's ashes had been wedged into the car boot between the cat basket and Silva's bag but something must have shifted because every time Miranda drove round a bend there was a thud from the back of the Passat. She risked a glance at her mother in the seat beside her but Clare had the *Guardian* in her hand and her crossword face on: teeth clamped on her lower lip and the pen tapping lightly against her jawbone. Miranda considered whether she should stop in the next lay-by – on the pretext of checking the cat – and rearrange things so Jack's urn would stop rolling around. He had never liked being a passenger. Being driven made him feel a bit queasy and even though he was now reduced to gritty grey dust she still felt his remains should be made as comfortable as possible.

'Granddad's got loose,' Silva said, kicking the back of the driving seat with her new pink Converses. Miranda gripped the steering wheel more tightly. Now Silva had drawn attention to the thumping, any minute now Clare would start a 'Do you remember the time he . . .' conversation which would certainly go on for the rest of the journey, with the only contribution from the back of the car being the click-click of Silva's thumbs-on iPad and the tish-tish of too-loud music leaking from Bo's headphones. Oh, and the roll-clunk of Jack.

'You *must* let Mum talk about him,' Miranda's sister Harriet had said on the phone after Miranda had lightly grouched that she'd heard three times, that day, the story of when Jack had climbed on to the Cornwall cottage roof with a broom handle to poke down a trapped rook. Well of *course* she let Clare talk about him. What did Harriet think she was going to do? Say, 'Hey, enough of the memories now, Mum, he's been gone six months; move on'? Sharing the role of listener would be a help, but Harriet was comfortably miles away being ambitious in television in Salford and newly blissed up with a footballer boyfriend. Their sister Amy was living in France (the youngest, still – at twenty-six – often referred to by Clare as 'the baby') and had copped right out, claiming she couldn't talk to their mother about Jack because it just *upset her too much*.

'Has he, darling? Is that the thudding noise?' Clare looked up from the crossword and turned to Silva. Miranda looked in the rear-view mirror and caught the full blast of Silva's glorious smile, directed at Clare.

These days it didn't often come Miranda's way. Silva, at the far end of being thirteen, was setting the tone for her teenage years and more often than not giving her mother the hellcat face.

'It doesn't matter, you know,' Clare told her grand-daughter. 'He can't feel it.'

'He might,' Silva said. 'You can't be sure.'

'I think we can, Silv,' Miranda said quietly, hoping Silva would take the hint that this was time to shut up a bit. Clare could still be tipped easily over the edge into tears. Soft, silent ones that simply fell from her eyes and down her face with no fuss and no noise, as if Clare were apologizing for her sadness. Somehow Miranda found this more heartbreaking than if Clare had hurled herself about in lavish displays of noisy grief. This was to-the-core mourning. Miranda couldn't share it, couldn't lighten that awful burden, whatever she tried.

'Are we nearly there yet?' Clare's childlike question, the sudden change of focus, startled Miranda. Also, Clare should know the answer; that she'd had to ask was strange. For most of Miranda's childhood, right up to when she was nearly seventeen, the family had visited their cottage in Chapel Creek every summer. Clare had once known, and driven, every inch of the A30.

'Well, we've passed Bodmin Moor,' Miranda told her. 'So no, not long now. An hour, tops.'

'This bit of road's new,' Clare commented, putting the newspaper down on the floor and her pen in her bag as if already neatly prepared for the journey's end. 'But then it's been nearly twenty years. Everything changes.' She sighed and dabbed a tissue at her eyes. 'Everything bloody changes.'

And yet some things don't, Miranda thought. Hot sunny weather always made her think of that last summer at Chapel Creek, and Steve. She hadn't seen him for twenty years and wasn't likely to now, but she did find he got into her head whenever the scent of the sea was in the air and the summer sun warmed her limbs. That was normal, wasn't it? You never forgot your first one.

As Miranda drove into the village, Clare was surprised she felt no sense of ownership when they passed Creek Cottage. It was so long now since she and Jack had sold the house, soon after that mad August when Celia from the next cottage along the creek had looked in through the window just at the moment when Eliot Lynch had got Clare backed up against the kitchen dresser and was kissing her lavishly. That illicit kiss was a memory she'd held on to in delicious secrecy for a long time after, getting it out to cheer herself up a bit when she and Jack went through the inevitable stale periods of ennui that punctuate long-term marriages. Eyes closed, late at night, and unable to sleep, she would remember the harsh graze of Eliot's stubble on her skin, the taste of Scotch and recent Gauloises. Ah Eliot, Clare thought as she noted the current owners had extended into the attic and installed white plantation shutters at 'her' windows, where are you now? He was still alive, that much she assumed, as his passing would have made the news and the obituaries. He hadn't had a book out for a few years, but that might be because he didn't need or want to write any more. Four of his blockbuster novels had been hugely successful films so he'd probably retired. It was likely: all those years ago he'd seemed to her already pretty ancient – baggy of body, unfit and a bit wheezy – but thinking about it he had probably only been in his mid-fifties, about the age she was now, possibly even younger. She hoped he was all right, that he still had his fast, feisty mind and those seductive traces of a Cork accent. Selling Creek Cottage had meant she and Jack lost touch with him and Liz, and also with Celia and Archie. It wasn't actually so surprising how those easy summer friendships hadn't translated to full-time ones. What had hippyish Clare and artist Jack really had in common with prim Celia and golf-mad Archie? 'We must meet up in London,' everyone would trill brightly each September as the cars were loaded and houses closed up at summer's end, but addresses were rarely exchanged and when they were it would be a Christmas card at the most.

'It's still very much a holiday homes place, isn't it?' she commented as Miranda turned off the village road and headed up the lane towards the hillside houses where Eliot and Liz and their children had spent their summers. Liz, Eliot's much younger second wife, had hated it here, Clare recalled: loathed the never-ending soft Cornish rain, the hearty sailing club set with their flapping, dripping waterproofs, the lack of fancy restaurants or chic London shops. She'd been scared of the blind rural dark at night and complained about roosters crowing long before sun-up and the spooky whoo-hoo of owls. She'd openly yawned her way through Celia's tales of tacking up-river against wind and tide and Archie's of the tricky par four on the fifteenth at Mullion.

'I don't suppose much has changed,' Miranda said, 'but probably lots of people will have had to sell up by now. House prices are still ridiculous here; I had a quick Google yesterday, just to see. Not much sign of the recession kicking in yet.' She turned the car in through a pair of blue-painted iron gates and pulled up in front of the house she'd rented.

'OK everyone, we're here.' Miranda's voice was bright and encouragingly upbeat as she switched off the engine and quickly opened her door. 'Help with the unloading, kids!'

Clare didn't move but sat looking out, puzzled. 'Here? But why are we *here*? Isn't this . . . yes, this is Eliot and Liz's house. Are we staying with . . . them?' For a crazy, panicky moment she imagined the two of them hurtling down the steps to greet them with hugs. Or rather Eliot hurtling – Liz would teeter down in her high shoes with a smile set like cement.

Miranda sat down in the car again to explain. 'I know it's theirs, Mum. Or was. I did tell you, when I booked it. They aren't here any more – they sold it years ago. Whoever owns it now has it as a holiday rental and it was the biggest available, the only one we could all fit into. You've forgotten, that's all.' She patted Clare's hand. 'There's the pool for the children and the lovely sunny terrace where you can sit and read in the sun. It'll be fine. And don't you remember how gorgeous the house used to be inside? It's changed a bit but it's still a stunner, I promise.'

Clare felt like a small child being gently coaxed. 'I'm not old enough for that sort of forgetting,' she said. 'I hope it's not the start of something.'

Miranda unfastened her mother's seat belt and got out of the car again. Bo and Silva were already out, racing up the path to the front door, arguing about bagging the biggest room. 'It's not the start of anything, Mum, it's just . . . the way things are for you right now. You'll recover in time.'

'But will I?' Clare asked, her eyes wide and wet. 'How *do* people? I don't even know where to start. I hate being like this. It's not *me*.'

'It's all right. You've started. *This* is the start.' Miranda opened the car boot and took out the cat basket from which fat ginger Toby stared at her with big confused eyes. Clare climbed out of the car and moved to take out some of the luggage, seeing the urn full of Jack lying like a tipped-over coffee flask beside Miranda's suitcase. For a horrible moment, she imagined how it would be if the lid had loosened on the journey and the contents had leaked out. She'd have had to ask Miranda to hoover them up. And then what would be done with them? When they went to scatter the rest of Jack on the sea, would they have to take the vacuum cleaner bag with them as well and turn out all that was inside? But then Jack wouldn't float away like a free, pale shadow on the water as he'd wanted but would be clogged with carpet fluff, wads of hair, crumbs and spiders. She quickly lifted her bag from the boot and left the urn where it was. That had been a mad train of thought, dangerously close to running way out of control. Perhaps Miranda was right. Maybe once they'd carried out Jack's request and consigned his ashes to the water he'd once loved she could start to feel a bit more sane. Right now, all that seemed to be in her head was a woolly feeling that real life was suspended for the duration, possibly for ever.

'Mum, I'm *not* sharing with Bo!' Silva shouted. 'He's like *soo* stinky? Boy-stink!' Bo was sitting on the stairs with his headphones still on and his head rocking slightly, oblivious to Silva's grievance and waiting to be told where to go and what to do. Fourteen years' worth of passivity, Miranda thought, wondering where her bright, active little boy had gone. Everyone had warned her you couldn't expect more from a boy at that age than a growth spurt and some grunting. How true.

'You don't have to share with Bo,' Miranda told her daughter, making her voice low and calm and hoping it was both soothing and authoritative. Also catching. 'There are five bedrooms; you and Bo have got the two up in the attic. Turn left at the top of the stairs and up the next flight. You have to share a bathroom but then you manage that at home.'

Silva gave her a look that told her a luxury suite and her own rainstorm shower had been what she'd expected at the very least. Spoiled brat, Miranda thought as her children hauled their bags up the stairs. She headed for the kitchen, from where she could hear the sound of Clare dealing with a kettle. Tea: perfect. Maybe after that she'd rally for the next round of jollying them all along.

'It's changed, hasn't it?' Clare said, rooting about in the cupboards, looking for mugs. 'Liz had it all country pine and pretty Provençal prints in here. Now look – all glass and granite. No soul. Where is *colour*?' She sat down heavily at the long pale wooden table on one of the Perspex chairs (Philippe Starck's Ghost chairs, Miranda recognized) and stared out of the window, but Miranda could see that she wasn't really taking in the view with any interest. In the distance the sea glinted in the sunlight, swift little flashes like fire-sparks. The leaves on the hillside trees that ran down to the river had a midsummer brightness to their shades of green, not yet gone over into their richer near-autumn maturity. Years ago, Clare would have had her oil pastels out and be making sketched notes about colours, then later sorting yarn samples for a piece of knitting and discussing designs with Miranda. But her knitwear business had been sold soon after Jack's dreadful diagnosis, and these days all that was left to show for her past success were her initials on the labels of garments now produced in bulk in Korea.

'Oh, but I love it! It's all fresh and sleek,' Miranda said, feeling hugely relieved that for the massive amount of money she'd laid out for this holiday the house had moved on from Liz's frilled chintz and dust-trap Austrian blinds to acres of walnut flooring, rough linen curtains and soft shades of bluey-greys on the walls she'd seen so far. On the rental company website there'd been photos of this kitchen, the sea view from the sitting room and a bedroom that looked blissfully like something from a swanky boutique hotel, but the lack of more detail had made her suspicious about what *wasn't* shown. Liz had liked rich earthy tones but also the surfeit of fabric that had been fashionable at the time: blinds *and* curtains, fancy tie-backs, throws on every sofa and chair in a losing bid to protect them from Eliot's tatty mongrel and the twins, who weren't allowed into the house at all unless their shoes were off and lined up by the back door. Miranda had a quick flash-back to that last summer when she'd been only sixteen, when she and Eliot's daughter Jessica had stumbled in after drinking cider with Paul from the boatyard and had tripped over the collection of shoes and gone sprawling and giggling into the utility room's baskets of colour-coded laundry. Was that before or after she'd stopped being pregnant, Miranda wondered. Probably after. She wouldn't have laughed so long, so freely and so plain girlishly if it hadn't been. Nor would she have been able to smell cider, let alone drink it, without being horribly sick.

'Anything to eat? Starvin'. When's food?' Bo swayed into the kitchen and slumped on to a chair as if the effort of coming down the stairs and walking a few paces was all too exhausting. The transparent chair looked too delicate for his apparent bulk but Miranda knew most of it consisted of baggy, fashionably falling-down jeans and oversized hoodie and that beneath was a long wiry body, heartbreakingly slender. His fingers clutched the edges of the hoodie's pulled-down cuffs as if afraid of having nothing to hold on to. She felt all tender inside. Her beautiful boy was adrift in that un-certain, awkward stage between child and adult, forever finding his judgement about the space he now took up to be that little bit out so that he stumbled, banged into things, jarred his skinny hip bone on edges and ledges.

No wonder he spent so long sitting still with computers and music – simply crossing a room was a complicated matter of spatial guesswork and hazards.

'OK, supper,' she said, feeling suddenly exhausted but determined, seeing as she was essentially the troop leader, not to flag. 'Shall we go to the pub? I'm not sure I can face cooking, not after driving nearly three hundred miles.'

'Pub! Yes! Can I have wine?' Silva appeared in the doorway, clutching the bewildered-looking cat.

'*May* I have wine,' Clare corrected her.

'May or not, no, of course you can't,' Miranda said, pouring Go-Cat into Toby's bowl and putting it on the floor for him. 'Even with food, I think the law says it's not allowed till you're fifteen.' She watched Toby eyeing his bowl suspiciously. He sniffed at the food for a bit and then tucked in, heartily scattering chunks of the biscuits across the floor as he ate.

'I bet *you* did before you were fifteen.' Silva scowled. 'And nobody will know. We're supposed to be on *holiday*. Nobody knows us here.'

No, they didn't. Not this time anyway. Miranda glanced up and could see her mother giving her a strange, speculative look. You could almost see the memory cogs starting up. Had this been a good idea? They could have stayed somewhere a few miles away, somewhere with no memories for them at all, and simply visited the beach here for a day just to do the ash-scattering then gone away again, barely touching the surface of the past. Still, too late now. She got up and started putting mugs into the dishwasher and then poured water into a bowl for the cat even though he would ignore it and – as at home – only drink out of the loo or the bath. It would be all right, being here. There wouldn't be anyone left here who remembered her, definitely not. All those teen-years holiday friends were long dispersed. And Steve, one of the very few permanent village residents they'd even spoken to, would have moved away as nearly all the local young did. He wouldn't still be running the ferry and taking his dad's lobster pots out in the boat these days. And he certainly wouldn't be showing silly, smitten sixteen-year-old girls what sex was like under the low-hanging trees on scorching lazy afternoons on Dolphin Beach. No. He'd be long gone.

TWO

'I don't remember this path being so steep,' Clare said as she and Miranda walked down the lane from the house towards the centre of the village and the creek. 'And we have to come back up it later. We should have brought a torch. I mustn't think like that – it's a bit old-lady and I'm not there yet.'

'Leave it out, Mum; you're fitter than most of my friends. And don't worry about falling over in the dark; it'll probably still be light when we come back but in case it isn't I've got a little torch on my key ring.'

Miranda was hungry and in need of a big glass of wine but she managed – just – to keep up a jollying tone towards her mother, trying as always to keep Clare's fragile spirits from collapsing. She'd got her computer set up in her room and checked emails in case there was a work crisis somewhere that needed dealing with from this distance but she hadn't unpacked a single item yet, apart from the box of essential food supplies that she'd crammed fast and haphazardly into the fridge and cupboards. She was conscious of Jack's urn still in the boot of the car and that no one was mentioning it. Still, on the plus side the evening was warm and sunny, the candlelike spikes of pink valerian and generous clumps of ox-eye daisies were massed on the warm dry-stone wall along the lane, brushing against their limbs as they walked along the narrow path the way they had all those years ago, and the children seemed happy, which had to be a massive bonus. She could hear them shouting and laughing together – a rare sound these days since Bo had taken up silence and Silva had discovered the power of mood swings. The two of them had walked on ahead and Miranda guessed they'd now be as far as the footbridge over the creek where years ago she had teased her little sisters that the trolls lurked waiting to pounce. Just as she was thinking how lovely it was that they seemed to be enjoying themselves at last, a loud splash told her first that the tide was up – rather than reduced to low-ebb mud – and second that someone had fallen in the water. The girly shriek that followed told her it was Silva. Bo would have simply sworn, loudly.

'Jesus, the little sods – *now* what have they done?' Miranda left Clare and sprinted the last few dozen yards past the clump of gone-to-the-wild rhododendrons to the little wooden bridge where Bo was leaning under

the rail with his hand stretched out, hauling out someone who wasn't his sister. Miranda ran to him, even
now her feet automatically skipping over the bridge's
fourth plank, the one that always used to feel softer than
the others, as if it was about to give way. Replaced now,
she quickly noted.

'What happened? Did you slip off the bridge? Are you
all right?' Miranda asked the soaking, giggling girl. She
was about Bo's age and as she emerged from the water
Miranda could see she was wearing a black wetsuit, so
falling in probably wasn't something too unexpected or
calamitous. Her long light brown hair stuck to the
neoprene like pondweed and the smell of the muddy
creek was already wafting from her. She didn't seem at
all bothered by her ducking.

'I was walking along the top of that wall over there,'
she said, pointing back to the cottage by the bridge, still
laughing. 'I'm getting really good at it.'

'Not *that* good.' Silva sneered. 'Do you fall in *every*
time?'

'Only when I'm not concentrating.' The girl smiled,
but only at Bo, who stared at his shoes.

Clare caught up with them and looked in the
direction the girl had pointed. 'That's Creek Cottage: *our*
house,' she said. 'Are you staying there?'

'No it's not, it's mine! Well, my mum's and mine, that
is. It's not yours.' The girl was frowning now, looking a
bit worried.

'It's OK, she meant it *used* to be ours,' Miranda explained. 'But it was a very long time ago, way before you were even born. When we had the house and I was about your age, I used to walk along that wall too, playing circuses, pretending it was a tightrope.' And climb over it too, she remembered. She'd go up the stone steps and over the wall late at night rather than using the gate with its noisy latch, to slide silently into the garden and in through the side door when Steve brought her back from the beach or the pub in his boat. The night would be so quiet you could hear every drop of water as it rolled from his oars when they dipped in and out of the stream. He could row so stealthily, without splashing; essential when you were being all secret. He'd told her it was an inborn skill, handed down through a long line of Cornish smugglers, and in the romance of the moment she'd pretty much believed him. Swans would loom out of the blackness from behind moored boats, their heads level with hers. Miranda was scared of their orange beaks which could snap at her face at any minute, but she never dared admit it to Steve. He'd had her down from the start as a spoiled town girl, ripe for teasing, and he wasn't wrong.

'Maybe you'd better go in and get dry,' Clare told the girl, who was now wringing her long hair out, the water splashing on to Bo's trainers. He didn't seem to mind. It occurred to Miranda that if Silva had done this he'd have had plenty to say.

'Lola! Have you done it again? You are a total pain! Come back here *right now*!' A woman was leaning out from an upstairs window, her hair tied up in a green scarf and a paintbrush in her hand.

'That used to be my bedroom,' Miranda said, almost to herself. She wondered what colour the girl's mother (who she assumed this must be) was painting it. It used to be a sort of pale straw shade, the same colour as her hair, which had been long, almost to her waist. She put her hand up to the in-between length she had now, half expecting to feel that an extra half-metre had magicked itself back.

'Yes, you'd better go in – you'll catch your death,' she told the girl, realizing this was the first time she'd ever said that actual phrase. 'You'll catch your death' was something only a mother said. *She* was a mother, and had been for nearly fifteen years, but right now she felt as if she'd been one for absolutely ever. That was about the urn full of ashes and Clare being so needy and about being the one who, for this trip, was the organizer, the coper, the one whose job it was to lead the cheers to gee up the team. It all made her feel as if she'd skipped, in one day, to a new level on the grown-up chart. Possibly to an age older than her own mother. These three weeks were going to be hard work. Why on earth had they chosen to come here for so damn long? A weekend could have done the job and then they could have flown off to France and rented somewhere near her sister Amy, as they had last year.

The woman at the window waved in a vague sort of way at them and for a second Miranda felt she knew her. But then she vanished back into the house, the moment passed and the girl, Lola, turned to go, calling back to Bo with another sparkling smile, 'Thank you for pulling me out. See you around, maybe?' He grunted at her, shoved his hands deep in his pockets and set off towards the pub.

'She was only ripping the piss, you know. She thinks you're well butters,' Silva called to the back of her brother as she scurried along to catch up with him. He turned briefly but didn't say anything and Miranda could see a pleased smirk on his face. Good, she thought, feeling a surge of love for her tall, gawky boy.

Every inch of the walk through the village to the Mariners pub was familiar to Miranda and yet also not, rather as the woman at the window had been. Across the creek, next to their old cottage, Celia and Archie's house looked much as it always had with its immaculate garden still full of roses. What had happened to their solitary son Andrew, Miranda wondered. Had he long grown out of his gawky awkwardness and worked out how to fit in with the world or was he still slightly out of place and finding the whole experience of life completely bemusing? She hoped he'd carried on with all the sailing he so loved. It had been the one area in which he looked perfectly comfortable and competent.

She'd ask around, she decided, see if anyone knew if the family still visited.

The old mix of thatched cottages and slate-roofed houses was the same (give or take the odd extension, and some fancy new windows) but every so often there'd be something different that jarred. The old red phonebox across the creek from 'their' cottage was still there but there was no phone in it now. Someone had put a metre-high garden gnome inside it and its fat plaster face grinned out at passers-by, looking a bit evil. The one village shop had been updated and extended and the old racks of postcards that used to hang by the door and the tatty plastic bins crammed with cheap beach mats had been replaced by chic wooden crates of vegetables. A promise that these were both local and organic was chalked up on a slate. A glance through the door showed more chalked signs offering home-baked bread, local cheese and a top selection of wines. Miranda wondered what had become of the previous stock. Had anyone actually bought up the old never-changing display of tinned mince and evaporated milk? Or maybe they were still there, defiantly surviving among the bantam eggs and balsamic vinegar. She'd find out in the morning.

'Do you remember Harriet organizing a mass shoplifting?' Clare asked as they passed. 'They were banned from the shop for the rest of the summer. We were mortified.' A small smile was on Clare's face and Miranda's spirits lifted a bit at the sight of it.

'For Amy's birthday party, yes. No one was allowed to buy presents, Harriet ordered all her guests to steal them, as a sort of dare.'

'They were such silly little things, doing just as Harriet said. You'd think they'd just get their mums to buy things and then pretend, wouldn't you? The parents of the village ones wouldn't speak to us after that. It's one reason Jack and I decided to sell up. The second-homers were always despised as outsiders as it was, without being extra hated for corrupting the village infants. It wouldn't be something the locals would forget in a hurry.'

Miranda laughed. 'Harriet wasn't to be messed with. Even at eight.' She wasn't now, either. What Harriet wanted, she got. Right now she wanted *not* to be involved with her mother's grief or with her father's final send-off and had refused to come down to Cornwall even for a weekend. 'Jeez, Manda, we've had the friggin' funeral. It's over; why drag it out?' All heart, that girl.

Not much had changed outside the Mariners pub either. The hanging baskets and the half-barrels by the door still had the same eye-watering colour mixes of orange geraniums and purple petunias with a few pink and white hanging fuchsias thrown in. The wooden picnic tables were still lined up along the creek edge and holidaying family groups were out early, bagging tables in the fading sun and trying to round up children to choose from the chalked-up menu before they ran off down the slipway to the water's edge to catch little crabs. Here and there, moody teenagers sat sullenly with their parents, picking lichen off the benches and glaring at soft drinks, desperate to be with someone they could actually talk to but too shy to make eye contact.

'What are those kids *doing* with the crabs?' Silva asked, staring at three little boys bending over the tiny creatures they had tipped out of plastic buckets on to the slipway.

'Racing them,' Miranda told her. 'We used to do that too. Harriet always seemed to get the biggest, fastest ones. I had to help Amy find some that could beat her.'

'Yuck. That's like well gross? They've been in like, *mud*?' Silva said as they chose a table near the water's edge and sat down. But Miranda could see she was looking at the smaller children with something more than curiosity. A little bit of envy, possibly? She was willing to bet that as soon as they'd eaten, Silva would be down on the slipway, up to her knees in the water with the younger ones. Miranda had felt the same at her age, caught between being too old to play like a child and a longing still to be one. Her sisters were much younger than her, so she'd taken on a bit of a nanny role at times, like the crab-fishing or the sand-castle building, and been able to enjoy it without feeling nervous she'd be sneered at by passing groups of cool girls.

'You see?' Clare said to Miranda, following Silva's gaze. 'You should have taken them on English seaside holidays as we did with you. They've missed out.'

'How can you say they've missed out? They've been all over France and Italy and to Florida and . . . well, loads of places.' Miranda felt annoyed. 'And don't you remember the endless rain? That Cornish thing . . . what's the word?'

'Mizzle; rain so fine you hardly know it's there,' Clare supplied. 'It was all part of the charm. We'd simply put the waterproofs on and go for a walk; use a bit of initiative. Anyway, it wasn't always wet. Remember that last summer we were here? It was blazing. And it's pretty fabulous now, isn't it? We're going to get a wonderful sunset.' She put her face up to the soft, late rays of the sun and looked, Miranda thought, the most content she had since, ten months before, Jack had first become properly ill.

'Food!' Bo's voice boomed out from beneath the eternal hoodie. 'Have we ordered? Can I have the T-bone steak?'

'You can. Mum and Silva, have you decided?' She glanced at the menu that was hung on the outside of the pub, behind them.

'The lemon chicken thing for me, please,' Silva said.

'Great. OK, I'll go and put the order in. And drinks? A bottle of red for us, Mum?'

'A bottle? But there's only the two of us.'

Miranda had an urge to say, 'Yes, and . . . ?' She could do with more than one glass, that was for sure. 'Tell you what, I'll order a bottle and we can take what's left back to the house with us. OK?'

'If you like. I'd like the lamb kebab, please, Miranda.' Clare was sounding defeated again. This was hard work.

The inside of the pub was dark by comparison with the brightness of the evening sun reflected from the glinting water. As her eyes adjusted and she gradually focused properly, Miranda looked around at the customers by the bar, wondering if she would recognize anyone. It was quite crowded, mostly with bemused-looking holidaymakers trying to make sense of the food-ordering system and getting small, tired children to choose something more than just chips. Over in the far corner a bunch of hefty-looking sailing types, men and women with Henri Lloyd jackets and voices that were used to making themselves heard from stem to stern, laughed and yelled to each other. She couldn't see anyone who looked even remotely familiar, but then twenty years on everyone would have changed so much. Some of the older villagers would surely be dead, others bald, aged, grey, run to fat or run away from the place altogether. What, she wondered, had happened to Steve's mother Jeannie, who used to be the cleaner at Creek Cottage? She'd been Liz and Eliot's cleaner too and Clare had been grumpy about this and furious that Liz undermined the balance of the local economy by paying her at London rates, though, Miranda considered now, why wouldn't she? It was a competitive market, and finding someone you could trust with a key during your long absences wasn't easy. She remembered there used to be stories (exchanged in horrified whispers) of cleaners who'd run a secret little rental scam using the owners' properties without their knowledge. Celia once told Clare that a woman in the village had turned up from London unexpectedly and found a couple cooking supper in her kitchen and the washing machine on. All the grown-ups had seemed so *old* to Miranda back then, but the chances were that that had simply been the typical view from any self-obsessed sixteen-year-old and Jeannie could well still be energetically cleaning holiday cottages on changeover days and stashing all those abandoned half-bottles of shower gel, washing-up liquid and gin into her old shopping bag like so much well-earned swag.

Miranda ordered the food, drinks for the children and a bottle of Australian Merlot from the barman, handed over her credit card for later payment and headed back to the terrace, still thinking about that long-ago summer and almost knocking into a man and woman in the doorway, on their way in.

'Sorry!' she called as she passed.

'Bloody trippers,' she heard the woman mutter. Miranda turned briefly to look at her, shocked by the rudeness. The back of the girl, all long lemony hair, a short denim skirt and tanned bare legs, vanished into the pub and the man, flicking his car key to lock a convertible Mercedes in the car park, gave Miranda a brief apologetic grin before quickly following his companion into the bar. Miranda took a deep and rather shaky breath and went back down the steps to re-join her family on the terrace. She hoped this wasn't going to happen every time she came across local strangers in this village: this unsettling certainty – as she'd had with the woman at Creek Cottage – that she'd known them before. Especially this one.

THREE

Andrew knew it had been too much to hope for, that he'd get to go to his parents' cottage on his own with Freddie. Geraldine had said it would be all right, or at least he'd thought she had. You could never quite tell with Geraldine. What she'd actually said was yes, of course he could take Freddie to Cornwall. She'd also added, in her full-strength headmistress voice, that in fact it was about time, wasn't it, and why had he waited till now, when Archie and Celia were about to sell it? So he hadn't been wrong to think that had been a definite yes, and in spite of wanting to argue that he'd been asking to take Freddie there for the past four years but she'd insisted they all do the Mark Warner holidays and Center Parcs instead, he'd been happy and excited at the prospect of showing off to his son the village that had been part of his young life. And yet now, instead of being back in Esher tidying up her garden to within a centimetre of its terrified life, Geraldine was in the car with them, barking instructions about which route to take and how many miles it was till Truro. She knew quite well how many years his folks had had this cottage and that he knew the way. She'd never even crossed the Tamar in her life and couldn't tell Bodmin Moor from Dartmoor. He'd told her he could drive it blindfold and that, of course, had been a mistake.

'You see, that's why I can't possibly let Freddie go with you unaccompanied,' she'd snapped. 'Not when you say things like that. You have a reckless streak.'

Andrew did *not* have a reckless streak. Anything but. He was caution personified. Everything he'd done in his grown-up life had been with careful thought and a considered weighing up of pros, cons and consequences. Except for one time: that colleague's wedding nearly sixteen years ago when after the toasts he'd gone looking for the gents and somehow ended up in the bride's sister's room having tumultuous, glorious sex on a pink chaise longue with the woman he'd been seated next to at the lunch and whose cleavage he'd been so longing to put his tongue into that he'd found himself dribbling champagne down his chin as he'd absent-mindedly licked at the glass on its way to his lips. Oh, those fleshy, plump mounds that so lived up to what the low-cut frock had promised. The almost shockingly oversized nipples. The fist-deep rolls of lustrous softness around her capacious hips. And then, a few months later came the sudden call with the revelation of pregnancy and an order that Andrew (plus substantial maintenance) was to be part of the child's life but only on her, Geraldine's, terms. Andrew, for Freddie's first years, had felt like those old-school aristocratic parents who are only shown their children for an hour of supervised stilted conversation over formal tea each day. Geraldine would invite him to her little house in Esher and allow him to bring a new toy (*not* plastic) and play with and read to Freddie who, Andrew was thrilled to find, really took to his part-time dad and seemed keen to love him in spite of Geraldine's strictures.

As he drove very carefully down the steep narrow lane into the village, Andrew had a flashback to his teenage years when he'd so longed to seduce pretty, smiley Jessica. Her family had sold up long ago, sadly. But as he pulled up outside Rose Quay's garage, he was appalled to realize that his body was also remembering his crush on her and that old familiar excitement was making itself very much felt. He waited for a few moments, hoping things would subside. He didn't want Geraldine to notice – and she *would* notice, as nothing got past her – and get ideas. Absolutely not.

Miranda thought about her ex-husband as she tidied her bedroom the next morning and hung up the last of the clothes she'd brought with her. Even ten years after they'd split up, she sometimes thought about how living with him had been, mostly to remind herself that, in spite of how hard it had been to raise the children on her own at the same time as working to establish her design business, she'd taken the right path. If Dan were here now, he'd be lolling in bed flicking through the TV channels, at the same time diddling about on his iPad and asking in the ickle-baby voice – which he wrongly thought she'd ever found cute – if any coffee was on the go. His clothes from the night before would be in a heap on the floor where most of them would stay, added to the next night and the next till she could stand it no longer and reminded him where the laundry basket was. That would trigger him to accuse her of being an old nag. What he really meant was that dealing with his dirty clothes was *her* job, just as it had been his doting mother's and, at his hugely smart boarding school, presumably Matron's. Poor Dan – it had been hard for him, slowly realizing during the time they lived together that slobbing about like someone too used to being pampered and waited on while she ran an increasingly demanding business and raised two small children was not an acceptable option for a grown-up. But it was no longer her problem. He'd gone back to his fond mama, who was thrilled to be proved so right: a woman who thought a man should be capable of a bit of basic housework could not be considered proper wife material. The clues had been there right from the first time Dan had taken her to meet his family. His mother had taken Miranda into her utility room and demonstrated the proper way to iron a shirt. Miranda had watched and smiled politely then said thanks but she didn't actually possess an iron. That would be why there'd been three among the wedding presents. Dan would have gone to work this very morning wearing a shirt his mother had meticulously pressed for him and socks that she had lovingly paired up before she put them in his drawer. If he ever found another woman to live with it would be over his mum's dead body, and even then it would have to be one who'd never heard of equal rights

Miranda folded some T-shirts and put them in a drawer and had a moment of wondering what Steve would be like these days. He'd only been nineteen the last time she'd seen him, an age that had seemed truly awesome to an impressionable sixteen-year-old. Steve was a grown-up, long out of school, working for real, running the ferry and the lobster pots. This wasn't just some student fill-in soft-handed occupation like bar work or being a call-centre temp, saving up for indulgent gap-year travel; this was proper working for a living. He'd been a quiet boy who didn't need to waste words when a smile and a look and an invitation to an evening trip out in his boat seemed to be enough to attract girls in droves. Almost certainly he'd be long-term married now – Cornwall was big on early weddings – and most likely father to a couple of children. If they looked anything like him, they'd be beautiful: all huge dark eyes and a smile to charm the toughest heart. That couldn't, she was now sure, have been him at the pub last night. He'd have long moved on. Australia had been a lot of the local boys' destination of choice, that and Indonesia, for the surfing, and then maybe London or Bristol in search of the work that wasn't available locally. No, that one last night was just some random man of a similar build and jawline. She hadn't really seen more of him than that. The place was sure to be full of them, typical stock from a fairly local gene pool. The teenage Steve had had long brown hair, which was always slightly sun-streaked with a touch of caramel, and his face was tanned from the sea's constant glare. He'd also had a moody youth's contempt for up-country people whizzing about the narrow lanes too fast in what he called 'fuckin' poncy drop-heads', so that pretty much ruled out – unless he'd had a radical change of heart – ownership of that little black Mercedes.

Oh, but the bliss of being single, she thought now as she plumped up the pillows and pulled the soft lavender knitted throw over the duvet. Later, she'd pick some of the pink roses she'd seen down by the pool, put them in a vase on the table by the window. How wonderful to have the scent of flowers and not some man's smelly trainers. This lovely room, with its glorious view towards the creek, the sea and the tiny offshore island beyond the first estuary beach, was going to be her private haven for the duration. Clare – when trying to get the teenage Miranda to clear up her room – had once quoted to her from Shirley Conran's *Superwoman*: 'Never come back to an unmade bed', and even during her most rebellious phase it had lodged in her mind. She might be a long, long way from obsessively houseproud, but when she needed space to escape to, the last thing she wanted was to open the door and find it depressingly scruffy.

But downstairs it was a different story. How, she wondered as her sequinned Havaianas crunched over toast crumbs on the kitchen floor, did a mere two children manage to make such a mess in such a short time? Mugs were on the worktop, resting in puddles of sticky spilled coffee. More plates, dishes and knives than could possibly be justified by a few slices of toast and a bit of cereal were drowned in a sink full of cold, grey scummy water with a scrunched-up J-cloth floating on top. The dishwasher was only inches away. Did they, Miranda asked herself, think it opened with a magic key that only a grown-up could be trusted with? As she opened the larder door, pulled a loaf of bread from the shelf and put two slices into the toaster, she resolved to be more assertive when it came to shared chores. Bo and Silva were *not* to be allowed to take after their bone-idle dad.

'What are we doing today? Can we just hang out by

the pool here or have we got to . . . er . . . y'know, do the Granddad thing?' Silva came in through the utility room door in her blue and white stripy bikini, dripping water and rubbing a towel across her wet hair.

'I hadn't really thought about it yet,' Miranda told her after a moment or two of considering the options. Beach? It was already pretty sunny out there. Were Bo and Silva too old for simply messing about on the sand, or was her mother right – that they'd missed out on the bucket and spade stage and might quite enjoy (though pretending it was beneath them really) some childlike fun in a place where none of their so-cool friends would see them.

'I think I'd better ask your gran,' she decided. 'I thought she'd say something last night about what she wanted to do about Jack's ashes but she didn't mention it and we were all so knackered from the journey that it didn't seem right to put any pressure on her. She's not up yet, so we'll have to wait and see.'

'No, Mum, she is up. She's in the garden pulling up random weeds just like this was her own place.' Silva suddenly sniffed the air like a cat. 'I smell toast. Can I have some?'

'You can. Though I see you already have. Or did the elves come in the night and make this mess?' Miranda started spreading her own toast with honey. No butter. She was sure her middle was starting to spread (should that happen before you were even *forty*?) and she wanted to let it know that this wasn't allowed.

'Must have been Bo,' Silva said, shrugging off all responsibility and looking in the larder for the bread Miranda had just put away. 'Gran's been up ages and down to the sea and she's swum out to the little island and back. She said we should have gone with her but I said what's the point of freezing in the sea when you've got a lovely warm pool right here.'

'She has? Already? And hey, put that bread back once you've finished with it, please.' Miranda glanced at the giant station-style clock on the wall. It was only just after nine. Maybe Clare couldn't sleep. Once again she wondered if this trip had been the best idea. After she'd had her breakfast she'd go and check the back of the car, see if the urn had been taken out and brought to somewhere in the house. It wasn't in the kitchen, though she'd half dreaded coming downstairs and seeing it sitting on the table when she'd walked in. Back at Clare's flat, overlooking the Thames in Richmond, the urn had been kept on the table beside her bed. Amy, sounding nervous all the way from south-west France, had asked Miranda on the phone if she thought Clare actually slept with it, 'like, *under the duvet*?' Miranda had told her not to be so ridiculous but, all the same, she'd slightly wondered too. Harriet had seen it one day when she and the footballer were on a weekend trip down to an away match and she and Miranda had gone to

Clare's with food supplies that Miranda didn't quite trust Clare to bother getting for herself.

'Ugh! It's completely *gross!*' Harriet had said in her usual tactless way, shuddering over-dramatically.

'It's not gross, that's your father,' Clare had said simply, very quietly.

Harriet had, for once, waited till she was out of range of Clare to mutter, 'It's just dust, not Dad,' but there'd been tears in her eyes. Not so tough, that time.

Perhaps, Miranda considered, Clare had taken the urn up to her room. She hoped not, because if she had it could be a sign that she wasn't after all ready to say goodbye to Jack's remains and they'd end up taking his ashes all the way back to London again at the end of the three weeks. Although she didn't – and never could – take Harriet's harsh line, it would surely be the right thing to do to dispose of the ashes exactly the way Jack had asked. That could be an emotional blackmail point, should the need arise.

'I don't mind what we do today, Silva, but I would like to look around the village a bit, see what's changed. We could see if they still let visitors be holiday members at the sailing club, so you and Bo would have something to do. Back in the old days we used to have loads of good times down there. You might meet some people to hang out with.'

'Uh? "Hang out"? Who says like, *hang out?*' Silva gave

42

her the utter-incomprehension look, though of course she knew perfectly well what it meant.

'OK, OK, I give up. It'll be just you and Bo on your own, then. Exclusively in each other's company for three whole weeks. I'm sure you'll manage to have a perfectly brilliant time, amusing yourselves, just the two of you. Together.'

Ha, thought Miranda, seeing Silva's eyes narrow – a clear sign that some cog-wheels were clunking around in her thought processes. That worked.

There was such a lot of garden here to deal with, Clare thought as she took out a few well-grown stinkhorn weeds along the hydrangea-lined path on her way back from swimming in the cove. She remembered how Liz and Eliot's gardener had always seemed to be around, pushing a wheelbarrow silently across the grass past where the rest of them were sitting on the terrace or by the pool with drinks. What a privileged and idle bunch they must have seemed to him, all the tedious domestic tidying being done for them while they lazed and sailed and were forever going out to eat at prices that would have kept the gardener's family for a week. She stopped now by the pool and pulled fronds of goosegrass out from between the clumps of agapanthus. She didn't have to, but when you saw something that needed doing there was no point in leaving it. Goosegrass was a bugger for strangling plants, clinging to them stickily and dragging them down till they were covered over and smothered. She couldn't bear to leave them to struggle when the stuff unravelled so easily with only a light tug. With a garden this size you'd need either nothing else to do with your time or a knowledgeable gardener – and more than just once a week for an hour or two. Outdoor space was only a good thing so long as it was manageable. One of her upstairs neighbours, after Jack had died, had said to her, 'Well, at least you have your garden. It'll be a comfort.' What a stupid thing to say, she'd thought at the time, feeling *that* close to whopping the woman hard across the head with a trowel. How could a garden possibly even come close to making up for the loss of the person you'd loved and lived with for over thirty years? And yet she'd found herself out among her plants in her little greenhouse on the morning of Jack's funeral, potting on the calendulas she'd grown from seed the previous autumn, absorbing herself in weeding and tidying and not thinking about anything but the job in hand. It was only an hour later that she'd stood in the chapel at Mortlake crematorium as the congregation sang 'Love Divine', picking compost from under her fingernails and trying not to look at the coffin.

Toby purred around her feet, rubbing his face against the plants and chewing at the flowers on a rambling clump of purple catnip. She stroked his ginger ears and wondered if he should have sunscreen on the tender tips to prevent skin cancer. The air was so thin and clear here by the sea. At Miranda's home in west London he was probably protected from burning by layers of sticky urban air, with its constant outfall of aircraft fuel, and at very low risk. She would sneak some Piz Buin on to him later when no one was around. They'd only laugh. She reached for another clump of the goosegrass and pulled it out to add to the pile on the path.

'My stepmother hated this stuff,' a voice behind Clare suddenly said. She looked up. The girl who had fallen in the water the night before (Lola? Lily?) was standing by the diving board close to her mother, who was pulling another long strand of the goosegrass from among the agapanthus. It was the mother (with her hair hidden under a scarlet scarf this time and a newspaper tucked under her arm) who was talking, and she came over to add her weeds to the pile Clare had heaped on the paving. 'Especially after Dad told us one of its names was sticky willy.'

The woman giggled; her daughter rolled her eyes and said, 'Gross, Mum. Like shu' up?'

'You don't remember me, do you?' the woman went on. 'I mean, why would you – it's been a long time. I hope you don't mind – I went down to the shop to get the paper and thought, I just have to come up here and see if it's actually you. When you were on the bridge yesterday I thought I kind of knew you but then I thought, as you do, no, it couldn't be, but then it nagged at me half the night. But you are Mrs Miller, aren't you? And that was Miranda who was with you?'

Clare looked carefully at her and hesitated only a few seconds. 'Oh, goodness, Jessica! Eliot's daughter! You're still here. How wonderful! And you have this beautiful girl too. You must come on up to the house and see Miranda – she'll be so thrilled!'

Jessica hesitated. 'Will she, though? We did sort of lose touch.' She sounded shy and almost as young as Clare remembered her. 'Are you sure it'll be OK?'

'I don't see why not. I'm sure she'll be delighted!' Clare assured her, then asked, 'You didn't end on a big falling out or anything, did you?'

'No, but . . . well, I did try to find her on Facebook a few years ago but all the Miranda Millers weren't the right ones.'

'That's because she's not really a Miller. Never was, really, though she tried it for a while when she was in her teens. Miller was Jack's surname and the one her younger sisters have. She had my maiden name and we never changed it to my husband's. I had her before I met him, you see, so she's Miranda Beck.'

'Ha!' Jessica laughed as she followed Clare up the steps to the house. 'That's funny – she's got the same name as all that kitchen design stuff that's absolutely everywhere. Mugs and trays and flowery plates and all that. Do people keep thinking it's her? Must be a pain.'

'Well, yes, they do.' Clare turned and smiled at Jessica.

'But it's not a pain because she *is* that Miranda Beck.'

'Crikey, is she really?' Jessica said. 'I mean, wow – she's done well! She's everywhere. There's like, Cath Kidston, Orla Kiely and . . . Miranda Beck. Impressed.'

She went quiet but her daughter Lola chipped in, 'Don't worry, Mum. I don't think you're an underachiever. It can't be that hard to paint flowers on a plate.'

'Gran's coming in. She's on the steps and she's got someone with her. It's those people from last night – you know, that stupid girl who fell off the wall. Better wake Bo up – that Lola girl's going to be *in da kit-chin* in like a *minute* and he'll be well vexed if he misses her.' Silva, now wearing a long grey T-shirt with its neckline roughly scissored off over her bikini, was opening the door to the terrace to let them all in.

'Aagh! Look at this mess,' Miranda said, beginning to cram the mass of dirty crockery and sticky knives from the worktop into the dishwasher. 'Why do people always drop by at a point of maximum messiness? Come on, Silva, move your body.'

'Why?'

'Because . . .' Too late. 'Oh, hi!' Miranda said, putting on a social smile as Clare came in ahead of the other two. 'Good swim?'

'Glorious. But look who I just found in the garden!' She turned and pulled Jessica into the room.

'Hello, Miranda. Been a long time. How are you?'

'Oh my God!' Miranda's hand went to her mouth. 'Jess! How amazing – I thought I sort of knew you last night, but it was all too quick. And I thought, no, it couldn't be.' She could feel tears pricking at her eyes. Jessica came forward and hugged her gently. Miranda sniffed and smiled.

'Come on, girls, let's leave these two to chat,' Clare said to Lola and Silva, who were scowling at each other across the kitchen. She chivvied them outside to the terrace. 'They've got twenty years of catching up to do.'

FOUR

'Is it me or is this *totally* weird?' Miranda said to Jessica as she switched on the kettle to make coffee. 'I mean, we're here in *your* house, you and me, but where did twenty years go? Or at least now you're in it I think of it as yours, like from before. I expect to see Liz coming through the door telling us off for treading sand all over the floor.'

'Ha! She so would. Not that she's around now – she and Dad got divorced ages ago and she's happy in Hampstead where there are *proper streets*. It is completely bizarre, you're right, cos there's me living in *your* old house,' Jessica said, prowling the kitchen, stroking her fingers along the back of one of the Ghost chairs. 'Mad, isn't it? Who'd ever have thought it would be like this, back when we were sixteen? Or even that we wouldn't see each other again after that summer?' She went to the window and gazed out at the view down the creek to the sea. Miranda watched her, quickly taking in how slim Jess was now, even though she'd been quite a curvy girl and had once said she was sure she was going to end up massive. She still seemed to like wearing several layers of tops at the same time, today a little floppy purple vest over a long pink T-shirt. She'd always had something on or in her hair, too – either mad colour, chopped-out gelled ends, bits of beaded ribbon or scarves like this one, with ends trailing down on her shoulders.

'So how long are you down here for?' Miranda asked, wishing she could think of something less banal to ask. But she had rather been put on the spot. 'Or do you live here full time?' Here they were making polite conversation like strangers. But then for twenty years they *had* been strangers. And even before that they'd only been holiday friends: in child terms, just by-chance play-mates, really. Close for those intense few weeks each year before home life, the routines of school and friends absorbed them again. Jess now was pacing restlessly by the terrace doors, looking down towards the pool where her daughter was sitting on the diving board dangling her feet in the pool. Miranda could see Bo perched on the end of a sun lounger, his body hunched over his knees and his hair wet. He must have got out of bed and showered in absolute record time, which had to be all down to the magnetic power of a pretty girl. There was no sign of Silva. Was either of those two making an effort to talk? She hoped so, but she wouldn't be surprised if Bo were sitting in contented silence, staring into space.

'We live here all the time. Been about a year now. Since . . .' Jessica suddenly stopped both talking and pacing, then said, 'Oh, but hey, look, why don't we do what we always used to do on the first day of the holidays?' She turned back to Miranda, smiling brightly. 'We should go down to our beach and catch up properly there. It would feel, y'know, more *us*. Even though it's all different, I sort of think of this as a parental house, for proper grown-ups.'

Miranda was about to pour the coffee and looked up, surprised. 'Oh, really? OK. You mean, go back and sit on our old rocks? At least *they* won't have changed, moved away or anything. I know – I'll do coffee in a flask and we can have it there.' She started opening cupboards. 'There must be one here somewhere. I'm sure it was on the list. Ah – here.' She pulled it down from a high shelf and looked at the design of stylized pink and purple pansies on it. 'Oh, and it's one of mine. D'you know, I actually designed this; well, not the actual flask, y'know, just the flowery bits.' She grinned shyly at Jessica as she rinsed it with boiling water, wishing she hadn't sounded as if she were showing off. 'I never thought I'd end up making a career out of prettying up kitchen kit. When you're a kid you just don't have any idea how life will turn out, do you?'

'No.' Jessica looked sad for a moment. 'No, you're right. You don't see any further than the next set of exams and whatever's happening on Saturday night. I quite miss that amazing lack of responsibility. If I'd only realized how fantastic it was. But then, I suppose everyone thinks that at some point. Nice pattern, though, Manda; you always were arty. Genes, I expect.'

'My mum used to live here, in the summers. Did you know that? So it's like more my house than yours,' Lola told Bo as she perched on the end of the diving board and splashed her feet in the water. Silva watched her from inside the little pool house where she'd discovered a fridge that contained cans of Coke, and noticed how Lola fluffed out her long russety curls with her fingers and Bo leaned further forward towards her. Silva took out three cans (secretly giving Lola's a crafty hard shake-up first) and walked across to hand theirs to the other two.

'It's so not your house.' Silva wasn't having any of this. 'But I didn't even know your mum knew mine. Why isn't she still living here, then?'

'Her folks sold it. Granddad's last wife didn't like Cornwall. She always wore heels and she needed a blow-dry and a manicure every couple of days, Mum said. Doesn't really go with country life.' Lola opened her can and gave Silva a look when the brown liquid fizzed out and dripped into the pool. Bo's didn't.

Silva smiled back at her rival, acknowledging the canny recognition of a war-declaration, and secretly sympathized with this unknown woman. She had long-term ambitions of her own to become high maintenance.

'Granddad likes it, though. He's coming down here tonight to stay with us. He's Eliot Lynch and he wrote loads of books and got really rich so he doesn't bother writing now because he doesn't need to.' She sipped her Coke and waited for Bo to say something that made it clear he was impressed.

'Bo doesn't read much,' Silva said, when nothing but silence was forthcoming.

'Does he like boats?' Lola asked her. 'I've got one. I'll take you out on it. We can go across to St Piran and go down the long beach to do surfing or wha'ever.' Silva was about to accept, deciding that for the sake of entertainment and something to do she would concede that Lola might be better than three weeks with her near-silent brother, when she realized Lola wasn't actually inviting her. OK then; game on, she thought, taking her old T-shirt off. She skipped neatly along the diving board past Lola and leapt with maximum splash into the pool.

The path from the back of the boatyard to Miranda and Jessica's old favourite beach looked just as it had twenty years before. As then, no one else was bothering with the tricky little hidden route to this particular stretch of sand, which was only accessible at shore-level during the very lowest tides. Holidaymakers rarely seemed to want to walk more than a few yards from the car park with small children, wind-breaks, beach mats and heavy cool-boxes of food and drink. That had meant it had always felt like *theirs*, apart from the occasional party who dragged a boat up the sand, cooked a swift barbecue while nervously watching the tide and then vanished again in a panic of ebbing water and outboard-threatening rocks. Nettles still grew thick and tall each side of the track, waiting to savage bare legs. Tree roots surfaced in the same old places, lurking to trip the inattentive walker, but Miranda's feet seemed to have some memory of them stashed away and she walked nimbly, easily avoiding the hazards. The path meandered steeply uphill (had Miranda always been this short of breath by the top? And had the sheer drop to the shore always looked this scary?) then down the sandy dunes and rock to the sea's edge. Alongside the sailing club, the little marina had been extended with new pontoons, and the ferry boat that went across to the extended resort of St Piran on the far side of the estuary was larger and smarter than the one Miranda remembered. Steve had manned the old one single-handedly and she wondered at what point he'd given it up and what he'd moved on to do. She could see it being loaded with passengers. The operation needed two people now – one to drive and another to supervise and take fares – and there was a ramp from the back of it down to the sand for easy access. Trippers didn't have to scramble in and out over its side any more which was just as well, as there'd be complaints about that sort of thing these days. Health and Safety would be grumbling about provision for wheelchairs and buggies, the generally infirm and those of a mind to take legal action in the event of a sprained ankle.

'Do you remember that lovely Paul who used to work in the boatyard?' Jessica was saying as they rounded the sandy point and came to the bit where they had to start picking their way over rocks to get to their favourite spot.

'I do. He was going to uni to do a degree in Peace Studies or something, wasn't he?'

'That's the one. I see his name in the *Guardian* some-times. He's . . .' Jessica stopped in the middle of the path and laughed. 'He's a war correspondent.'

'Oh, the irony!' Miranda said. 'Or at least it sounds like one. Maybe it's not.'

'No, I suppose not, really. Reporting it doesn't have to mean you agree with it. Don't suppose any of them are exactly thrilled to be in a war zone. It just seemed funny, that's all. I had very nice sex with him over on the island one night. He'd nicked some rich bloke's Riva for the evening to take me out in. He told me it was the boat equivalent of picking me up in a Ferrari.'

'Smooth talker then. And you never said. I thought we told each other stuff back then?'

'No, well, sorry. I could have told you, thinking about it. But then the moment passed. I was scared Andrew would find out. I know I never fancied him or anything but he was like a puppy around me at the time and I didn't want to hurt his feelings.'

'Considerate of you,' Miranda teased. 'Oh, God, sorry, that sounds bad. No, you were actually. You could keep a secret. You kept mine. I'd have kept yours.'

'I know. Well, I do now. Sorry.'

Miranda concentrated now on not slipping on the damp stone. She was sure she and the others used to skip across these rocks without a thought for falling over, but now it all seemed alarmingly hazardous and she tried to avoid the slimy green weed that had been left by the tide clinging to the wet-black surfaces of the granite. Pools between the stones swished with tiny transparent freshwater prawns and little trapped fish, waiting for freedom on the next high tide or to be caught in the nets of small children.

She felt strangely nervous, as if this trek to the rocks was leading up to something important rather than being a fun re-enactment of one of their adolescent rituals. Was it five or even six years in a row, or even more, that their group had met each summer (and some holiday breaks in between too)? Must be about that long that she and Jess, Jess's brother Milo and their neighbour Andrew, the slightly gauche only child of seemingly ancient parents Celia and Archie, had come down to sit on these sun-warmed stones in the sunny early evenings to chat about nothing and everything.

'This is the place, isn't it?' Jessica looked puffed as she crumpled her body down on to the dry top of a rock in the shelter of the craggy cliff and reached up to tighten the silky Paisley scarf that hid her hair. She offered the newspaper she was still carrying to Miranda, who refused it and sat on her own rock, pretty sure it was dry enough.

'Lucky this is all still here,' Jessica said. 'You think this sort of solid rock stuff is for ever but then you get surprises. I couldn't get down to Pentreath beach after Easter because of a rock fall. And even at Kynance there's a heap of rocks at the bottom of the steps that didn't use to be there. I always tell Lola not to hang about close to the cliff face. I can see it becoming some kind of phobia in my old age.'

Miranda squinted out at the sea. The sun was bright and the water shimmered and dazzled and the little island looked deceptively close in the sunlight. She remembered swimming out to it and feeling a flash of panic yards from its shore that she wasn't going to make it. Jess's brother Milo had swum up alongside her, realizing she was scared, and she'd got there and back again safely enough, but never again had she tried it at high tide when there was so much deep water to cross.

For a few moments there was silence between the two women. Miranda wanted to fill it immediately with questions that would cover all the missing years, but she realized that just wasn't possible because, well, where to start? Instead she poured coffee and handed a cup to Jessica.

'You look just the same,' Jess said quietly, looking at Miranda intently. 'You've got two children and yet you're still all little and lovely and your hair hasn't darkened with age at all. It still looks like a piece of a barley field.'

Self-conscious under Jess's gaze, Miranda put her hand up to her head. 'It's thicker, maybe a bit coarser, I think. Or perhaps that's because I have it shorter now. My mother always says that anything below shoulder-length on a woman over thirty is a bit desperate.' She laughed. 'I think she's talking about years ago, though. Mid-thirties is about the new twenty-two now, isn't it?'

'Maybe. But I hope that doesn't mean Lola's going to be a stroppy teen for the next ten years.' She groaned. 'Are yours like that? All charm one second, vile and moody the next?'

'Silva's just coming up to fourteen but she's certainly heading that way, yes. Bo is . . . well, he doesn't say a lot. Sometimes I wonder what he *is* like. If he doesn't come out of the brooding silence soon, I won't know a thing about him by the time he's twenty.' She felt quite gloomy at the thought. 'This is surreal. Here we are, haven't met since we were sixteen and we're talking about our *own* teenage children. *So* mad.'

'I know.' Jess picked up a pebble and aimed it at a rock a few yards away. 'We used to sit here for ages moaning about our folks and making plans that would only give them grief. Remember Andrew's party?'

'I do! Poor Andrew, what we did to him. He thought he was just getting *you* round for the evening when Celia and Archie were away for the night and you pretended you'd thought he was having a proper party. We invited *everyone* – talk about bad. He looked quite bewildered.'

'We did clear up after, though.'

'No we didn't! You and I went off to Truro for most of the day and came back when it was nearly all done. I think my mum did a lot of it. She said your brother was very handy with a vacuum cleaner.' She thought of the elegant Milo with his slender wrists and his floppy blond hair. He was the one person she'd ever seen who made smoking a cigarette look like some kind of ballet move. She used to stand in front of the bathroom mirror at Creek Cottage after they'd been to the beach, practising his smoking style with her toothbrush between her fingers. It wasn't as if she even wanted to smoke. She just wanted to copy his pretty mannerisms.

'Well, Andrew was in no fit state to be useful, was he? That was the hangover from hell he'd got. Also, I don't think he'd been near a domestic appliance in his life. Celia would have considered it *unmanly*. The family still own the house, you know, but I haven't seen anyone there in all the time I've lived in the village. There's sometimes a car, but no sign of life, though I did see a cleaning company's van last week.'

'I wonder what he did with the photograph we sent him.' Miranda giggled suddenly. 'I thought you were brilliant, doing that. Such a crazy thing to do.'

'Topless in a photo booth – what the hell was I thinking of? The things you do . . . Poor Andrew. It was a bit unkind, winding him up like that. I know he couldn't see my face in the shot but I kept thinking he'd be sure to know it was me who sent it. Not nice of me. I'm not proud of it.'

'Hey, don't beat yourself up – I'm sure it gave him hours of fun!'

'Eeeuw! *Don't!* Hey, that sun's getting hot.' She put her hand up and untied her scarf, pulling it off and scratching her head.

'Wow, that's *short*,' Miranda said, looking at Jess's coppery inch of fuzzy hair. 'You always did do mad things with your hair. I like it – it suits you.'

Jessica smiled at her. 'Ah, well, it wasn't a choice thing. Chemo did it for me.' She took a deep breath. 'I had a mastectomy just after we moved here. All OK now, though. I'm fine. And it's growing back.'

Miranda stared at Jess's chest. 'Growing *back*?'

Jessica hit her on the leg with the folded newspaper. 'My *hair*, you loon, not my breast. If only! You know, I'd give a lot to see that stupid little photo I sent to Andrew. It's probably the only one of me that exists with my tits out and now here I am with only one of them, or rather one plus a reconstruction. They kind of match, the two of them, more or less, and I'm grateful not to be dead or anything, but it's all a bit awful really. Maybe it's karma for the photo. I try not to think of it that way, but sometimes in the middle of the night when I was halfway through the treatment I couldn't help thinking it.'

'Jeez, I'm sorry, Jess. You're so young to have gone through that. Not on your own, I hope?' She wanted to ask about Lola's father but Jessica hadn't mentioned a partner. Would it be tactless to ask? Jess hadn't asked her about Bo and Silva's father either, come to think of it.

'Pretty much on my own. Dad came down and stayed and took care of Lola, made sure she got to school and ate properly. Milo came down too – for a week. But he pined for his boyfriend so I sent him back to Hoxton.' She laughed. 'He's a bit too exotic a flower for Cornwall these days. Man-bags and those tight ditsy trousers that stop short of your bare ankles aren't really the thing here. One of the yachty lot made kissy faces at him in the pub and Steve bundled him outside and gave him a lecture about homophobia, but it turned out the bloke did actually fancy him, just had a clumsy way of going about things.'

'Steve? Who is . . . ?'

'Oh, you remember Steve!' Jess said. 'Or you should do. Didn't you and he . . . ?'

Miranda smiled. 'Yes. Y'know, just for a few weeks. Not long. I mean, I was only sixteen. Silly sixteen.' She looked along the beach to where the sand piled close to the small cave near the headland. That had been the spot. A sunny afternoon, a bottle of local cider, a gorgeous, desirable older boy telling you how beautiful you are – what more did it take to persuade a girl to part with her virginity? 'So he's still around then?' she asked, trying to sound completely don't-careish. She was surprised how hard her heart was thumping. It had no reason to – it must be the coffee. She put her hand up to feel it beating, half expecting her ribs to be the actual soft spot that she kept for that first lovely boyfriend.

'He is. I heard he'd been away for years but came back to take over the family business. It's all expanded and he not only owns the ferry operation but the fish side supplies posh restaurants from here to London. He's done OK, your Steve.'

Miranda laughed. 'Not *my* Steve! But hey, I'm glad. Hope he's happy. A bit like you with Andrew, I was pretty ashamed about how I treated him. It was just a holiday thing for me, just something to do, but then one night he said he loved me. I was vile – I laughed, mostly because I was too embarrassed to know how to react. Thinking about it now, I remember how sweet he was, but I'm sure he ended up thinking I was a nasty little up-country snob.'

'He probably thought we all were. Most of the locals thought that about us second-homers. You couldn't blame them really, the way we all swanned down here in the holidays and took over the place but never took any interest in things like local politics unless we wanted some councillor to back a planning application or something.'

Miranda watched as a family who seemed to be entirely clothed from the Boden catalogue came and set up camp on the spot where she'd had sex with Steve. A sudden feeling that she might cry surprised her. She turned her face away from the wind and wiped the ridiculous moisture from her eyes.

Jess shivered. 'Shall we go back to the house? The children will either have become best friends for ever or be killing each other by now. Lola can be tricky so I wouldn't like to call it, frankly.' She reached to pick up her newspaper and it fell further down the rock towards Miranda, who glanced at the big photo on the front page.

'Oh, bloody hell! Look at this footballer being chucked out of a club; he's my sister Harriet's boyfriend. She lives with him,' she said, feeling cold. It looked like an all too usual story – Premier-League player staggering drunk out of a club, draped over a well-stacked, very young blonde wearing more hair extensions than clothes. Poor Harriet.

'Ooh, give us a look. Ha! So your little sis is a WAG? And there's me still thinking of her with plaits and a chocolatey face. Wow, she's foxy-looking.' Jess scrambled across to peer at the page, 'Eeuw, nasty,' she commented, reading the first few lines of the story.

'Ah, no. This girl he's with,' Miranda said as they set off back up the path to the top of the cliff, 'she isn't Harriet.' Just then the phone in her pocket beeped and she took it out to read a text that had been sent half an hour before. Down on the beach beneath the cliff there had been no signal. *Coming down on plane tonight. Meet me at Newquay? H.*

'Well, you'll see for yourself about the plaits and the chocolate-face,' Miranda said. 'Harriet's coming to stay.'

FIVE

Miranda made up the bed for Harriet in the room next to hers and put a vase with a mixed bunch of sweet peas, cornflowers and ox-eye daisies from the garden on the table next to the bed. She wanted to leave a selection of books out for her too but, looking on the shelves in the sitting room at the selection that other holidaymakers had left behind, she found it hard to choose something that would be neither tactless (there were quite a lot of fun romantic comedies) nor depressing (someone had been keen on gloomy Scandinavian crime). Harriet was a great one for abundant tears and the boyfriend situation was looking bad enough without Miranda's accidentally setting her off. In the end she chose a book of the Mitford sisters' letters and Keith Richards's autobiography. Surely either of those would be an absorbing distraction if Harriet were afflicted with misery-filled sleepless nights.

'I am *homeless*,' she had wailed down the phone, adding with maximum Dickensian drama, 'You must take me in!' Miranda had offered her the keys to her Chiswick house, thinking perhaps Harriet might prefer the distractions of London to the quiet of Cornwall, but she had started howling again. 'But I need to be with *you*! I need my *family*!' So of course Miranda agreed to collect her that night from Newquay airport. Somehow, on the drive back to Chapel Creek, she was going to have to persuade Harriet that however desolate she was feeling, it might be an idea to give some thought to their mother. Being dumped by a wayward faithless boyfriend whom she had only recently moved in with wasn't really up there with Clare's loss of her husband. Harriet might have to think a bit before claiming that every single bit of life's unfairness had landed on her and her alone. But all the same, it could be good to have an ally in the house. Maybe Miranda could even start to feel a bit more like relaxing, more as if this were actually a pleasurable break, if she had someone else to share Clare with. Harriet was a persuasive sort – she might even manage to get their mother to deal with Jack's ashes sooner rather than later. It would be such a relief to get whatever ceremony Clare wanted out of the way so they could get on with trying to make this a proper holiday. In the meantime, still in her capacity of team leader and default dogsbody, Miranda had to think about food for them all. Bo had gone off with Lola to

Jess's house, leaving Silva trying to look as if she didn't care in the slightest about having chosen to stay behind.

'Are you sure you didn't want to go with them?' Miranda asked when she came back from the beach and found Silva floating on a pink inflatable crocodile in the pool, her iPod plugged into her ears.

'Like, *no*?' The emphatic negative told Miranda that Silva was indeed regretting her decision. She looked lonely, a bit lost, and was possibly heading for a full-day sulk. When Clare offered to take her over on the ferry to St Piran, Miranda was absolutely *not* going to let her say no.

Miranda locked up the house, texted Bo to tell him where she'd hidden a spare key in case he came back, and set off to the village shop. She was hoping to do some serious stocking up and decided that using the village shop would be far more interesting than a trip to the nearest supermarket, nine miles away. She needed quite a lot of supplies and wasn't sure if the shop did deliveries (where was Ocado when you needed it?), but there was an old-fashioned wicker shopping trolley being decoratively chic in the hallway so she took the umbrellas out of it and almost laughed as she considered how she wouldn't be seen dead with such an item back home on the Chiswick High Road. The shopping trolley of shame, she thought, practising manoeuvring it on the path and doing a little dance with it, thinking along the lines of Fred Astaire with a cane, before she headed off down the hill. Although maybe back home among the thousands of fit young fashion-forward mummies pushing top of the range baby buggies it would count as retro enough to look kind of edgily ironic.

The shop was busy. It had been extended a long way back from how Miranda remembered it and was no longer gloomily dark-shelved, tatty and a bit forbidding but all light wood fittings, smart rubber flooring and pale turquoise paint. A big heap of wicker picnic baskets was down by the deli counter, each of them name-labelled for customers. The place seemed to be doing a tremendous trade, making up gourmet picnic lunch orders for those who were too holiday-relaxed to want the bother of putting together a sandwich or two for the beach. Good call, whoever had thought of that. Children hovered around their parents, scooping up extras in terms of fancy crisps (no Monster Munch here) and heritage apples displayed in wooden trugs. Someone was also being very enterprising with ready-cooked food and the shop's freezer was crammed with home-made, hand-labelled lasagne, fish pies, organic chicken casseroles and aubergine moussaka.

'Bloody 'ellfire, they see you coming, here,' a northern-accented voice commented to the shop in general. A stout woman in a navy and white striped top peered into the freezer cabinet and held up a pack of monkfish goujons. 'Would you look at the price of these, and they're not even Bird's Eye. I didn't expect to have to take out a bleedin' mortgage for a packet of fish fingers.'

Miranda couldn't see any wire baskets so used her shopping trolley to collect what she needed, piling in an extravagant few packs of ready-cooked frozen boeuf bourguignon that they could have the next day. For tonight, she chose a fish pie for Clare and the children, realizing she'd be off doing the airport run for most of the evening and wouldn't be home for supper. She grabbed brown paper bags and loaded them with tomatoes, mixing up a chic selection of red, stripy and yellow ones, plus knobbly pink fir apple potatoes, a stack of grubby-looking mixed salad leaves, avocados, chicory and some dark, crinkly *cavolo nero* which she was pretty sure Silva would eat so long as the word 'cabbage' wasn't mentioned. Just as she was studying the deli counter in search of ingredients for a sandwich she could eat in the car on the way to Newquay, a man came in from the back of the shop and spoke to the assistant, whom Miranda recognized as the rude blonde girl who'd snapped about 'bloody trippers' at the pub the night before. And he was the one she'd thought resembled Steve. She edged away to a safe distance to get a good look without his noticing her. If it wasn't Steve, it was someone incredibly closely related to him. It if *was* him, she didn't particularly want him to see her, not just yet anyway. In fact, to be honest, not without fair warning and a good go at her make-up.

'Cheryl?' he said. 'I just dropped off your order out back. Three dozen oysters, ten lobsters ready cooked-off and five more kilos of langoustines.' Miranda hung back behind a party of browsers who'd gone silent, possibly mesmerized by the £3.50 price tag on the small lumpy loaves of sourdough bread. 'They're in the left-hand fridge. Anything else, just give me a bell.' The girl – Cheryl – looked up and smiled. 'Thanks, Stevie, babe,' she said, almost purring at him.

So it *was* him. That unsettling, briefly glimpsed lookalike from the pub really *was* Steve – or *Stevie babe*. Yuck. Miranda, from behind the stocky frame of the fish-finger-seeking holidaymaker (now grumbling about the lack of white sliced bread), had a good stare as he fondly tweaked the girl's thick, untidy blonde plait and went through to the back of the shop again. He'd aged well, she'd give him that. Twenty years certainly hadn't given him a paunchy middle or cost him his hair, which was still quite long but in a cool Johnny Depp sort of way, not lank and neglected. His broad smile at Cheryl showed gleaming teeth, bright against the tanned face she remembered from way back. Still curious (OK, frankly nosy), Miranda crossed to the shop's doorway and peered out, hoping to take in some more of how he was looking without his seeing her, but as she stepped outside a white van with a big blue curly fish painted on the back was already pulling away. Damn.

'Oy! Excuse *me*!' The sharp, accusing voice of Cheryl cut across the shop and Miranda could almost feel it whamming into the back of her head. She turned round. 'Yes, you, lady over there with your wheelie basket full of *our* goods. Don't think I haven't been watching you!' Cheryl was now coming round from behind the deli counter to the shop floor and heading Miranda's way, looking furious and determined and as if she didn't intend to stop till she'd got close enough to give her a smack in the mouth. Miranda backed away, alarmed in case she did plan exactly that. She felt a small longing for the peaceful anonymity of Waitrose on the Chiswick High Road, where nobody would ever storm across the shop floor to show you up in front of your fellow customers. 'Don't you even *think* of buggering off out of here without paying!' Cheryl's face was close enough to Miranda for her to smell minty chewing gum and see that beneath heavily applied foundation her chin had a lumpy little outcrop of spots. The entire shopful of customers had parted to make way for small, bustling Cheryl and every one of them was staring as she reached into the shopping trolley and started pulling out Miranda's vegetables.

'I wasn't stealing them! I was only . . . I was just

looking outside for . . . something,' Miranda protested feebly as she moved away from the door and hauled what was left of her basket of supplies back inside, trailing behind Cheryl to the check-out queue, feeling mortified. No *way* had she been about to shoplift, but she got the impression that any further denial wouldn't be accepted.

'You use these next time, right? Or you're barred!' Cheryl pointed to a pile of baskets cutely wrought from chicken wire and bamboo. Miranda had assumed they were for sale: the shop had all sorts of similar goods on offer – mugs (not Miranda's designs, she noted), tea towels with local scenes, kitchenware, scented candles, standard gift-shop items.

'OK. Sorry.' Miranda wondered how much more contrite she was expected to be and was getting an unbanishable picture in her head of Cheryl in bed with Steve later that night, the two of them laughing together about stupid thieving grockles.

Cheryl went back behind the counter, pulled on some latex gloves with the firm snapping movement of a therapist about to undertake a tricky colonic irrigation and continued deftly putting together a crab sandwich for a woman in the skinniest white jeans Miranda had ever seen. Miranda, too embarrassed now to line up to ask the girl to make her a sandwich for later – not to mention frightened of what might 'accidentally' find its way into it if she did – quickly unloaded her food at the check-out and shakily groped in her bag for her credit card.

'Some people just have to try it on, don't they? Can't trust anyone . . .' Cheryl was still grouching at full volume to the rest of the shop as she handed over the crab sandwich.

'I'm not bloody surprised.' The sliced-bread woman's northern voice rang clearly through the shop. 'At these prices, love, I'd say it's you lot committing daylight robbery, not your customers.'

Clare and Silva walked along the pontoon to the ferry and boarded the boat to cross the estuary to St Piran. Clare accepted a steadying hand from a stocky boy in board shorts and a cap. 'Three quid, return. Each,' he said, adding a grudging, 'Please,' as if he'd just remembered the rest of the training manual script.

'Three pounds? Good grief, it used to be about fifty p,' Clare told him. She handed over the cash, and as they went to sit down on the long side bench she murmured to Silva, 'I wish I hadn't said that. I sound like one of those people from my mother's generation who say things like, "In my day it was sixpence in old money and you'd still have change for a bag of chips."'

But Silva was leaning over the side and staring down into the sea. 'Fish,' she said. 'Look at these fish, Gran. The water's so weird.'

'Is it?' Clare turned and looked down at the sea as the

boat started to pull away. It was just . . . sea, surely? 'What's weird about it?'

'When you look at it from the shore, it's all grey and brownish, pretty much like the Thames at home. But here where you're right on top of it and looking straight down, it's like abroad-sea, all turquoise and different shades where the rocks are and really clear. I don't get it.'

'It'll be something to do with refracted light,' Clare said.

'And that is . . . ?'

'I haven't a clue, darling,' she said, laughing.

'You're laughing, Gran,' Silva pointed out as the boat revved up and pulled away across the water.

Clare looked at her, smiling. She could feel her hair being blown back from her face and bits of it whipping round again to hit her. Tears came into her eyes but for once they weren't the crying sort, just from the breeze.

'I am, aren't I? It's being here, I expect. It's something in the air.'

'I'm glad. And Gran?'

'Yes, Silva?'

'You mentioned chips. Please can we get some?'

'I don't see why not. But let's look around a bit first, yes? I was reading something about a new gallery and I want to find it if we can. I'd like to see what kind of paintings are selling down here. How did you and Bo get on with that Lola girl? Do you think you'll be friends?'

'Dunno.' Silva shrugged. 'She winds me up. She winds Bo up too but in a different way. I think she thinks I'm just a kid and not worth the hassle, you know? Bo fancies her.'

'How can you tell?'

'He smiled. Bo *smiled*. It was totes sick-making. He smiled at everything she said, like she was saying amaze stuff he'd never heard before. It was like, *so* embarrassing. I had to go back in the house.'

Clare wanted to hug her, but with Silva's tolerance level for embarrassment being clearly pretty low she thought better of it. All the same, she felt enormous sympathy for the girl, who was seeing herself potentially becoming sidelined by her brother during this holiday while he followed this Lola around. She remembered Miranda at the same age, or maybe a bit younger, being rather lost in the village till she met Jessica, Milo and Andrew. Her little sisters were way too young to be proper companions and she'd sometimes seemed to Clare still to be the only child she had been for her first eight years. Bo and Silva were very lucky to be close in age, really, she thought. But she also knew better than to point this fact out to Silva right now.

'It's changed a lot over here,' she said as the two of them ambled between the shops and cafés on the St Piran beachfront. 'There didn't use to be much, just holiday homes, a few retired people in bungalows, some run-down shops and the one big old pub with rickety metal tables outside. Now look, the shops are all arty and bright and the pub's gone all boutique hotel and bistro. Your mum used to come over here some nights in a boat with her friends.'

'Did she?' Silva, not that interested in what went on long before she was born, stopped to look at a window display of surfwear and wetsuits. Its customers streamed in and out – a file of confident and fit-looking boys in board shorts and flip-flops, swishy-haired girls with deep-tanned long legs in cut-off shorts or tiny dresses. Local, Clare would guess, not tourists. Or the locally detested second home owners as she'd once been, coming down here every summer and taking over, cluttering up the narrow lanes with big cars towing boats. This was one of the places that made it into the outraged press each summer, when over-privileged children partied late at night in the sand dunes with too much drink and too much noise. Town-boy holiday-makers were lurking on the beach looking awkward and out of place in old trainers and the falling-down jeans they all wore up-country. The girls kept their city-pale legs covered, wearing black leggings under tiny shorts and surely sweltering horribly. She felt a bit sorry for them – all their street-smart was no use here. You needed water skills: surfing, sailing, even just basic bodyboarding, to fit in, and you needed, even if only by moving a few yards up the beach, not to be lumbered with your parents.

This place was far busier than Clare remembered. The gift shops, the new galleries and the chic cafés brought a constant stream of holidaymakers pouring off the ferry, looking for something to entertain them, something to buy. Young girls sat queuing on the harbour wall for henna tattoos and hair-braids while their parents sat on benches munching pasties and trying to fend off the greedy seagulls.

But it was the galleries that interested Clare. 'Your granddad used to sell paintings here when he first decided to give up teaching,' she told Silva as they walked up a narrow lane just off the seafront. 'It was here he decided he wanted to be a full-time artist, while . . .' she hesitated, 'while he still could.'

'Was he ill right back then as well?' Silva asked. 'That was years ago, wasn't it?'

'No, he wasn't ill then,' Clare told her, 'but he made a big decision the last summer we were here. He'd got to a point where he thought that if he didn't give up teaching and do full-time painting *now* he never would. So he did. It was a risk, but I'm so glad he took it. You always regret passing up on what you really want. Remember that, if your teachers ever push you to give up subjects you really like best.'

'Good choice,' Silva agreed, nodding as if she knew. Perhaps she did, Clare thought. At nearly fourteen you can't imagine *not* having all the options in the world.

'It was. He did well at it. But his first sales after that decision were for hardly any money. They were typical seaside scenes and he had an exhibition at a little gallery in Chapel Creek. When we drove past it yesterday it looked as if it had turned into a tea room.'

'There're a lot of dogs,' Silva suddenly said, moving out of the way of a black spaniel, pulling at its lead. 'Everyone here's got a dog.' She sounded grumpy and a bit bored. Clare took hold of her arm and pulled her across the road to a gallery where the window was full of bright harbour scenes.

'But that's the thing about a holiday that isn't abroad. You don't have to worry about leaving the dog. And people do worry. Even you've brought your cat.'

'Only cos he's old. Mum didn't trust the cattery.'

'Aha, now this is the place I wanted to see,' Clare said. 'Tell you what, Silva, why don't you go and bag us a table at that Sail Loft café by the ferry so we can have some lunch and I'll catch up with you in about ten minutes? Order yourself a drink while you wait for me, yes?'

'OK.' Clare watched as Silva sauntered off down the road, her hands stuffed deep into the pockets of her denim shorts. Jack had loved her very much, this child of Miranda's, to whom he was no blood relation. And now he'd never see her grow up, not be there to give her a hug and a cash bonus for exam success, not go to her graduation – if she chose to go to university, that is. He wouldn't be able to help teach her to drive as he had Miranda. Silva and Bo had always been called him Granddad. But Miranda hadn't called him Daddy; Clare hadn't ever suggested she did. He'd always been Jack to her, at first because Clare hadn't known whether the relationship would last, and by the time they'd actually decided it would, and they'd married, the habit was ingrained. How ridiculous, she thought now. The man who'd raised her daughter since she'd been three and she'd denied him and Miranda that small measure of closeness. She'd never know if it had made a difference. Too late now.

She waited till a few browsers left the gallery and then went inside. There was something she had to do. It wasn't only Jack's mortal remains that needed to be set free. She had twenty-three of his early Cornish paintings that needed a home. And this gallery was where she hoped they'd find one.

Silva walked back to the harbour-front and had another look in the beachwear shop. She'd clocked the surf-crowd earlier and envied how they all knew each other and wished she were part of a group of friends like that. If Bo went off and hung with the Lola girl she'd be mostly mooching about by herself for three whole weeks, which was like *for ever*. *Not* fun. Her best friend Willow had gone to Florida for a month to stay with a bunch of cousins and she kept putting up all these photos of beach party fun on Facebook and in most of them there was a boy with his arm round her. You couldn't not be envious. Silva wasn't the only one – every single one of their mates had been madly clicking on 'Like' under the pictures. She imagined Willow on a beach at sundown, out of sight of her parents, snogging the boy's face off. He didn't actually look all that but at least she'd have something to tell when they got back to school. What was Silva going to have? *It was great. I hung with my mum, my aunt and my gran.* Not that she didn't love her family, but the summer you become fourteen you want it to have something a bit more . . . memorable.

She went into the shop. A couple of the boys from before were still there, talking like experts about wet-suits – something about gauges and percentages. She listened in as she flicked through a rail of discounted T-shirts, noting the ya-ya drawls of private-school accents. Maybe they were from London as well. She wished one of them would notice her and . . . well, anything really. Just a smile would be something, especially from the streaky blond one with the gold ear stud, just so she felt she was worth a look. But they were a couple of years older than her, at least. She was probably invisible. Willow wouldn't be – she'd make sure they clocked her, just flicking her hair about and maybe bumping into one of them. But then Willow was the oldest in her school year – she'd be fifteen in September, practically *adult*. Silva was the baby of their group and had only got her periods just after Christmas. It was hard keeping up with a best friend whose fake ID was never (according to Willow anyway) challenged in clubs. In fact it was hard keeping up with a friend who even *went* to clubs.

The boys were talking about something called sex wax now. What *was* that? It sounded weird. Where did you put it? Was it like . . . bikini waxing or something? She'd never be able to ask because she'd look like a numpty for not knowing. Whatever it was it must be gross.

Silva hoped her gran wouldn't be too long because although she'd said she was OK with going by herself to the Sail Loft, she actually felt a bit shy about sitting at a table alone and actually ordering something. You'd look like a loser, sitting all by your lonesome. She probably just had time to try something on, maybe a little skirt or one of the flowery dresses that she wouldn't wear back home but which looked so cool on the girls here. Another boy (nerdy geek style this time, though with nice grey eyes) came in with a tall stringy dad and they started looking at wetsuits.

'You'll need a life jacket as well, Freddie,' the dad was saying, pacing about and being loud. 'And some gloves and, hey, how about this hat?' The dad put a baseball cap on back to front and smirked at himself in the long mirror on the wall. The surf-boys made faces at each other.

'Dad . . .' Freddie mumbled, looking embarrassed. Silva glanced at him, feeling sympathetic. He smiled shyly and she could feel herself blushing so she grabbed a dress and rushed into the changing area, pulling the curtain shut behind her.

The dress was a terrible choice. She put it on and pulled the loose fabric back at the waist. She must have picked out a size twelve or something – it was way too big for her. She unzipped it quickly and just as she was pulling it over her head the curtain was abruptly pulled back.

'Aha, it's occupied. Sorree!' The boy she'd wanted to notice her was now staring at her body, which was exposed to the whole shop. 'Aw, everyone, look at these cute li'l pink knickers!' He was laughing loudly and taking his time putting the curtain back again. Silva flung her shorts on, hands shaking as she fastened them, and hurtled out of the shop, almost tripping over the big, white-trainered feet of the Freddie boy. She ran up the lane and into the courtyard of the Sail Loft, collapsing panting into a chair at the far back close to the hedge and in the face-cooling shade of a big umbrella.

'Don't you want to sit in the sun?' Clare arrived seconds later, when Silva was still trying to erase the cringeworthy picture of the gorgeous but horribly teasing surf-boy – along with everyone else in the shop – staring at her Hello Kitty underwear. I must have looked about *nine*, was all she could think. What a great start to the holiday.

SIX

Miranda was running late. She'd never been to the little airport at Newquay before and although it looked easy enough to find on the map, once she was off the main road there were too many winding lanes to make the trip a fast and smooth one. At least the urn full of ashes was no longer rolling about in the boot of the car. Clare must have taken it out some time during the day. Miranda would have to ask her where it was, if only so that Harriet wouldn't fling open a random cupboard door and start screeching if she found her father's remains where she'd expected the biscuit tin to be. Bo and Silva, bless them, wouldn't even think to comment. How much more adaptable and unconcerned children are, she thought. Or maybe it was just hers. And maybe they simply had no curiosity . . . She mustn't over-analyse – that way lay another dollop of single-parent self-recrimination. They were fine.

And of course, now that Miranda at last had the St Mawgan air base in sight, Dan was phoning for the fourth time and she couldn't ignore him any longer otherwise she'd end up having to take a call from him later when she'd got Harriet in the car. If that happened, Harriet would do the thing she did where she kept asking why on earth Miranda ever even spoke to him. OK, so he was an idle, useless sod, but he was the idle, useless sod who was father to her children. She couldn't expect her sister to understand that you never quite escaped those. She pulled over into a farm gateway to find out what was so urgent.

'I was chatting to Bo on Facebook,' he said, sounding cheery. 'He says you've rented a nice big fancy place down in Cornwall. Sounds idyllic.'

'It's not *that* big,' Miranda told him, wary about what might be coming next. 'It'll be full once Harriet's got here.' Damn, she thought, it might have been better not to mention Harriet was coming. Straight into his trap.

'Oh, right. Well, hey, if you've got room for your sister, you can find a sofa or something for your children's father, can't you?' he said. 'I'd really like to come and see them on their holiday. One big happy family and all that.'

She thought about the last time they'd tried that one, because, in the interests of bringing up the children without their seeing only lasting rancour, she had given it a go. They'd gone for a weekend in Barcelona where she'd discovered that Dan, for once in his life pulling the macho 'I'll organize everything' card, had booked them all into one inadequate family room in a truly nasty hotel, in which he'd assumed, staggeringly, that she'd share a bed with him. Still, at least being re-acquainted with Dan's bathroom habits had squashed any guilt she'd occasionally felt about leaving him and depriving the children of a live-in father. As a hygiene role model, she'd told him as they boarded the plane home, frankly she'd do better to shack up with a zoo animal.

'No really, Dan, there isn't the space. Truly.'

'Well, if you've run out of rooms we can always bunk in together, you and me.' Dan chuckled at her down the phone. Miranda opened the window and took a deep breath of fresh evening air. Did the concept of 'divorce' mean nothing to him?

'I don't think so, Dan, do you? I've got Mum here who's still feeling fragile, Harriet who's just been dumped by her boyfriend and the children who need entertaining. Sorry, but I don't want to have to look after you as well. Tell you what,' she went on quickly before he could think of another weaselly argument, 'why don't you have them on their own after we get back? There'll be another week or two of the summer holidays left. Maybe you could take them somewhere?'

'Gee, thanks. I get palmed off with a few leftover days, do I, while you get them for most of the holidays?

Remind me, don't we have some sort of proper child-care arrangement in force?'

Through the windscreen, Miranda could see a plane touching down on the runway. She had to get going.

'We do and I've never argued about that, as you know. But you also agreed to this trip, for the sake of my mother, remember? And now the children are older they get a say as well, surely? And they really wanted this. Please, Dan, don't be difficult.'

'But I can't afford to take them away, not right now.' No, well you wouldn't, not while you're spending most of your life on the sofa eating Pringles, watching *Cash in the Attic* and wondering why the living the world apparently owes you isn't actually forthcoming, Miranda managed *not* to say, saving the thought for possible emergency use later.

'OK. Then how about you have them to stay with you?' she suggested, switching the engine back on and indicating to pull out.

'Well, you know I would, but Mum finds teenagers a handful,' he countered.

'Now that I doubt,' Miranda said, laughing. 'After all, she manages to cope with you.' She made the goodbye a swift one, drove the last half-mile to the airport, quickly parked and hurtled into the terminal as the first passengers were coming out.

'Manda! Where *were* you – I've been waiting *ages*!' Harriet looked close to stamping her foot with indignation. It was a gesture that would, Miranda immediately thought, go well with the pretty fifties-style lilac full-skirted shirt dress and five-inch wedge shoes she was wearing. She'd always had a great dress-up sense of style and now only lacked a cute pillbox hat and little white gloves.

Miranda hugged her and she immediately burst into noisy sobs, which meant that Miranda could hardly point out that she knew Harriet hadn't been waiting – she'd just seen her walk across the tarmac from the plane right that minute.

'Oh, don't cry, darling,' she said, patting her gently as if soothing a fallen-down child. 'It's all going to be fine, I promise. Now, where's your luggage?'

'Over there.' Harriet sniffed and pointed to a carousel on which several large matching pink cases were going round by themselves. Most people had grabbed theirs quickly and already raced out.

'Fine. Shall we get them?' Miranda didn't think this was a good sign. Had the footballer's defection left the girl completely incapable? The indications pointed to 'yes'. So that would be someone else in the house who would need careful handling, then. She left Harriet mopping her eyes while peering into a small mirror and loaded the bags on to a trolley. They were very heavy and there were rather a lot of them. Had Harriet brought everything she owned? Miranda had assumed this was just a flying visit to lick her wounds and gather a bit of strength. With difficulty, and with Harriet trotting uselessly alongside, she shoved the unwieldy trolley – which of course had to have a wonky wheel – out towards the car park. One lone man stood outside the terminal, staring round and looking confused, a squashy old leather bag on the pavement at his feet.

'There's never a feckin' cab round here when you need one, not unless you sprint like a bloody gazelle through this damn place,' he grumbled in the general direction of Miranda. It was happening again, she realized: yet another person who looked somehow familiar. Or maybe it was something to do with the voice. A bit Irish, a bit London. Except yet again it actually was someone she'd known, and amazingly he looked hardly different at all from the last time she'd seen him. Barely older somehow (how did that happen?), still shambolic, a bit like a cleaned-up tramp but in a bobbly soft grey cashmere sweater.

'I don't suppose by any remote feckin' chance you'll be travelling anywhere near a back-of-beyond place called Chapel Creek, will you?' He smiled at Miranda, who'd stopped mid-trolley-struggle.

'Come *on*, Miranda. Don't talk to him,' hissed Harriet. 'He was drinking on the plane.'

'And don't tell me you weren't,' Miranda murmured back. 'I know gin-tears when I see them.'

'Yeah, and so what? You'd feel the same in my shoes.'

This was probably true. Miranda gave her hand a sympathetic squeeze.

The man was still looking hopeful, still giving them the smile full of Irish charm.

'I actually know you,' Miranda said. 'Aren't you Eliot Lynch?'

The smile turned into the broadest beam and he laughed. 'I so am! Jaysus, I haven't been recognized on the street for a long time now. You've made my day, so you have. You'll be a reader then?'

'Er . . .' How to say without hurting his feelings that yes, she was a voracious reader, but not really of his sex-and-spies genre. 'I remember you from years ago, over at Chapel Creek. I was friends with Jessica and Milo? Down here in the summers?'

Harriet was scowling, picking at her nails. 'Can we get going? Please?'

'I can give you a lift, Eliot. I've seen Jess today – she said you were coming. I'm Miranda – do you remember us all?'

Eliot looked at her for a few long seconds, 'Oh, my Lord. Miranda. Daughter of the lovely Clare and all grown up so pretty. Tell me, is your mam well? I always had a soft spot for her.'

'She is.' This wasn't really the moment to elaborate, Miranda decided; she could tell him about Jack later on the journey. 'And she's in Chapel Creek. We've rented your old house for a few weeks. Come on,' she said, as his face showed he was taking this in rather slowly. 'The car's this way. Shall we get going?'

'I'm not going to do this every day,' Miranda warned everyone the next morning as she bustled around the kitchen cooking a huge late fry-up breakfast for them all. 'It's just a one-off treat and a sort of welcome to Harriet. After this you can all fend for yourselves in the mornings. Bo, please will you take knives and forks and stuff out to the terrace table? It's warm enough to be outside. Has your gran come back from her swim yet? She did say nine thirty.' And that had been pretty much all she'd said as she was leaving the house by herself when Miranda came down the stairs.

'Would you like me to come and swim with you?' Miranda had asked, thinking her mother might like some company, but Clare just gave her a sad little smile, shook her head and closed the door softly behind her. When Miranda had got back the night before, Clare had already gone to bed, so she'd had no chance to tell her about meeting Eliot. Bo and Silva had been curled like cats on opposite sofas, half asleep and watching a film full of old-school car chases. Harriet, pleading emotional exhaustion, had carried just one of her smaller bags upstairs, leaving Miranda to follow with the two heaviest.

'Pretty room,' Harriet had commented, getting her phone out and checking for a signal. She went to the window and pulled the curtains firmly shut, then opened one of them the tiniest chink and peered out.

'Is there something out there?' Miranda asked, going to take a look. She remembered how bats used to swoop low over the village and she pulled the fabric back a bit.

'No, don't! There might be paps,' Harriet hissed, grabbing the curtains and hauling them tightly shut.

'Paps?'

'Paparazzi.' Harriet went and sat on the bed. 'You've no idea how it's been since Pablo was all over the press with that . . . that *slag*. They hung around outside the flat. I'm sure they followed me to the airport. They could be *here*.'

Miranda pictured the hedges and lanes of Chapel Creek crammed with photographers with their little ladders and giant lenses, hoping for a glimpse of the Wronged Girlfriend. It was possible, she conceded as she wearily went off to bed. After all, it was August; Cornwall was sunny instead of raining for once and there'd been no big cat sightings or schools of stranded whales yet to bring the newsmen hurtling across the Tamar for a few days of seaside fun. But somehow she thought it wasn't likely.

'Gran is back,' Silva said now. 'She's in the sitting room watching the news on TV.'

'Really?' That was something Clare had never been known to do at home as she'd always considered watching television before six p.m. to be the ultimate in slovenliness. But then Miranda hadn't shared a house with her mother for so many years, how would she know how she organized her days now? Maybe she and Jack had got to a point where they started every day with a news round-up followed by a good rage at the *Jeremy Kyle Show*. She went in to tell her breakfast was on its way and ask her what she'd like. Clare was staring blankly at the TV, where two brightly smiling women on a pink sofa were squealing over-excitedly about elaborate cupcake icing. She switched off as Miranda came in.

'Mum? I haven't had a chance to tell you. Last night at the airport we met Jessica's dad. You remember Eliot Lynch? We gave him a lift – he's come to stay with Jess for a while.'

'That's nice, darling. I don't suppose he remembered us, though, did he? It was such a long time ago.'

'Oh, but he did. And he specially asked about you.' She giggled. 'He said he'd had a soft spot for you.'

'That's sweet of him.' Clare was smiling and looking a bit pink. 'Maybe we'll run into him in the village. He must be ancient by now.' She sighed. 'But then none of us are the same.'

'Actually, he looked in amazingly good condition, considering what he used to be like. Way better than you'd expect. Maybe he's had work done,' Miranda suggested, holding the door open for Clare.

'Cosmetic work? Oh, don't be silly!' Clare laughed,

sounding almost girlish. 'He'd be the last person to do that!' Miranda looked at her, thinking how the years fell away from her mother's face when she had these odd moments of looking carefree. Perhaps, Miranda thought, these moments would gradually get more frequent and then eventually join up so she could feel properly happy again. Who knew? Clare was far too young to be blighted, to grieve this deeply for the rest of her life. What it must be like to have had someone you loved so, so much. Miranda had loved Dan for several years but, looking back, she couldn't honestly swear she'd ever had that true soul-mate feeling about him. Would she ever, about anyone? What chance did a mid-thirties divorcée with two teenage children have out there in the dating pond against beautiful, free, twenty-something gorgeousness such as her own sister?

Harriet paced about the kitchen, wearing a pink satin robe and a pair of fluffy tiger slippers, opening and closing the fridge and being generally useless. 'I hardly slept a *minute*,' she said, chewing a nail. Flakes of pink varnish fluttered to the worktop and she flicked them to the floor. Miranda felt mildly annoyed. The rental agency had promised them a cleaner twice a week but there was no need to be carelessly untidy. All the same, so as not to be seen as a nag, she said nothing and carried on turning the mushrooms in the bubbling butter. At least Harriet, in her misery, wasn't refusing to eat – usually she would be horrified at the idea of a cooked breakfast. 'The camera hates a porker,' she'd once said when Miranda had dared suggest she might like a bacon sandwich, as if just one would signal the end of her quest to be the next Kirsty Young. Perhaps it would encourage Clare who, before they came down here, had found it hard to get more than a few tiny mouthfuls of food into her body. Last night's fish pie had all gone, though, she noticed, though it might have gone into Bo (whose skinny body could still put away a truckload of food every mealtime) or into Toby the greedy cat who hovered in the kitchen as if waiting to trip up anyone carrying food.

Harriet, now sitting at the table and looking droopy, continued with the story of her night. 'Just when I could feel myself drifting off at last, the birds all woke up and bloody *sunlight* started to come in.'

'Oh, *naughty* sunlight. How very dare it!' Miranda said, as she laid strips of bacon on the grill pan. 'I'm sorry you didn't sleep, though. Maybe a day of fresh country air will help.'

'Don't go all Enid Blyton on me, Manda. Don't forget, I'm broken-hearted.'

'Shh! Don't let Mum hear you say that, please. I know you're hurting now and I'm sorry for you, but try to remember that in your case nobody died.'

'Sorry.' Harriet yawned again. 'But honestly, it'll take more than some messing about in boats and coast path walks to get my life back on track. What time do the papers come?'

Bo looked up from his iPod. 'They don't. You have to go and get them.'

Harriet looked puzzled. 'What, like from the shop? Don't they deliver? I need *all* of them. The tabloids, anyway.'

'Why?' Silva asked. 'Are you like *in* them? Is it because of your love-rat footballer in night-club drug arrest shock thing?'

'Silva!' Miranda warned, turning her face back to the cooking to hide the threat of laughter.

'I was only . . .'

'Well please don't,' Harriet told her. 'You have *no idea* what it's like to be at the centre of a huge news story like this. It's . . . awful. Just . . . terrible.'

'So why do you want to read about it then?' Silva's question didn't seem too unreasonable, if a little abruptly put. Miranda shoved the bacon and tomatoes under the grill and sliced some of the shop's rather solid (yet four pounds a loaf) bread for toast. For a second, as she sawed at it with the knife, she felt a bond with the northern holidaymaker who'd bemoaned the lack of white sliced.

'Because, Silva darling, if people are going to talk about you then it's better to hear what they're saying rather than just wonder about it. Knowledge is power.'

'Are they actually talking about *you*? Isn't it just the footballer and the drugs and the other girl?'

'Look – does it matter? My *life* has been taken apart, that's the important thing. I've come here to get away and to hide. That's all.'

'So what does everyone want to do today?' Miranda asked as they sat down to eat breakfast under the terrace sunshade. She looked at Clare, hoping this would be the cue for her to say something about Jack's ashes and what exactly she'd decided to do about them. 'Anybody got anything they really feel like doing?' No answers were forthcoming. Bo shrugged and put a massive forkful of bacon and mushrooms into his mouth. Silva looked miles away. She tried again. 'Do you and Bo want to go and see about sailing lessons or something? Or just go off and do your own thing?'

'Dunno. Maybe,' Silva said unhelpfully. This was hard work, Miranda thought as she sipped her tea. How on earth did those people who used to work at holiday camps ever get the punters excited about the daily events? Still, at the worst they could all just hang about the house and swim in the pool now and then. Doing nothing here wasn't exactly a hardship.

'OK – I'll just leave you all to make your own minds up,' she said. 'Nothing organized. But Mum, if you decide you might like a long walk around the headland and lunch in the next village, I'll be happy to come with you.' She couldn't see Harriet doing more than lying on a lounger down by the pool, pecking at her phone every few minutes and sighing a lot.

'Another day, Miranda, that'll be lovely. But today we will all go to the beach,' Clare declared. 'There's nothing more uplifting than being next to the ocean. It puts things into perspective. We will all go together and have a proper family time on the sand, with a flask of tea and a picnic lunch.'

It was an order. There'd be no arguing, it was clear. Also, there was no mention of the ashes. Miranda looked at her, feeling concerned, but only one small tear fell to Clare's cheek and she quickly dashed that away and started spreading marmalade on a piece of toast. Somehow, Miranda would get her alone later and pin her down about whatever arrangements she had in mind.

'Yeah, beach! Tan! Sea!' Well, at least Silva was up for Clare's decision. 'And can I take that crocodile from the pool with me? He'd be more fun than a bodyboard. And he's my new best friend.' She glared at Bo.

'I can't go out in public,' Harriet stated flatly, gazing out towards the sea.

'Why on earth not?' Clare's voice was sharp. 'Can't you do this one thing?'

'Because people will *stare*.' Harriet was giving her a look as if this was so obvious it shouldn't need saying.

Clare laughed. 'Oh, don't be so melodramatic, Harriet! No one's going to be looking at you.'

'Oh, thanks, Mum! Don't forget my entire career was about people *looking at me*. I was on TV, you know.' Harriet stood up and stalked off in a big huff back into the house, the effect being more comic than anything else, since she was still wearing the stripy tiger slippers.

Miranda and Clare looked at each other. Clare spoke first 'Did she say, "was"?'

'She did. She's either quit or been fired, hasn't she?'

'If it's about the footballer, that wouldn't be fair. It's hardly her fault. You'll have to ask her, Miranda.'

Yes, Miranda thought with a certain amount of resignation as she collected up plates to take back inside, she rather thought it would be down to her. She'd put it on the list.

SEVEN

The party for the beach took some assembling. Bo found a bodyboard in the utility room and claimed it as his own, much to Silva's annoyance. She sat on the stairs, blowing more air into the pink crocodile and getting in Harriet's way as she went up and down to her room and back, changing her clothes twice and eventually coming down with a large basket containing sunscreen, books, her iPad and several changes of shoes. And just when everyone was actually going out of the door, Miranda's phone rang. 'You'll never guess what!' Jess sounded excited.

'Hi, Jess – what won't I guess?'

'Andrew's here!' she squealed, '*Andrew!* I saw him, just now. He's hardly changed *at all*. He was doing something to a boat at the end of his garden, with a gawky-looking boy of about fifteen. There was this big woman too, sitting on their old swing-seat with a cigarette.'

'Really? Wife, do you think? Can't be his old mum, can it? Celia was as skinny as a stick and thought smoking was a deadly sin.'

Jess giggled. 'Too right. She'd go ape. I can't imagine Andrew with an actual wife, can you?'

Miranda couldn't. Not the old Andrew anyway; not sweet nerdy Andrew who never seemed to fit with his own generation. Was that down to having older and very traditional parents maybe? He'd liked sailing and windsurfing, Mozart and chess. And he'd liked Jessica. But most of typical teen life seemed a mystery to him. If he had a teenage son, she could imagine him being dragged by the lad into Abercrombie and Fitch and, mystified by the pounding music, the half-dark and the barely dressed sales assistants, asking himself: *Which new circle of hell is this?*

'Well no, to be honest, I can't. His mum must have set him up with some nice home counties girl. It can only have been an arranged thing.'

'Maybe he's better at being a grown-up than he was at being a teenager, poor boy. I'm going to run next door in a bit and surprise him. Or do you think that's not a good idea?' Jess sounded nervously excited.

'It's a great idea. I mean, after all, it would be rude not to be friendly to the neighbours, wouldn't it? I'd love to see him again too. Perhaps I'll go round later as well, when we get back from the beach.'

'I suppose a proper grown-up neighbour would take

a cake.' Jess sounded as if she were almost talking to herself now. 'But he'll have to make do with a bottle of wine. I don't really do baking.'

'Oh, now come on, Jess, unless he's changed *massively*, he'll be so thrilled to see you he won't mind if you take him a bag of carrots. Hope it goes well and he's not too terrified to hear we're both in the village.'

Jessica giggled, sounding like a teenager again. 'I'll be gentle with him. Actually, what I really also wanted to say was, thanks for dropping my old dad off last night. He says he'd love to get together with you all again, especially your mum, so would you like to bring her round here tonight for a drink in the garden? Would be fun. We can peer through the hedge and spy on Andrew's big woman.'

Miranda thought for a moment. 'It would be good, yes . . . but hey, as the weather's so brilliant and there are so many of us, why don't you bring him and Lola up here for supper? I could barbecue something down by the pool.'

'Ha – that used to be Dad's job. Do you remember him wielding a fish-slice and prodding at meat as though it was still half alive and likely to bite him?' Jessica laughed. 'OK, that would be great, thanks. What time? Sevenish, while it's still warm out?'

'Seven's fine.' Miranda had a sudden thought. 'And if it goes well with Andrew and you don't completely scare him off, why not invite him and his lot up here too?'

'Are you serious?'

Miranda wondered for a second if perhaps she was being a bit rash, taking on catering for so many, but then it could be fun for the younger ones and three more guests wouldn't be any trouble – assuming it was only three and he hadn't brought down a party of extras. She'd trust Jess on that – if she saw there was going to be a numbers problem she'd be tactful and it would just be drinks. The table down by the pool was massive and simple outdoor food was a lot easier to manage for large numbers than fancy kitchen cooking. After all, nobody expected a gourmet event from a barbecue. 'Yes, why not? I'm only here for a few weeks – might as well make the most of it. And the son, if that's what he is, might enjoy meeting up with our kids. It'll be us all over again, a generation on.'

'Hell yes, how mad is that? OK, you're on! What shall I bring? A couple of salads or something?'

'Excellent. I'll get things that can go on skewers because that's really easy, and I'll marinade them first in something or other. Prawns and chicken and stuff. Or is Lola vegetarian?'

'No. Well she wasn't yesterday, anyway. Today, who knows?'

It would mean another trip to that damn shop, Miranda realized as she locked up the house. She only hoped that if she put on sunglasses and a hat, scary Cheryl wouldn't recognize her.

*

Silva knew she was lucky in that unlike so many at her school, who were always finding bits of themselves to complain about, she quite liked her body and didn't at all mind being seen in her bikini, the bottom part of which was even smaller than the stupid childish knickers the surf-god boy had copped a look at in the changing room. She tried not to think about that little episode as it made her insides go tight with embarrassment. Ridiculous to feel like that, she knew. They were only *pants*. But in a bikini, on a beach, you'd kind of given permission for people to see you. Surprising someone at a private moment in a curtained cubicle was just plain *rude*. That blond boy would probably be out there among the surfers currently bobbing like seals on the wave break out in the bay. She wondered if he'd remember her if she saw him in the sea. Probably not. She wasn't sure if she minded that or not. Why was life so confusing? Did you get it all sorted by eighteen? Harriet was twenty-eight and a like *totes* mess so maybe not.

The family settled high up the beach, making a camp on the lower slopes of the soft dunes. Clare had stridden ahead, surveyed the beach and chosen the spot, keen on its access to the café. There was also a surf shack close by where the lifeguards had their base, with a board outside advertising wetsuit hire and lessons.

'Do you two want to learn how to surf?' Miranda

asked Silva and Bo, who had pitched their beach mats at a bit of a distance from the rest of them. She could understand that. She did the same at their age.

'Maybe,' Bo said, looking back at the rail of wetsuits for rent that were hanging from a rail outside the surf shack. 'I mean, how hard can it be? It's only like skateboarding but on water.'

'Bloody hard,' Harriet told him. 'Years of practice is what you need just to be able to stand up on a board.'

'Don't put him off.' Clare looked up from her book, 'The young don't get nearly enough exercise. It'll do him good. '

Bo huffed a bit and plugged his headphones in, lay down on his mat and closed his eyes. He was still wearing a T-shirt and long baggy shorts and had a fringy scarf round his neck. The bodyboard lay beside him on the sand and didn't look as though it was going to be getting wet any time soon.

'Nice one, Harrie,' Miranda murmured to her sister. 'It'll give him something to do. And it's not as if he and his mates haven't spent years hurtling down the streets on skateboards. It's what counts for serious sporting activity in the smarter suburbs. That and trying to blag cans of Stella from the corner shop.'

'I'll do surfing,' Silva said. 'I'll be good at it.'

'OK, I'll pay for the lessons, for both of you. You just go and book it. And have you got plenty of high-factor sun cream on, Silva? Do you want me to do your back?'

'Got loads on, Mum. Like, chill. If I spray on any more I'll look like a fish finger if I get sand on me.' Silva turned over on to her front and settled to sunbathe with one arm round the pink crocodile.

Miranda looked round at them all, feeling like a mother hen checking on her chicks. Harriet had made a kind of nest in the sand and was cosied into it, reading her Kindle. She was wearing a little pink hat and white-framed sunglasses and her already (fake?) tanned body was glistening with factor 30. So she's relaxed at last, Miranda thought, with the same feeling of relief she remembered from the long nights of trying to get her babies off to sleep. Even Clare looked peaceful, her brow unfurrowed and her eyes not full of ready tears, leaning against a rock with the crossword from the day before, looking out to sea. Miranda wanted to ask her about the ashes and when (and how) they were going to deal with them, but yet again this didn't seem to be the moment. You couldn't exactly start discussing something so potentially painful when everyone was chilling on a beach full of happy people relishing the sun. It would completely wreck the mood and she'd be the one who copped the blame.

She tried to settle to reading her book but kept being distracted by thoughts of Steve. In theory, it was ridiculous to be completely fine about seeing Andrew again after all these years and yet to feel terrified of running into Steve. But of course it was different. She hadn't had sex with Andrew. She hadn't been brutally callous about chucking him, hadn't laughed in his face when he'd hoped she was serious about him, or treated him like some holiday flirtation she'd used when she was bored and he was convenient and then discarded without a backward glance once her usual friends showed up. She wasn't proud of herself for any of that. What a spoilt, snobby little horror she must have been at sixteen. And he'd been a very lovely boy. What could have been more romantic than rowing her to moonlit beaches with a bottle of wine and peaches from his family's tree? She hoped he'd found someone thoroughly lovely and forgotten all about her. And the village might be small but he was working and hardly likely to be trailing around it with the holidaymakers. With luck, she wouldn't bump into him again, but the thought that he *could* be round any corner, that she could come face to face with him at almost any time in the shop or the pub, upped her heart rate from sheer apprehension. She distracted herself by resorting to thinking about work, to the date in her diary three weeks from now when she'd be meeting a team from a Europe-wide chain of upmarket boutique hotels who wanted an exclusive range of designs for fabrics for blinds and cushion covers. The designs and some samples were ready with a range of colour-ways; spread-sheets with all the costings were done and in theory it was a done deal. It was just a matter of whether the buyers liked the final details. It could only take one silly intern making a flippant comment, saying the bluebell pattern looked like seahorses or something equally irrelevant and the whole thing might collapse. No pressure then. No matter that this project made the difference between whether she had a major chunk of income for the next few years or not. No, no pressure at all.

It was barely half an hour later that Harriet became bored and fidgety, taking off her hat and then fussing with her wind-blown hair.

'It's a bit cold when the breeze strikes up,' she grumbled. 'I think I'll go back to the house and sit by the pool. I haven't got the newspapers yet, either. I need to go to the shop before they sell out.'

'You can't wait till after we've all had some lunch? I thought we'd get some hot dogs or something from the café,' Clare said. 'I'm hoping they do crab sandwiches too. They always used to.' She squinted across to the board outside the café but the writing was all curly and fancy and couldn't be easily read from a distance.

Harriet shuddered. 'Sorry, Mum. That would be a total carb overload for me. I just couldn't. Tell you what, though, I could get a load of food for tonight. Didn't you say you wanted prawns, Miranda? I could get them at the village shop, and I'll marinade some chicken as well. Have you got any couscous? That would be easy, with lemon and loads of coriander and parsley. I saw some herbs growing in pots on the terrace up by the kitchen. The house owners will never know if we use them.'

'That would be great. Thanks, Harriet,' Miranda said, feeling almost tearfully grateful for the unexpected offer of help. 'And,' she added, wondering if she should even mention it, 'I do hope there's nothing in the papers, Harrie. Whatever Pablo did, it's not your fault.'

'Oh, I expect they'll find *something*.' Harriet sighed and collected her belongings together, crammed her hat back on and hid her eyes behind her sunglasses again. 'When both members of the couple are well known, they like to spin it out. I should know. Or at least, I should *have* known.' She gave Miranda a sad little half-smile, waved to the rest of them and started walking back up the beach, her head well down.

'She'll walk into someone, staring at the ground like that,' Clare said, watching her middle child going up the village path on espadrilles that had a serious heel. 'Is she actually properly famous? I've been so out of touch with things the last year or so, I haven't a clue about my own daughter's career. I'll make more effort from now on.'

'She co-presents something regional, a middle of the afternoon TV show about local interest things, but I expect she's hoping for a sofa spot on a national breakfast show any time soon,' Miranda told her. 'But I don't think she's troubled *Heat* magazine yet. Or at least she hadn't till the footballer. I'll ask her tonight about the job thing. Right now, I just feel sorry for her. I don't think she's only upset about losing Pablo.'

'I'm sorry for her too. But she needs to keep it in perspective. She's only twenty-eight – she's got years to meet someone who's right for her. She mustn't let this one rotten apple poison her life,' Clare said, flipping over the page in her book rather forcefully. Miranda took a deep, calming breath. Competitive misery between Clare and Harriet – was that going to be the pattern from now on? Please not.

Silva, on her raffia beach mat, had drifted sleepily into a reverie in which the inflatable crocodile was wearing a black swimsuit, the regulation sort they had for swimming at school. She shifted her head slightly and actually found herself opening an eye to check the big plastic toy in case it wasn't actually a dream. A shadow fell across her face and she squinted up at her brother.

'Silv? You coming to the shack with me to book the lessons?' Bo pulled his headphones out of his ears and looked out to sea where the surfers were still lying on their boards. The sea was fairly calm just then, not giving enough waves for good rides. He looked down at Silva and laughed. 'Oh my *God*! You should see your back and your legs! Didn't you put like *any* stuff on you?'

'Course I did. I sprayed it everywhere. Like, y'know,

where I could reach. Maybe I missed a teeny bit?' Silva tried to squint round and shrieked at the sight of her thighs. 'Nooo! I look like someone's painted me bright red!' she squealed, pulling a towel over herself and hiding under it.

'Yeah, and you've got a white stripe down your back where your hair was lying.' Bo wasn't helping, almost doubled over with laughter.

'I need to get in the sea. I'm so hot.' She fanned her face with her hand and scrambled to her feet.

'In the actual freezing sea? Wow, that'll sting!' Bo teased cheerily. 'Good luck with that.'

'Shut *up*, bruv!' Silva's face was thunderous as she picked up the crocodile and ran down to the sea's edge, pounding as fast as she could past families camped behind wind-breaks and children playing beach cricket so she didn't have to risk seeing people pointing at her scarlet and white striped body and laughing at her.

Annoyingly, Bo had been completely right. The first splashes on her feet and ankles told her the sea was close to icy. She felt a big stab of envy for Willow in Florida who would almost definitely be lying *right now* on a big stylish surfboard, trailing her hand in warm water, with turtles floating about in the clear blue below her. No wonder almost everyone in the sea here was wearing a full-on wetsuit; only the stupid holiday crowd had to brave the chill in just swimwear and *skin*. A big wave washed over her legs and Silva caught her breath.

But if she didn't want to hear Bo jeering 'Told you so' she had to get right into the sea so she pushed the crocodile in front of her and launched herself at it, gasping as another wave swooshed right over it and soaked her scorched thighs.

The crocodile wasn't easy to manoeuvre. Ahead of her Silva could see very small children being helped by parents to ride on blow-up lilos and sharks and dolphins and getting giddy with laughter, whereas here she was looking hopeless and inelegant trying to get on top of the crocodile and floundering around. The idea had been to lie on it, paddle out a little way and then ride back on the soft waves that broke on the shore, but it wasn't that easy. At last, she managed to grab the thing and push herself aboard and wallow for a bit on the water. She felt a sudden moment of panic, not knowing whether the tide was going out or coming in. Suppose she was washed out to sea, really fast? You read about people. There were stories every year where the lifeboat rescuers said how stupid someone had been, letting their child drift miles out on a beach toy. She could easily be out of her depth already and she turned to look back to see if the beach lifeguard had noticed her. The twisting movement dislodged her from the crocodile and she fell off into deep water and turned to swim back to the shore, furious with herself for being so shaken. When her feet hit the gritty seabed she staggered upright and breathed properly at last.

Ridiculous, she thought: she was a really good swimmer, always in the school team, with life-saving qualifications too. She'd have been fine; it was just English sea was so *wavy*. Now she'd lost the crocodile and her mum would be cross because it belonged with the house, not to her. She stood for a while, squinting out at the sparkling sea, wondering where the stupid toy had gone.

'Hey, don't forget your little friend.' A boy's voice beside her sounded teasing. A surfer stood beside her, his arm round the upright crocodile as if it were a human he could lean on. 'Oh, it's you!' he said. 'Hello Kitty!' He looked down at her bottom and grinned.

Oh lordy, the pants boy from the shop. And here she was all red-stripy and shaken and her hair all seawater mussed-up. Great.

'Say thank you nicely to me for rescuing your mate here,' he said.

'Thank you,' she muttered, staring at her feet and holding out her hand for the crocodile.

'Is that it?' he asked, pulling the croc back against him. 'Isn't my heroism worth a snog?'

'*What?*' Silva's quick brain thought two things: first that she should tell him she was actually only, like, thirteen but second that she couldn't wait to tell Willow. How impressed would *she* be? At some point this holiday, she'd have to get a photo.

'Only joking,' he said, which disappointed her. 'Here's

your pet. You need a lead for him, like we have for the boards.'

'Yeah. Like, right.' Leads? As for dogs? Then she noticed his surfboard lying on the sand just ahead of her, with a curly blue cable like old-fashioned telephone wire. 'What do you tie it to?' she asked, and wondered, as he cracked up laughing, what she'd said that was so funny.

Eventually he stopped laughing. 'Only my ankle,' he said. 'But respect for having a great imagination. What's your name? Or is it really Kitty?'

'Silva.'

'Right. Silver. Like gold.'

'No. Silva as in trees and stuff. Wood. Latin.' She shrugged, 'Y'know, like *parents*.' They were walking up the beach now and Silva hoped Bo wasn't watching. She'd never hear the end of it.

'I'm Jules,' the boy said.

'Like diamonds?'

'Oh, you're a sharp one, aren't you? My kind of girl.' He laughed, reached out and tugged the end of her wet hair, then ran off back to the sea. She stood and watched for a while as he plunged into the water on his board and started paddling strongly out across the shallows to join the others waiting for the perfect break. *My kind of girl*. Nice.

'Oh, she's going to be so sore,' Miranda said as she

watched Silva hurtle down the beach. 'I should have checked her properly, not just asked. I should have known she was only telling a half-truth.'

'She'll be fourteen in a week or so,' Clare reminded her. 'She can take a bit of responsibility for herself.'

'But sunburn's so dangerous. And this cool breeze disguises the sun's strength. I'm never this careless when we're abroad. You forget the UK can be just as bad.'

'She'll be all right in a day or so. It'll go brown and she'll look very pretty. You can't do anything about it now apart from slap on the after-sun so there's no point fussing.' Clare put her hand up to shade her eyes as she looked out at the sea. 'Sorry. That sounded a bit bossy.'

'It's fine. And, Mum, while it's just you and me here . . . When do you want to do the thing with . . . you know the thing . . .'

'Jack's ashes.' Clare frowned. 'You can say it, you know.'

'Right.' Miranda took a deep breath. 'OK, so tell me what you've got in mind.'

'I've got nothing in my mind at all, to be honest. I thought that when I got here it would be obvious what we'd do. I thought we'd just hire a boat and go out at sunset and scatter him on the calm evening water and it would all be easy.'

Miranda waited for her to go on but Clare seemed to have run out of steam. 'Well . . . isn't it easy? We could rent a little boat, couldn't we, and just do exactly that?'

'Well, no. It's not that simple. The boatyard have rules now. You have to have a powerboat licence, otherwise you have to get someone who's qualified to take you out. The lifeboat people will take you out and do it if you give them a donation, but I don't want to do that, not with a stranger. It would be . . . you know, *wrong*. Intrusive.' Clare sniffed and reached into her bag for tissues. 'We'll have to think of something else. But it won't be what he asked for.'

'How about off the beach?'

'Oh Lord no, definitely not off the beach! It has to be out in the middle of the estuary, in proper deep water. I don't want him floating about on the shoreline with the seaweed and stuff. When the tide goes out and leaves hunks of fishing twine and plastic bottles and rubbish, I don't want to be imagining he's stuck there among it all.' Clare laughed at the idea of it. 'He'd hate that. We'll have to ask around, find someone who's got a boat big enough for us all. The place is full of them – it shouldn't be hard.' She looked at Miranda, still a bit blurry-eyed, and Miranda had a flashback to the little private funeral she and Jessica had conducted one warm evening on their favourite beach. Two clam shells had been taped together with very little inside to show for a tiny life. Harriet and Amy had thought it a great game, like when they'd buried their pet hamster at home. Andrew had tagged along and wondered what they were doing. They'd told him – and the little girls – it was a baby bird. He probably wouldn't remember anything about it now but Miranda would never forget.

'I'll ask around,' she promised her mother. 'It'll be fine.'

EIGHT

When Miranda got back from the beach, Harriet was stretched out topless on a lounger by the pool looking like a movie star waiting to be photographed. She had what looked like a glass of Pimm's on the table beside her and was keeping her face in the shade of the huge cream canvas umbrella. She'd been swimming and drops of water sparkled like crystals on her perfect skin.

'You look incredibly glam,' Miranda told her, plonking herself on the next lounger. Miranda, by contrast, was hot and sweaty from trudging up the steep lane and felt worn out and suddenly a lot older than her years.

'I don't feel glam. My hair is minging and my period is due.' She prodded her perfectly flat golden stomach. 'Look at this: I'm disgusting and bloated.'

Miranda laughed. 'Oh, will you listen to yourself. Mum once told me – when I was about your age and grumbling about stretch marks from the babies – that one day I'd look back and really wish I looked that good again. Just look in the mirror, Harrie, and smile at yourself, for heaven's sake. You are gorgeous.'

'Christ, have you been at the hippy crystals again? Those two years in Totnes really rubbed off on you, didn't they? Totnes – where shoplifters are warned that thieving will give them bad karma and it's the law that every window has to have a dreamcatcher.'

'So you loved it, then. Obviously,' Miranda said, kicking off her flip-flops and going to sit on the pool steps. She dangled her feet in the cool water, glad to rinse off the sticky salt from the beach, which was making her ankles itch.

'It was all right, actually,' Harriet conceded. 'I suppose pretty much anywhere's OK if you feel, you know, OK. And anyway, me and Amy were still too small to notice where we were really.' She sat up and took off her sunglasses. 'I got the food,' she said, 'Lots of it. I couldn't carry it all, just the papers, the salad, and the chicken, which is marinating right now. It's all in the fridge.'

'Brilliant. Thanks for that.' Miranda flung her dress across to a lounger and jumped into the pool. 'Oh – this is heaven!' she said, turning on her back and letting her hair get properly wet. 'What was it you didn't get?'

'Prawns. The man is bringing them later.'

'Man?'

'The girl in the shop didn't have enough prawns so she said the man would bring them.' Harriet stood up and yawned. 'They'll be here, she promised. Before six, she said. I didn't like her and I wanted to get out of the shop quickly with the papers.'

'Why's that?' Miranda was only half concentrating. It definitely wouldn't be Steve with the prawns. No. It would be some kid that Cheryl sent along, just dropping off the box. It wouldn't be Steve. After all, pretty much exactly half the population of the entire village fitted the description of 'the man'.

'She recognized me, Manda. I could tell. She looked at me in a funny way. You get to sense these things. And I had to give her my name and where I was staying for the address for the delivery. So I gave her your name, but she looked at me like, *yeah right.*'

'Oh, I'm sure it doesn't matter.'

'Are you? Suppose she tells the press? The village could be swarming with paps by the morning.' Harriet ran her fingers through her long streaky hair and picked up her bikini top, putting it back on and staring at the shrubbery as if she expected to catch sunlight flashing on a camera lens. From the way she was holding in the absolutely not-bloated stomach and sticking out her front, Miranda could tell that on the sly Harriet might not object to the attention that much, especially if a press photo showed her from a tasty angle.

'So is there any more footballer gossip?' she asked, rolling over and over in the gorgeously clear water.

Harriet pouted and picked up her bag. 'Not a thing. Anyone would think it wasn't important.'

Miranda looked at her. 'But . . . it isn't really, is it?' Oh Lord, she thought, did that sound callous? But surely Harriet realized she was well rid of Pablo. Unfaithful and a habitual coke-head? Could that really be something anyone would want?

'Oh, you have no idea!' Harriet flounced up the first few steps to the terrace, then turned back, 'You do realize I have nowhere to live now? And not only that . . .' She stopped abruptly. 'I'm off for a shower. I'll see you later.'

'Not only what, Harriet?' Miranda called after her. Harriet just kept on walking. No job, was Miranda's best (and also worst) guess. If only she would just *tell*.

So. Eliot Lynch was coming to what used to be his own house for supper. It all felt a bit time-warpish and unreal. Clare sat on the bed and looked at herself in the long mirror that hung inside the wardrobe door. Jess had said he remembered them all well. But she wondered if, in his head over the years, they'd become just the collective Miller family, one amalgam, like a lot of separate ice-cream scoops that had been half melted and then refrozen into one barely distinguishable block, or would he really remember her most of all? Twice he'd kissed her, with passion and enthusiasm – the first time against a gnarly old oak tree when they were all out on a chilly Easter walk – and thrilled her madly. Strangely, at the time she'd felt no guilt and she didn't feel any now in retrospect, even though she was picking at her conscience as if it were an old scab to see if it was at all active. Nothing. In fact she'd been feeling numb about everything, and accepted that was the way it was to be from Jack's death onwards. And yet now here she was wondering if she maybe would feel something again one day. That was new – the idea of seeing Eliot again brought her the closest to some kind of excitement she'd felt for ages. A few weeks ago she didn't even feel curious about the possibility of any kind of emotion. There was no future in her head at all. She could see nothing but the day-to-day plod of pointless living without her life partner alongside her. For the first time it occurred to her that Eliot might simply have been a serial snogger and spent all his grown-up life taking chances for minor grapplings with unlikely, off-limits women. Most likely he considered it merely a generous gesture, the handing out of the odd near-innocent frisson to those he thought might be in need of it. Not a good thought, and she banished it from her head. No one likes to think they're nothing special, even if the special is only for a moment. But either way, she was looking forward to seeing him. It would be . . . fun.

She stood up and looked at her reflection, checking out what Eliot would see that evening. She'd been plumpish, mother-shaped and soft-bodied twenty years ago, fighting the hopeless war on cellulite with pointless creams and body brushes. Grief had made her thinner now and sharper-edged, and her clothes hung off her. When was a woman ever happy with the way she looked? It would be interesting to see what twenty years had made of Eliot, who must be pretty ancient by now. Some men flab out and become mostly stomach. Eliot had been well on the way to that, though he'd been surprisingly lively and agile at the same time, leaping on and off boats, sailing more than competently with Milo and Jess. Other men, though, lose volume and muscle and become stunted and bony. Was it also progress that she hoped this hadn't happened to him? Who knew? She reached into the bottom of the wardrobe and stroked the urn of ashes, whispered a brief 'hello, darling' to Jack and then closed the door on them. Time to put on her black linen trousers, a strappy little vest top and her favourite drapy long cream cardigan and go down and help Miranda with the supper. It really wasn't fair to leave it all to her.

When Miranda walked into the kitchen it looked yet again – as if it had been ransacked by someone desperately searching for a massively valuable truffle. What was it with this family? It wasn't as if they'd been raised with a fleet of slaves in attendance. It was almost like having Dan on the premises again. Perhaps there was something about her that made those who lived with her think it was perfectly all right to be complete slobs. Helpful as it was that Harriet had managed to put together a tasty marinade for the chicken from white wine, oil, lemon and garlic, with thyme from the plants on the terrace, it was hard to see how she'd managed to muck up so many dishes, spoons and surfaces to make something that was essentially quite simple. Why was there sugar all over the worktop? What had she used that for? Why were there so many used tea bags in the sink when the pull-out bin was right alongside? A puddle of olive oil shimmered on the table with the pepper grinder fallen over and lying on its side in it. Squeezed-out lemon halves were in a heap by the sink and pips bobbed about on the murky waters of the washing up bowl. She almost shuddered at the thought of what it must be like in Harriet's flat. Or Harriet's *ex*-flat. Did she leave trails of grated cheese between the fridge and the table there too, as she had here? Maybe the footballer had kept staff to do the cooking and clearing up. Toby the cat was doing his best to help with the floor, licking up the spilled cheese eagerly and battling Miranda's attempts to shoosh him out of the way. She just hoped he wouldn't go upstairs now and be sick on one of the beds.

Time was getting on. Where were the prawns? Had Cheryl forgotten, or even 'forgotten'? She wanted to go up and have a quick shower and get changed but she seemed to be the only one around and couldn't risk missing the delivery in case 'the man' took them away again. She could hear water from Harriet's shower running down the drain outside so there was obviously no chance of getting her down to help with the mess, and the huge clock on the wall showed it was already close to six. People would be arriving before she knew it. Miranda clipped her damp hair roughly up on her head and set about making the place look less embarrassingly disgraceful. She didn't want Eliot and Jess to think she wasn't taking care of what used to be their house, even though they'd sold it years before and probably wouldn't even notice.

She shoved a piece of one of the squeezed lemons down the waste-disposal and switched it on, just for a moment breathing in the fresh scent of the fruit and feeling – a rare one this – like a properly competent cleaner. She switched the noisy gadget off and rinsed her fingers under the tap.

'Where do you want the prawns?' A male voice came from the terrace doors and Miranda jumped at the sound.

'Goodness, you startled me!' She turned round to greet her visitor and came face to face with Steve.

'Oh . . . hi. Um . . . Steve,' she said, rather pathetically.

'Hello, Miranda. I thought it was you when I saw you at the pub the other night,' he said, sounding depressingly as if she were the least welcome person who'd ever dared enter the village. No smile, just a cool, cool gaze.

He put the white polystyrene box of prawns on the table and backed away again towards the door.

'I see you've made yourselves at home, then,' he went on, raising his eyebrows at the mess by the sink that Miranda was still clearing.

'I think we're supposed to, aren't we?' Miranda replied, feeling a bit miffed at what sounded like criticism. Twenty years on and he was commenting on her *housekeeping*? How dare he? And how dare he look so damn gorgeous?

'Sure. Home from home, these rental places. I've seen worse. So how are you?' At last, a small shimmer of a smile.

'Well. I'm well. Thank you. How about you?' Miranda asked, feeling strangely trembly. She tried to tell herself not to be so silly but very swiftly through her mind went an uncontrollable flash of wondering: what if instead of looking as if he wanted to get the hell out of the place as fast as possible he took one step forward and kissed her right now? In fact, wouldn't the friendly thing to do be to give him a hug and a quick hello kiss herself? That's what she'd have done if, say, he'd been an old art college connection. But his grey eyes looked cold and wary. If she approached him she had the feeling he'd be hurtling down the terrace steps in a heartbeat.

'I'm fine,' he said, leaning a tanned arm against the doorframe. 'Thriving, I think they call it.'

'Still doing fish,' she said, cursing herself for stating the obvious.

He grinned, at last, the deep-tanned corners of his eyes crinkling like a fan. 'As you see,' he said, pointing at the prawns. 'Still here, still doing fish, as you call it. So you lot are all back in the village, then. Been a long time, hasn't it? Why are we graced with your presence again all of a sudden?'

'Well . . . it's mostly because . . .' she began, meaning to explain about Jack, but there was a flurry in the hallway and Harriet raced in, all freshly showered and prettied up in tiny denim shorts and a little turquoise top that made her tan shimmer. Most of her seemed to be gorgeous leg.

'Ooh, a nice man visitor!' she cooed. 'Sorry, am I interrupting something?'

'No!' Miranda and Steve both snapped at the same time. Miranda glared at her and she smirked.

'Ah, got it – you're the prawn man. Are you staying for supper? It's just a barbecue. One more wouldn't be a problem, would it, Manda? There's tons of food.'

'There is,' Miranda agreed and then rather recklessly said, 'And yes, please stay if you'd like to.'

'No thanks, I've got things to do. But nice of you to ask,' he said, now looking a lot less frosty. Well, what man wouldn't, faced with Harriet at her most luscious? Miranda was appalled that she was feeling a bit jealous. What did it matter that Steve was seeing her at her most dishevelled and messy? It was hardly as if he had any interest in her now. Nor she in him, of course. How long was guilt supposed to last? She had a massive urge to apologize to him for how she'd treated him all those years ago, but he'd probably think she was mad because he'd have long forgotten about her, and certainly long got over her. He must have had hundreds of girls like her, back in the day. Either way, any kind of real conversation couldn't happen here and now. Not with Harriet dancing around being in the way and – unmistakably – flirting as if it were her default setting.

'Aren't you going to introduce me, then?' Harriet said.

'Oh, er, yes. Harriet, this is Steve. Steve, this is my sister Harriet.'

They shook hands rather awkwardly and Miranda had the depressing sensation that she could well be witnessing the first encounter in Harriet's next doomed romance, or maybe not doomed. Her brain flew at breakneck speed through the scene where a beaming and triumphant Harriet showed her a diamond ring, asked her to be matron of honour and requested her help in choosing a wedding dress, to watching her sister walk up the aisle towards a radiant Steve and being handed the bridal bouquet of golden roses to hold during the vows. Mad.

'I remember you,' he was saying to Harriet, smiling at her. 'You were about nine, running around and playing in the creek. Or was that the other sister? I seem to remember there were two of you little girls.'

'Can I get you a drink, Steve? I've got beers and wine.' Miranda needed a glass of something herself. Maybe if they had an open bottle on the table between them they could talk for a few minutes, catch up a bit. If he wanted to, that is. Actually, he probably didn't, not with her. He only seemed animated when looking at Harriet.

'No thanks, Miranda, I've got some deliveries to do. In fact I'd better get going.'

'Oh, no, don't rush off!' Harriet put her hand on his arm. 'This is so funny! So we knew you back then? Wow!' Steve looked quickly at Miranda and she felt her face going warm. He remembered, all right. She wondered if he thought of her sometimes too. On that little beach, on the odd hot afternoon.

'I expect you knew lots of people,' Steve said, more to Miranda than Harriet.

'I didn't. Not at all,' she replied, feeling a bit cross that he seemed to be insinuating that she'd put herself about among the boys. Unless he didn't mean that at all. She didn't know what to think. Maybe she'd better just get on with skewering the prawns.

'Thanks for bringing these,' she said to him as she opened the box, 'it was really kind of you. I could have sent one of the children down for them.'

'Your children?' he asked.

'Yes. Two, boy and girl. And you?'

'None so far,' he said.

Clare came in from the terrace at that moment,

holding a big bunch of flat-leaved parsley. 'Miranda, I've picked almost all the parsley there was. I hope the owner won't mind. Oh – sorry, I didn't know we had a visitor.'

'It's OK, I was just leaving. And I'm sure the owner won't mind at all; the stuff keeps on growing however much you pick. I'll put in a word for you.'

'You know the owner, then?' Miranda asked. She'd been curious about who'd bought the house from the Lynch family and she'd been meaning to ask Jessica.

'I suppose you could say I don't know him that well,' he said, giving Miranda a sly-looking sideways smile, 'but a long time ago I slept with one of his girlfriends.'

And before Miranda could make sense of any of that and come up with a suitable reply, he'd gone.

'Strange young man,' Clare said, looking in a drawer for a sharp knife. 'What on earth was he talking about?'

Miranda took the slide out of her hair and let it fall round her face. It was one way of hiding the fact that she'd gone all confused.

'No idea, Mum,' she said, crossing her fingers to cancel what might, once she'd untangled what he said, be a lie. 'No idea at all.'

NINE

Silva didn't want to wear jeans but she didn't have much choice, not with her legs looking as if she'd been attacked by a spray gun full of red paint. No way could she let anyone see them. So – here was a fabulous warm evening with the sun still blazing on the pool terrace and she had to swelter in denim. It was that or her flowery maxi-dress, but that would look a bit too try-hard. That Lola would probably say something snide, like asking whose wedding she was on her way to be a bridesmaid at.

She'd put masses of after-sun on all the red skin but it was getting sore all the same, kind of crackly and itchy at the same time. She'd even let Harriet rub some freezing cold cream on her back, but only after she'd made her promise not to tell Miranda how bad it was. She hoped her skin wouldn't all peel off. If that happened you were back to the beginning but even more extra-delicate. She should have just got a fake tan like Willow had before she'd gone to Florida. Willow and her mum had gone to You're Gorgeous! and had full-on spray tan, mani-pedi and a max-wax. 'It's like the most agony *ever*,' Willow had said about the waxing after she'd told Silva in horrible detail just where on her body she'd been defoliated. 'And you have to keep doing it for the rest of like your actual *life*.' Something to look forward to then, Silva thought now as she plundered the drawer in which she kept her T-shirts in search of the perfect long pink one. She pulled it on and went into the bathroom to look at herself in the mirror and make sure that what she was looking at – now that she'd put on a bit of soft grey eyeshadow and enough mascara to make her eyelids droop – was not some *child*. She leaned far forward so her head was down by her knees and brushed her hair downwards so it flapped against her legs, then flicked it back again to max up the fluffiness. The result pleased her and she was aware, for a weird few moments that made her hold her breath, that this was one of those moments of big change. This time last year she'd been hardly any different from herself at eight, playing rounders on a French beach with her other aunt, Amy, and some random kids, giving no thought to anything but the here and now, not even considering that she might not always be a child: the future just didn't exist. But today she looked different. No longer a little girl – and it wasn't just that she was getting tall and was curvier. And it wasn't just for this evening either, not really. This was more a practice run for the rest of the holiday and then the rest of her life. One thing was clear. No way, next time she ran into him, was the Jules boy going to be thinking of her as the little Hello Kitty girl.

Miranda was surprised how twitchy she felt in the moments before Jess and the others were due to arrive. And Andrew and his family *were* coming. Jess had called and told Clare while Miranda was in the shower. She'd had a few moments of thinking she must have been mad to invite them all, but knew deep down that it would be fine. Gentle, shy Andrew could hardly have grown up to be a total monster and there was masses of food, as Harriet was one of life's generous over-caterers and had bought enough to feed half the village.

'You're faffing, Miranda. Surely you're not feeling nervous, are you, darling?' Clare asked as Miranda kept tweaking at things on the long wooden garden table beside the pool, moving glasses, straightening forks, counting plates, washing a big pebble to hold down the heap of paper napkins.

'Not nervous, not really. OK, maybe a tiny bit. It's fine being with Jess again – that's easy, and we were good mates years ago – but Andrew . . . he was quite odd in some ways. I wonder what he's like now? He might have gone in for extreme politics or joined a religious sect for all I know. Could be really, y'know, interesting, but there is the outside chance it won't be interesting in a good way.'

'Well, I always liked him, and he's probably just as lovely as he always was,' Clare said, 'And I'm sure he'll be perfectly normal. At the worst he might be a bit dull, but in the grand scheme of things we can put up with more or less anything in life for a few hours, so you've no need to fret about it.'

'I'm not fretting. It's fine.' Miranda felt a bit sulky. Was her mother telling her off? How old did you have to be before *that* stopped happening? Clare seemed quite twitchy herself, actually, and was already halfway down a glass of red wine. Miranda poured herself some Pinot Grigio, deciding a sharpener might be a relaxing thing and would stop her thinking about that surprisingly wicked smile Steve had given her as he left. Before that moment he'd been almost hostile. Maybe it was the sight of the gorgeous Harriet that had cheered him up. She topped up the wine with fizzy water as a sense of responsibility kicked in. It would be hugely bad manners to drink too fast and end up slurring over her guests. The thing he'd said had puzzled her too. Working it out, it seemed to mean he was actually the owner of the house. How bizarre was that? Or did he mean something else completely? She'd have to find out. Asking him was the obvious route to information, but the chances were he wouldn't want to see her again, let alone have a proper conversation with her.

'Mum?' Silva was calling down the terrace steps. 'There are people coming up the lane. Looks like loads of them.'

'Thanks, Silva. And can you give your brother a shout? He's probably in front of the telly or on my computer or something. I think he's only really happy when he's completely still.'

'Will do.' Silva ran in through the kitchen doors, shouting for Bo.

'Did you notice? Silva's looking different. Older, suddenly,' Clare commented, staring up at the now-empty terrace. 'She's got make-up on and her hair is all shooshy. She's growing up.' She sounded almost surprised.

'She's all right. She's just making a bit of an effort, that's all. And I can remember that early teenage stage. You're neither one thing nor the other. I expect she's just trying to keep up with Lola.'

'All the same, she's not usually one for make-up, is she? And thirteen?'

Miranda gave the hot barbecue coals a cross prodding. 'Mum, it's her choice and I'm not going to pick fights with her over things that don't really matter. I'm saving that for later, like making sure she never gets into a dodgy minicab and so on. It's not as if she's plastered in the stuff. All her friends wear it – she can't help being the youngest in her year group and feeling the need to keep up. Anyway, hey look, they've arrived.'

And there, suddenly as if twenty years hadn't passed, were Eliot, Jessica and Andrew, along with Lola plus the large woman Jess had presumed was Andrew's wife and a tallish sliver of a boy who was the image of the younger Andrew but with longer and floppier hair than either Andrew's mother or the quasi-military powers-that-be at his old boarding school had ever allowed him to have. Miranda waited as Andrew loped towards her and then reached out to hug him. He seemed a bit bewildered by this and was tentative about where to put his hands as she kissed him on each cheek, so he held them out to the side as if surrendering to a gunman in a bad Western movie.

'Andrew, you look *exactly* the same as you did all those summers ago!' she said, stepping back to get a proper look. He seemed taller than she remembered. He must have shot up by a few more fast inches between being seventeen and fully adult. He still looked as if his mother dressed him, too, as he was wearing a navy blazer with brass buttons, the sort his own father had worn, and she guessed it was more M&S than Paul Smith.

'You look . . . um . . . just like *you*,' he managed to say at last, smiling shyly and showing the perfect teeth that had taken eighteen months of painful brace-wearing to achieve. 'And this is . . .' He ushered the boy forward but the woman with them stepped in front and got in first, holding out a plump hand to Miranda.

'I'm Geraldine. Please don't call me Gerry,' she said, smiling but clearly not joking. She had the over-posh voice of a headmistress who had once met and much admired a fierce duchess. 'So kind of you to have us all here like this. And you on holiday as well. It looks as though it's been lot of work for you.' She sniffed at the air and frowned. 'Of course, barbecues aren't ideal. Shockingly carcinogenic; did you know that? They should be made illegal if you want my opinion.' She was peering past Miranda to where the food was set up ready to cook and the salads were out on the long table, still under cling-film to keep the bugs off. Her eyes narrowed as she gazed. What was she doing, Miranda wondered. Calculating portion sizes from across the pool?

'Not such hard work really; it's just simple stuff,' Miranda said, deciding she'd avoid the issue of barbecue safety. 'When we came back to the village I never imagined for a minute I'd find old friends here. It's all pretty exciting. Now – drinks? Can I get you some wine? And I'll introduce you to my crew.'

'I'll sort some drinks for everyone,' Harriet volunteered, steering the teenagers in the direction of the table and telling them in a bossy aunt voice not even to think about alcohol. Lola was scowling at this but moving close to Bo. Andrew was gazing at Harriet and her long brown legs in a wide-eyed way Miranda recognized from years before. She caught Jess's eye and they both giggled, remembering.

Luckily the young ones seemed already to be circling in that unsure way animals do before deciding whether they can trust each other. They'd find something to say eventually, and as Harriet handed out Cokes they started to look a bit more comfortable. Freddie, son of Andrew, was eyeing Silva and looking as if there was something he desperately wanted to say. Miranda hoped he'd find the words soon, as he looked as if he might collapse from shyness. Eventually she overheard him blurt out, 'You were in that shop.'

Silva said, 'Yeah. I remember.' Then both of them stared at the pool and went embarrassed and silent. All would be well, Miranda thought as she put bowls of bread on the table, all would be well in time.

Geraldine drifted across to have a closer look at the food while Andrew was meeting Harriet, Bo and Silva. She didn't seem, Miranda thought, interested in any of the humans.

'I hope there are no nuts in the salads,' Geraldine barked. She picked up a fork, peeled back a piece of cling-film and prodded at Harriet's couscous. 'Freddie reacts to nuts.'

'No I don't,' he grunted, going pink.

'You do.'

'Once. I choked on a peanut. Own fault. Not an allergy. And it was once,' he said to Bo, who nodded sympathetically.

'Shall I get you a plate?' Harriet asked Geraldine, looking miffed at having her cuisine questioned.

'Not yet. But you'll understand I did have to check.'

'You only have to ask,' Clare told her.

Miranda poked at the barbecue coals again to see if they were hot enough. She hadn't planned to start cooking immediately because she wanted them all to take time to catch up and get to know each other a bit. Mingling, circulating, all the words that she associated with the kind of very grown-up parties her parents' generation had had, not the more casual suppers she and her own friends back home liked. Now she thought it seemed best to get it all under way. With plenty of food and drink on the go, perhaps they'd loosen up a bit, especially the teen boys who were doing that half-hunched thing with hands in pockets and shoulders rounded as if trying to protect their bodies.

'You OK with this?' Jess half-whispered. 'What do you think of the terrifying Geraldine?'

'Terrifying's about right. I thought she was going to plunge a fat fist into Harrie's salad. Why? And what's she doing with poor Andrew? How did that ever happen? She embarrassed that sweet boy!'

'She's not doing a lot, that I found out this afternoon. They aren't married or even together; they just somehow produced Freddie. My guess is it was an accident, possibly even a one-off. Or one-*orf* as Geraldine would say.'

'I just can't imagine . . .'

'I know. And I'm trying really, really hard not to.'

They laughed. Miranda gave Jess a quick hug. 'I'm so glad you're here. I thought so much about you and us all before we came down here. Now it seems kind of *meant*.'

'Have you seen Steve?' Jess asked, giving her a beady look.

'Um – briefly. He brought the prawns up from the shop. He looks, y'know, quite good. He looks very well, I mean.'

'You've gone pink.'

'I so have *not*. It's the sun,' Miranda said. 'We were only kids at the time, don't forget. Just a long-ago holiday fling. Come on, you can help me with the barbie. Let's get these people fed. Bo, could you light the citrus candles, please? They'll fend off the mosquitoes.' She should probably have bought dozens of them. One tiny bite and Geraldine would probably be round accusing her of giving her malaria.

'I like your hair. Suits you all fluffed up.' A compliment was about the last thing Silva expected to hear from Lola and she looked at her for a moment, half expecting there to be a 'but' to follow.

'Thanks,' she said after a few moments, realizing that Lola seemed to mean it.

'Which shop did you see Freddie in?' Lola went on. 'I heard him say earlier that he'd seen you.'

'Across at St Piran. The surf place. He was in there with his dad.' She immediately felt tense at the thought of Jules whipping the changing room curtain back. At the risk of being teased ever after, she told Lola about it, laughing about being caught in her Hello Kitty knickers.

'That'll be why Freddie keeps looking at you. He's seeing through your clothes to your underwear, in hope. Oh, and the Jules boy, I know him. He fancies himself more than he fancies anyone else so I wouldn't bother having any ideas about him.'

Silva laughed. 'I don't think about him at all,' she said, crossing her fingers in case the god of teenage lies sent her a thunderbolt.

'Good. You're way too young anyway,' Lola said, turning her attention to her food. Silva chewed on a piece of garlic bread and wondered if she'd been warned off. If so, she felt quite flattered that Lola, who must be about fifteen, would think Silva was potential competition at two whole years younger.

'I was sorry to hear about Jack,' Eliot said to Clare a bit later. He was sitting next to her at the grown-ups' end of the long table.

'Thank you,' Clare said, then added, 'Sorry, I always think that sounds such a ridiculous response. I don't know why people always say "thank you" when someone says they're sorry about a death. I mean, what are they being thankful for?'

Eliot smiled. 'Sure, you know, it's just a tradition, isn't it? The ritual of acknowledging the passing. And besides, I *am* sorry he's gone. He was a top bloke. I liked him. I would have liked to see him here again.'

'Ah, but if he was still alive we wouldn't be here. We've come back to . . .' She hesitated and took a deep breath, determined not to get all tearful here at the table and embarrass herself and Eliot. 'We came to scatter his ashes on the sea. He loved it here, and that was what he wanted. I think he couldn't quite bear to come back once we'd sold the cottage, even though that had been his idea in the first place.'

To her surprise, beneath the table Eliot took her hand and squeezed it tight. 'So that's why you're here in my old house,' he said, looking dolefully at her. 'And there was me thinking you'd come to seek me out after all this time.'

'Well *you're* in *my* house!' she said, laughing at his face full of pretend disappointment and feeling grateful to him for lifting her mood. 'And I had no idea you'd be here. Though . . .' and she squeezed his hand in return, 'I am glad you are. You're looking in great nick.'

'Better than you expected, you mean!' he chuckled. 'Don't be shy of saying it, now. It's the truth. And I look better than I deserve considering I was drinking myself to the grave. I cut the whiskey. There was one episode too far when I fell down the steps getting off a plane in Dublin.'

'But you haven't given up drinking completely,' she said, watching as he picked up his wine glass.

'No. Just the amber glory. I stopped it before it stopped me. I had my lifetime's allocation all in a few short years, but it's over. I like a glass or two of wine, the odd beer, and I don't smoke any more. Unlike some.' He nodded across the table to where Geraldine was pulling a pack of cigarettes and a lighter out of her bag. She put them on the table and looked around.

'Freddie – *not* the bread!' she called along to the far end where he and the other young ones were sitting together. 'You know how you bloat!'

To their credit, none of his companions so much as sniggered. Silva even gave Geraldine one of her moodiest glares.

'Hey, give him a break!' Jess said. 'It's only a bit of garlic bread. How much can it hurt? He can't be allergic or he wouldn't touch it, would he?'

'I do *know* my son,' Geraldine told her firmly. 'And it's just as well I'm here. I knew I wouldn't be able to trust Andrew to have him to stay here on his own as he wanted. It's a bit of an experiment and *not* one that's likely to work if he doesn't keep a closer eye on the boy.'

'How old is he?' Harriet asked.

'How old?' She looked across at Andrew, who looked alarmed. 'About thirty-seven, I think. Why do you ask? I doubt he's *your* type.' She looked Harriet up and down with disapproval.

Harriet giggled. 'I meant Freddie.'

'Oh, he's nearly sixteen. A dangerous age for a boy. If they're going to drift to the bad, that'll be the age they start. You have to keep a *very close eye*. By which I mean . . .' she gave a stern look down to the far end of the table where Bo was using his fingers to feed a prawn into Lola's mouth, which was prettily upturned like a kitten accepting a treat, 'you have to keep a very close eye on *who they mix with*.' She picked up her cigarettes and lighter and said to Miranda, 'Do excuse me. I'll just go and find the facilities.'

'Through the top terrace doors, into the hallway and behind the stairs,' Miranda called after her. Geraldine didn't reply and Miranda guessed she'd prefer not to have been told, so she could have a good nosy around the house.

'I hardly dare ask this, Andrew,' Miranda turned to him, 'but I just wondered about your parents. Are they . . . all right?'

'Depends what you call all right,' he said, looking pensive. 'Mum got into computers down at the library and went off to live with someone she'd found online that she used to know at school. Dad's well enough, still mad on golf, but he's joined a sort of holiday club and keeps going off to Spain for months at a time with a load of old women who fuss over him.'

'Wow! Go Celia! Who'd have seen that one coming?' Eliot, across from them, was chuckling delightedly.

'So what's he like, this bloke she's shacked up with?'

'He's a woman actually,' Andrew said. 'Quite nice. She rides a Harley-Davidson and she's got every single Elvis record *ever*.'

'So you're OK about that?' Clare asked. 'That's good.' She tried to picture prim Celia, who must be at least seventy-five now, on the back of a Harley, wearing biker leathers. Celia had collected china cats, always wore Jaeger and would faint if anyone swore in her hearing. Clare, failing quite a lot with the imagined transformation, extended her vision to one of Celia and her partner pulling up at the Ace Café on the North Circular for strong tea and a full-on fry-up breakfast, but it was barely possible. Celia had been a scones (pronounced to rhyme with stones) and crustless cucumber sandwich woman through and through.

'Oh, yes. But they want to sell the cottage here, which is why I'm down. I need to see what the local market is like, get a feel for the prices at ground level.' He blushed. 'It's what I do, you see. Estate agent.'

Geraldine returned from the loo and stamped across the terrace towards the table. 'I see you've got a microwave in that kitchen,' she announced. 'I wouldn't have one if you paid me. It's like having a nuclear waste dump in your home.' She settled herself at the table and lit a cigarette.

'We're only renting the place for three weeks,' Clare

reminded her. 'We can hardly start taking the kitchen apart.'

'I'd want a refund, for the danger,' Geraldine said, adding, 'You don't mind if I smoke, do you? I don't see anyone still eating.'

'Er . . . well . . .' Clare glared at her. 'Maybe not at the table?'

'Oh, we're out of doors. It'll disperse.' Geraldine inhaled deeply.

Suddenly through the dusk there was flash from a camera and Harriet jumped up so fast she knocked her chair over. She screamed and flung a pink napkin over her face. 'No photographs! Get OUT!' she shrieked. Miranda got up quickly and moved towards the culprit, who was aiming his phone at the table, ready to take another shot.

'What the hell are you doing? Who are you?' Miranda demanded.

'Harrie, babe? Come on, be nice now,' the young man said, pushing past Miranda.

'Oh my God, it's Pablo Palmer!' Freddie said. 'Pablo Palmer, *here*!'

'Who? Who is this young man?' Geraldine demanded crossly.

'A footballer. Scumbag. Harriet's ex,' Silva told her.

Geraldine's eyes lit up with interest. 'Oh really? Golly, how delightfully vulgar.'

Harriet took the napkin away from her face and

glared at the newcomer while at the same time smoothing her hair down and making her mouth go prettily pouty.

'So, you gonna introduce me then, babes?' he said, smiling round at everyone.

Miranda looked at Harriet. 'Do you want him to stay or to go?'

'Go.' She turned to Pablo. 'You're a lousy bastard. I never want to see you ever again.'

'You heard her.' Eliot stood up and approached them. Miranda thought this pretty brave, seeing as Pablo was well over six feet and as fit as only a player in the premier division of any sport can be. Andrew hovered by the table, half out of his seat but looking wary of getting involved. Sensible man, Miranda considered.

'No way. She doesn't want me to go really, do you? I've missed you, baby,' he said, moving close to take Harriet in his arms. She resisted for a moment but then settled against his body, just as another camera flash cut through the dusk. She pulled away quickly.

'What the fuck . . . ? What's going on, Pablo?'

'Oh, this is my good friend Duncan. He drove me down here. Say hello, Duncan.'

Duncan's camera looked a lot more professional. 'Hope you don't mind,' he said to Miranda, 'just couldn't resist that lovely reconciliation. Sorry to intrude on your party.'

'Yeah, but hey, it's worth it,' Pablo said. 'I came all this way because I needed my little Harrie-babes back and I couldn't wait.'

Harriet looked at him for a few minutes, then went and stood next to Clare. 'No. Just for a second you nearly got me there. But I was right first time. You're up to something and I don't trust you. Just go away. Please.'

TEN

'So that went well. Not. Talk about clearing the place fast,' Miranda said in the kitchen as she snapped the half-charred wooden skewers into small pieces to put in the bin. It felt quite therapeutic and once she'd finished them she looked around the heaps of dirty plates and dishes on the worktop, hoping there were a few she'd overlooked. There were. Snap, snap, snap. It was ridiculously satisfying.

'Come on, Mum, it was ace! You should have seen Lola's face when Freddie told her which team Pablo played for. *Excellent.*' Silva had seen Lola grab Bo's arm and hiss, 'He's like, *famous*. Do you *know* him?' Bo hadn't exactly replied but had nodded in the vague way boys do, using most of his upper body, more an acknowledgement of the question than a direct answer.

'Yes, well, I'm glad you think so. Look, you and Bo did a brilliant job bringing everything up from the pool, so why don't you leave your gran and me to do the dishes? There might be something good on TV.'

'What I'd like to know is how did that Pablo know Harriet was here?' Clare said, when her grandchildren had left the kitchen. She was rinsing debris from plates and lining them up in the dishwasher. 'Do you think she's been talking to him or texting all this time? Did she say anything to you?'

'No. Nothing. She gave me the impression he'd dumped her for someone else and moved that someone else into the flat in less time than it took to change the sheets. Why he's suddenly changed his mind is anyone's guess. I hope she doesn't go running straight back to him. He seems a total sleazeball.'

'A sleazeball with no manners.' Clare sniffed. 'You don't just barge in to someone's house like that and take over without so much as a hello. Even his friend with the camera had the wit to apologize for gatecrashing. I don't think this Pablo even noticed the rest of us. He's not the sort I want for my daughter.' She put a heap of cutlery down on the worktop, went to the window and peered down towards the pool. 'They're still out there – he doesn't seem to have got the meaning of the words "go away". He's actually in the pool floating about stark naked. Harriet's lying on a lounger, would you believe, as if she's perfectly content. The other man's not there, or at least nowhere I can see him.'

'We mustn't watch them,' Miranda said. 'You know what Harrie's like about being watched.'

'She means the so-called media, not her own family. Suppose he hits her? Or gives her drugs? Isn't he on suspension for cocaine?' Clare looked agitated.

'If he hits her I don't fancy his chances of ever becoming a father. And Harriet's drug of choice is champagne, not cocaine. Don't worry about her, Mum. She's all grown up.'

Miranda felt exhausted. It had actually been quite a fun evening although she and Jess and Andrew would have felt more relaxed without the overbearing Geraldine. All the same, that larger-than-life presence had given her and Jessica something to giggle about. As Jess left, the two of them promised to wangle some time with Andrew alone, maybe with a picnic on their old beach, to find out how he and Geraldine had ever managed to get together. Freddie seemed quite a delight. Shy and rather serious but friendly. He'd said he'd join Bo and Silva on the beach in the morning for their first surf lesson.

Clare opened the terrace doors. 'It's still very warm, isn't it? I'll leave these open for a bit, let some fresh air in,' she said, going back to the sink.

Miranda wasn't fooled. 'You won't hear anything from up here, you know,' she teased her.

'I will if there's any shouting,' Clare said, giving her a wicked look, and as if on cue there was a crash of something heavy falling and a noise of breakage.

Miranda and Clare ran outside. Harriet and Pablo – who was out of the pool now and still entirely naked – were standing each side of a large broken pot that had fallen off the wall by the steps. Earth and bright flowers were scattered across the paving. 'Oh, but come *on*, babes! You know you want to!'

'Which bit of "no" don't you get?' Harriet shrieked. 'You're a lying, immature git and you've cost me my *job*!'

Pablo picked up a heap of napkins that were still on the table and started ineffectually drying himself with them, rubbing his cock and grinning at Harriet. 'You're missing this, aren't you? Come on, admit it.'

'Fucksake, Pablo, put it away. It's my job I miss. They've *suspended* me. And it's your fault.'

'You don't need a job, babes, not when you're with me.'

'I'm not *with* you. Just . . . go, will you?' Then, as he took a step towards her, Harriet added, at top volume, 'Pablo, just *sod off*.'

'She'll break the windows, screaming at him like that,' Clare said. 'But good on her.'

'OK, OK, I get it. You need time to think. I'll give you the night,' Pablo said, pulling his jeans back on. 'Duncan! The car!' he hollered in a voice that was clearly used to being heard from one goalmouth to another on a breezy pitch. Toby the cat came pelting up the steps, ears back.

'Go on down to her, Miranda. Make sure she doesn't chase after him,' Clare ordered.

'I don't think she will,' Miranda said. 'Not after that.' They watched from behind a big hibiscus as Pablo jogged off down the drive and the sound of a sporty car screeching away too fast cut through the silent rural night. Duncan blasted the horn four times as a farewell. Miranda went to the top of the steps, 'Cup of tea, darling?'

Harriet looked up at her, and Miranda was saddened by the amount of misery in her beautiful little face. 'No thanks, Manda. A bloody big vodka and tonic is what I need right now.'

'Shall I make myself scarce?' Clare muttered to Miranda. 'So you can talk?'

Miranda, weary to the point of falling asleep as she stood, like a horse, nodded. 'I'll finish up indoors. You go up and get some sleep.'

'Don't let her change her mind about him, will you?' Clare whispered as Harriet came up the steps.

'I won't. Goodnight, Mum.'

Clare gave Miranda a brief kiss and smiled rather wanly. 'When do your children stop giving you such worry? Still,' she squeezed Miranda's arm, 'at least I don't have to worry about you. You're the balanced one. I know I can rely on you not to go to the wild.'

In the kitchen Miranda sat down on one of the Ghost chairs, feeling horribly forlorn. So was this it? She was so sensible and reliable that 'going to the wild' was never to be an option. The thought thoroughly depressed her. She wasn't much given to the pursuit of the wild, but she hated to think it was not available, and would not be an option should it turn up and invite her.

Silva hadn't given much thought to the wetsuit-rental element of the surf lesson. She knew she'd have to wear one, because all surfers did, but it hadn't crossed her mind that this could be a problem. Jake the instructor was one of the classic streak-blond beach sorts and in charge of the surf shack. 'Hmm. You're a tricky size,' he said to her, looking her up and down and then flicking through the rack of neoprene suits. 'Most of the girl ones seem to be out apart from the really big ones and you don't want it all baggy. But hey,' he said, moving across to the other rack, 'try this.' He pulled a suit off its hanger and threw it across to her. 'It's a boy's fit but quite small. You'll be OK.'

'Thanks.' Silva said, looking at the thing and feeling doubtful. She wasn't sure about this. When she saw the experienced surfers jogging down the beach they looked as if their wetsuits were almost as supple as their skin. This one felt heavy and thick, and when she dropped it on the sand to take her shorts off it looked like a dead, deflated animal hide, a chunk of old elephant. And she was going to put herself into its skin. Who else had been in there before her? Andrew had told them the night before that the trick was to wee in your wetsuit once you were in the sea, as it kept you a bit warm or something. She'd thought he must be joking but Freddie said not. Surely that wouldn't work for long? And how hygienic was it to wear something some stranger had peed in? Too yucky. But she wanted to give surfing a go and she'd gone off to sleep the night before picturing herself out there in the sea, floating alongside Jules, who was looking at her as if she was the only girl he'd ever like in his whole life. And even if he just said hello again and smiled a bit, it would be something to tell Willow.

'And we use these boards for the lessons,' Jake said, handing what looked like a slender piece of yellow foam to Bo. 'They're easy to handle for beginners. We should have you up on the board by the end of the first session. You wouldn't get that on, say, a Mini Mal.' He grinned at Bo, clearly expecting him to know what he meant, but Bo was looking past him, waving to someone up the beach. Freddie was ambling down towards them, slow and lanky, already in a wetsuit and carrying a board. Lola was with him, but in jeans. Oh, great, Silva thought, an audience. This was going to be a disaster. Lola would be laughing for days.

'So Freddie's a surfer,' Silva commented to Bo as she grappled with the wetsuit and tried to haul it up her legs while at the same time keeping the embarrassingly scarlet-burned backs of them out of range of Lola's all-seeing eyes. It wasn't easy.

'His dad's big on windsurfing and sailing. He taught him loads of stuff. Freddie said it was the one thing his mum would let Andrew take him to do without her tagging along,' Bo told her. He seemed to have got into his wetsuit with no problem and Lola moved close and pulled the zip up at the back for him. Silva turned away – the small gesture looked like too intimate a moment for witnesses. Her *brother*. Eeuww.

'Hi,' Freddie said, dropping his board on the sand.

Jake scowled at him. 'It's a two-up lesson, man. Can't take any extras today, sorry.'

Freddie backed away a bit. 'Just saying hello,' he told Jake. 'Maybe I'll just get in the water.'

'See you after our lesson, in the café?' Silva said, not wanting him to feel bad.

'Yeah, sure. And good luck. Don't give up!' Freddie said, picking up his board and sprinting towards the sea.

Lola leaned on the surf shack and had a good look at Silva. 'Er . . . is that wetsuit, um, OK, fit-wise?' She was looking down and Silva followed her gaze towards crotch-level where the neoprene was too loose and felt weird.

'There were no girl sizes left,' Jake said, giving Lola a warning look.

'Ha – I thought there was something missing.' Lola laughed. 'You've got all that space in there for a massive cock. You want to stuff a couple of socks down.'

Silva felt like crying and turned away to pick up the foam board. How great was this not being. Here she was in a fat, man-shaped wetsuit that was so long she had to roll it up at the ankles and wrists and felt as heavy as a dead cow. And there she'd been last night, thinking Lola was her friend and fantasizing about Jules. He was probably one of the ones out there on the break line right now, him and the rest of them all lined up to laugh at her. She had two choices: either rip off the suit of shame and storm off back to the house or ignore Lola and get on with it. She looked across at Bo, who came over and gave her shoulder a quick shove. That was his version of a big hug and she felt grateful.

'Are you a surfer?' Bo asked Lola as he picked up his board and started following Jake to the sea's edge.

'No way. I do boats *on* the water but not stuff *in* it,' she said.

'Right. Well, we'll see you later then,' he said, walking away from her and not looking back.

'So where did Pablo go? Back up north?' Miranda asked Harriet as they walked down to the beach café together to get coffee and watch the children's surf lesson.

'No. He's staying at the Pengarret hotel at Tremorwell. Five stars and a spa, he told me, ocean-view suite. He thought that would be enough to get me to go with him. I so don't get what he's up to. Last week he didn't seem to give a flying one if he never saw me again. Told me to put up or get out.'

'Did you see it coming? Had you been rowing? I mean, you've only been together about six months.'

Should be the honeymoon period still, Miranda thought, if the relationship had any long-term possibilities at all. Clearly it didn't. Even she and Dan had managed several years and two quick-succession children before the terminal rot started and he took to sneaking out to have sex with the girl from behind the counter at the KFC and coming home smelling of chip fat.

'He asked me to marry him on our second date,' Harriet said. 'It was dead romantic but he was pissed and to be honest so was I. I told him to ask me again in the morning but he didn't. Nor on any other morning but we were OK, you know? Mostly. Everywhere we went, he got recognized, people coming to talk to him.'

'Most of them girls?'

'Shit yes, so many girls. And he's younger than me. Only twenty-four. I suppose it's what you get. It was like being with a rock star or something.' She sighed. 'It was fun. But over. Definitely.'

They'd reached the beach. Miranda glanced up to the road at the top of the hill and saw a little black Mercedes, top down, racing towards the village. Beside the driver – who might or might not have been Steve – was a woman with the kind of blonde hair that wafts about like something from a shampoo advert. Cheryl? In a way she hoped it was – at least if she was out with Steve that would mean Miranda could go to the shop later without having to sneak around waiting to be accused of shoplifting.

'Will Pablo be sacked from the team?' she asked Harriet as they pulled up a couple of chairs on the café's little terrace. A girl came out immediately and they ordered coffee and a couple of Danish pastries.

'Should we order for Mum as well? I thought she said she'd be down,' Miranda said.

'She said she had things to do and not to wait,' Harriet told her. 'And Pablo was suspended, not sacked, not that it matters much at the moment, not till the season starts. And he got fined about the same as I earn in a year but he didn't care. He's too good to be fired. And anyway – he's just a footballer, not the next Archbishop of Canterbury. No one expects them to behave. No one except an idiot girlfriend – ex-girlfriend – like me, that is.'

Miranda gazed out at the shoreline. The sun shimmered on the wet sand, reflecting the few clouds that dared to collect in the vivid blue sky. Another glorious day, though the weather forecast that morning had said it would get stormy over the next few days. Bo and Silva were making learning the art of surfing look like hard work, all that falling off the boards and hauling themselves back on. Beyond them, the skilled practitioners slid effortlessly across the waves, bending and turning and gliding in on the water right to the sand then stepping off their boards as casually as if they were getting off a bus. Miranda recognized the gangly figure of Freddie, looking more lithe and skilled than she'd expected. The gawkiness she'd noticed about him now made it seem as if being on land wasn't quite his natural habitat.

'You should give it a go, Harriet,' she said, nodding towards the sea.

'Why just me?' Harriet replied. 'Why not you as well?' She gave her sister a hard look. 'You're not thinking you're too *old*, are you?' She laughed. 'Miranda, you *are*, aren't you! My *God*!'

The coffee and pastries arrived and Miranda played with the spoon and the sugar for a few moments, 'Not *old*. Just, you know, not the right sort of mindset. For surfing and stuff. It's just not me.'

'It's not me either. I don't have the shoes for it.'

'Shoes?' Miranda looked down at Harriet's high-soled pink espadrilles.

'Oh, you know what I mean. I like to dress up, not down.'

There was a shriek from the water's edge and the two of them looked up in time to see Silva gliding along a wave, standing on the board. She looked awkward, but she was actually doing it. She landed on the beach and waved at them. A few of the experienced surfer-boys in the water behind her applauded.

'She's got admirers,' Harriet said, taking a huge, unladylike bite from her pastry.

'Has she? No, they're just being friendly,' Miranda said, watching her daughter proudly.

'No, she has. Look at her. She's stunning – that cloud of hair and her pretty body. That blond boy, the one who can surf best, he's been watching her the whole time.'

Miranda laughed. 'She's way too young for all that; she's still a child.' Was it only the night before that she was arguing with Clare that it was fine for Silva to wear make-up? Her daughter's teen years were turning out to be as confusing for Miranda as they were likely to be for Silva. One minute she was recognizing the emerging woman in her, the next trying to keep her in little-girlhood.

'She's a teenager – she'll be in her second year of it by the end of next week, and, yes, a child in most ways but not too young to be noticed by boys or to notice them. I remember all that – going to school on the bus and hoping Mark Brymer would get on and sit next to me. It's all just beginning. Honestly, Manda, you don't get it, do you? She's not too young and you're not too old. And in your case I don't just mean for surfing.'

Miranda sipped her coffee and watched as Bo, too, managed to ride a wave without falling off. He didn't get a round of applause.

*

'They're a bit old-fashioned but I can find space for half a dozen and we'll see how they go.'

Bloody woman. Clare shut her phone down and felt furious on Jack's behalf. He'd sold paintings to many a hotel chain, to greetings card companies and to major stores that sold prints all over the world. OK, so he wasn't madly avant garde or Turner Prize material, nor would he have been made a Royal Academy member, but he was *good* and the volume of sales should tell anyone that he painted what people liked to have on their walls. And here was this snotty woman from that obscure little gallery in St Piran giving her verdict on the photos of Jack's work that Clare had sent to her as if she had the job of considering pieces for a major show at Tate Modern. How dare she? Jack had been *known* and here was a chance for this poxy little venue to take some of his earlier works and offer them at more than tourist prices to the many, many generally loaded summer visitors in this damn place. She should be biting Clare's hand off.

Clare strode fast and furiously down the path, heading for the beach, hoping to catch the end of the children's surf lesson. She'd pick up a *Guardian* from the shop on the way and do the crossword after lunch. Perhaps it would calm her down a bit.

She walked fast past the old phone box with the hideous grinning gnome inside and looked across to where Creek Cottage stood with all its doors and windows open. There was no sign of Eliot but Jessica was outside, hanging T-shirts and jeans on a washing line. She saw Clare and waved, calling out, 'Thanks for last night. We all loved it!'

Clare waved back, feeling a bit cheered, and went up the steps into the shop where she found Geraldine poking through a box of oranges and being watched by a glaring Cheryl, who was piling her hair up into a pony tail. 'They're all the same colour, you know,' she was saying. 'That's why they're called oranges. I wouldn't bother expecting to find something different in there.'

'It's all about texture,' Geraldine boomed. 'Don't you know anything about fruit?'

Cheryl shrugged. 'Don't eat it much.'

'No, I can see that,' Geraldine replied. 'You'd have better skin if you did.'

Cheryl retreated behind the deli counter and Clare heard her mutter, 'Piss off.' You couldn't blame her. Clare went to the newspaper rack and pulled out the single copy of the *Guardian*. A couple of *Daily Mail*s clattered to the floor and Geraldine turned round at the noise. Clare picked them up and stuffed them back into place.

'Aha – our hostess from last night,' Geraldine said. 'I suppose I should thank you.' She didn't. 'That was quite a *disturbance* as we left. When we got home we could still hear the cacophony.'

'Er . . . sorry about that, but at least it wasn't for long.'

'No, but sound does carry so in the country. And especially across water.'

Cheryl was taking notice again and leaned on the counter top. 'So you're another from up at the big rental, then?' she said to Clare. 'God, you're a bunch and a half, aren't you? One slapper, one shoplifter . . .'

'Shoplifter?' Clare said, astonished. 'But that was twenty years ago!' How could this girl know about Harriet's childhood misdemeanours?

'Shu'up, twenty years? I was hardly born. No, it was a couple of days ago. She didn't get away with it. You don't get away with anything, with me,' she said proudly, arranging a selection of pork pies and various coloured olives on a dish. The words 'serving suggestion' popped into Clare's head, rather incongruously. The girl put together a classy counter display, she'd give her that. The array was close to Harrods Food Hall standard. No wonder the shop got away with the monstrous prices.

Geraldine laughed. It was a deep and alarming sound, rather like the sudden boom of a bittern across silent Norfolk marshes.

'No mercy with criminals, that's what I say. A small crime is just a big crime but, er . . .' Clare and Cheryl waited while Geraldine's brain searched for words, 'but smaller,' she finished feebly. 'That doesn't make it any less serious.'

'Anyway, that noise last night. All the shouting and the car revving and stuff. There've been complaints from people coming in here today. Holidaymakers come here for peace and quiet,' Cheryl told Clare. She looked ominously serious. 'I think you'll be *getting a visit*.'

'Oh, really? Who from?' Clare asked, putting her newspaper on the counter and wishing like mad that the village had more than one shop. She was going to have to nab Miranda's car in the mornings in future and drive round to Tremorwell for supplies, or make the twenty-mile round trip to the nearest Tesco.

'From the agency you rent from. About standards. They're keen on standards here. It's about not having riff-raff upsetting the residents. You'll likely get a *warning*.'

'Ha – that'll be a yellow card!' Geraldine guffawed. 'Like footballers. How perfectly apt!' Even Cheryl giggled. She was quite pretty when she smiled. Clare wished she'd do it more often.

'Anyway, it was very entertaining last night,' Geraldine conceded in a way that implied Clare should be very grateful for her presence at their gathering. 'Now, let me just have twenty Rothmans and a *Daily Mail* and I'll be on my way. Freddie has apparently gone to the beach and I want to make sure he's got hot porridge waiting for him when he gets back. He chills easily.'

'Unlike her,' Cheryl muttered as Geraldine wheezed down the shop steps and set off back to Andrew's cottage.

'So, is it true?' Cheryl switched her smile back on.

'Is what true?'

'That Pablo Palmer is here in the village.' She looked excited. 'We get famous people down here. Kylie was here doing a video last summer. And the year before, I heard Johnny Depp was buying a house across the water. He didn't, though.' Her smile faded for a moment but then returned. 'So is he?'

Harriet had probably looked this thrilled when she'd first attracted the footballer's interest. Would she have seen past the fancy restaurants and red-carpet events and the flashy cars? Clare hoped her daughter had more to her than that. If she'd meant what she'd said to Pablo the night before, it looked as if she did.

'He was here but I don't know where he is now,' she said, 'but if I find out he's still in the area I'll let you know.'

'Wow, thanks!'

'Nothing to thank me for,' Clare said, picking up her newspaper and starting to leave.

'No, there is, trust me. Nothing much ever happens round here.' She reached across to the basket of fruit Geraldine had been mauling. 'Here, have an orange. On the house. And keep me in the loop, won't you? Please?'

ELEVEN

Miranda hadn't intended to look at her emails more than once every few days but felt she had to keep an eye on them in case something to do with work cropped up. It shouldn't – there was never much going on in August – but you never knew. The meeting with the hotel people that she had scheduled for when she got home was the only important thing at the moment work-wise and she was completely prepared for it. She was nervous though, stomach-churningly so. In the dawn hours, half waking, she sometimes couldn't help wondering: suppose they'd been leading her on a bit and were actually still seeing several other designers and making them, too, assume they were the only one in the frame for this job? She'd been assured they were well past that stage, but still the possibility of its all going horribly wrong had to be somewhere in the reckoning. It didn't bear thinking about but it would be tempting fate not to.

She brought her Macbook down to the terrace, put it on the table in the shade of the cream canvas umbrella and switched it on. While it warmed up, she looked out across the higher lanes of the village, seeing if she remembered any more landmarks from all those years ago. Mostly on the hillside the houses had been ugly white bungalows or even wood-clad near-shacks back then, almost all of them occupied by retired couples keen on regimented floral displays and a well-striped lawn in their gardens. Clare had been sniffy in those days about all the straight lines of luridly vivid petunias and begonias. At the time, Miranda didn't think she'd noticed differences between types of gardens. Gardens, when she was a child, either had flowers or they didn't. They were overgrown and scruffy (all the better for making camps and hiding in) or they weren't. The details didn't register. I'm all grown up, she thought: I know that I prefer a lush, tumbled planting with soft colours to something all controlled and in shades that pain the eyes. When did that happen? Did it creep up with time and parenthood, in the same way that cheap red wine, after you're twenty-five or so, starts to give you vile headaches?

Miranda blinked as the sun reflected a fierce ray off the solar panels of one of the hillside houses. Several of them had the panels and she imagined the ecology versus aesthetics battles the owners had surely had with the local councils over that. Or worse, the mind-crushing talks with pushy salesmen who'd convinced these elderly targets that the reduction in electricity bills would easily cover the massive initial outlay. A few of the tatty old buildings had been completely rebuilt, or 'de-bungalowed' as Andrew, in estate-agent-speak, had pointed out at the barbecue. In twenty years, how many of the then-ancient-seeming retired had died long before they recouped the financial benefits from that solar heating? She shivered a bit, thinking of Jack, and wondered if, that time they last drove away from Creek Cottage, it had even once crossed his mind he might only come back here as a pile of grey ash. Grey ash which was – she now knew – resting in the bottom of the wardrobe in Clare's room. There was time, she told herself; they had ages to go here yet. There was no rush to get the scattering done, although she did hope Harriet would still be around for it. She had a sharp moment of missing Jack, a harsh little ache inside. When she thought of him she could swear she smelled paint. How much worse must her mother feel? No wonder she was being slow to dispose of the absolute last of him.

Miranda tip-tapped at the Mac and quickly skimmed through her Inbox. Nothing much immediately stood out as needing attention. There were tempting end of season sales bargains to be had from Toast and Brora. Dan was there asking about the children and telling her again that having them to stay could be a problem, but then there was a message with a scarlet urgency mark flagged up beside it – something from Coopers-Lee, the very company she was pinning much of next year's income and a growing of her reputation on. Please, she prayed as she opened the message, *don't* let them be cancelling the whole shebang.

'Aaagh!' she yelled, as she read it.

'You really are a noisy lot, aren't you? Or are you that terrified of seeing me again?' A man's shadow loomed across the table.

'Steve! God, you made me jump. Where did you come from?'

'The side path. Sorry to have startled you. *Was* that a reaction to me or did a wasp get you?'

Miranda quickly skim-read the relevant sentence of the email again, hoping it would say something different, then closed the computer down. This could be dealt with. It just needed some thinking about. 'No, it's just something in an email. Work stuff. It's OK. Or it *will* be OK. Actually I was expecting a visitor, but not you, someone from the agency.' She smiled at him. 'That noise issue you just mentioned – we've been warned we're getting a telling off. I expect we'll be evicted and have to pack and leave by nightfall. Cup of tea?'

'Thanks. That would be good.' She was conscious of him close behind her, following her into the kitchen. Something about him made her feel awkward, a bit uncoordinated. How would they get past this atmosphere between them? It crossed her mind that she might be the only one who felt it. He seemed perfectly relaxed – and why wouldn't he? Again she wondered about how she should have interpreted the remark about sleeping with the owner's girlfriend. *Had* he meant her? Which also meant . . . She fussed about with the kettle and tea bags and found some ginger biscuits in the larder.

'So the telling off you'll be getting from the agency. That'll be about last night's rumpus,' he said, leaning comfortably against the worktop and watching her. 'About shouting and swearing and loud car horns in the middle of the night. You're a disgrace, you lot. Not the sort we want in the village.'

She looked at him sideways. Nice hair today, she thought; it looked just-washed, slightly baby-bird fluffy. But as for what he'd just said . . . he'd never been much of a one for showing obvious rather than subtle humour, but surely he wasn't serious?

'Oh, come on, it wasn't the middle of the night. Barely ten o'clock, for heaven's sake,' she protested, feeling a bit put out. He wasn't remotely close to smiling. 'Sorry, but did you come here to have a go at me just because of a bit of village gossip?' She picked up the boiling kettle.

'Careful. That kettle spits a bit.'

'It docs, doesn't it? Not the best designed item in here.'

'Sorry,' he said. 'And yes, I did come here for exactly that. But better to get me than agency Angie. She's *fierce.*'

At last, a smile.

The pennies that had been in mid-air since he'd brought the prawns round finally dropped into place. 'So you *are* the owner of this house? I thought you just might be from something you . . . er . . . said. But then I thought, no. Unlikely.'

'Unlikely? For a simple village boy who fishes for lobsters? Actually, I am,' he said, taking a mug of tea from her.

'Awkward.'

'Is it? It shouldn't be, should it? Shall we sit outside? Too nice a day not to.' He led the way back to the terrace (*his* terrace) and they sat together on the bench (*his* bench).

'I wish I'd known,' Miranda said, watching a small boat sail away from the end of Andrew's garden.

'Would it have made a difference?'

Miranda shrugged. 'Before I booked it? I don't know. It would be ridiculous if it did, but . . .'

'I know. I do get it. But it's been a long time. More than half our lives, if you think about it that way.'

'Don't – that makes me feel old! So it's you who's come here to tell me off? And when we're evicted and we end up camping in a lay-by for the night on the moor and being eaten alive by the Beast of Bodmin, you'll be the one to blame?'

'Yep. That's it in one. Someone complained that the racket woke them up so you're to be put out for the panthers.'

'That Cheryl probably. She's taken against me.'

'It wasn't "that Cheryl". She was out last night.'

Miranda had to ask and it was out before she could stop herself. 'With you?'

He gave her a surprised look. 'Actually yes, with me.'

Miranda laughed, mostly at herself. Where on earth had that ridiculous little niggle of envy come from? Steve was someone she'd thought of many times over the past two decades but hadn't seen in all that time and yet here she was feeling mildly possessive about him. She could imagine her mother, if she knew, dismissing her as a silly girl, just as she had when Miranda had told her she was going to marry Dan at only twenty-two. Again, she wouldn't be wrong.

'So you own this house but you live somewhere else?' As soon as the words were out Miranda wished she hadn't bothered to ask. He'd be living with the Cheryl girl and now he was going to confirm it and make her even more . . . what? Jealous? How could you be jealous about someone you had absolutely no claim on, no relationship with and no plans for one either?

'In my mother's old cottage during the summer months. She's gone to live with her sister in St Keverne. I live on my own, which is fine by me. At the moment.'

'Good,' Miranda said. 'I mean . . . good that it's fine.'

He finished the tea and got up, 'Look, it was great to see you and I'm sorry about the warning from the agency. I won't let them chuck you out, I promise. On one condition.'

'It's OK, I get it. There won't be a repeat. Though for heaven's sake, you get worse racket than that on the Chiswick High Road any old night. It was just my sister's stupid ex-boyfriend. He's at the Pengarret hotel now, or was after he left here. With any luck he's gone back up north.'

'Oh, I know he's still around. Cheryl's very excited about him.'

'Really? Tell her from me not to waste her energy.'

He laughed. 'You can't tell Cheryl anything, trust me. And the no-repeat thing is not the condition.'

'It isn't?'

'No.' He looked hesitant and shuffled about a bit, hands thrust in the pockets of his jeans. Suddenly she could see him looking just as delightfully boyish as when he was nineteen. 'It's . . . would you, um . . . would you like to have lunch with me on Thursday? I have to go over to St Ives for a meeting and, you know, I just wondered if we could do a bit of proper catching up. If you want to, that is.'

It was possibly the last thing Miranda was expecting. He was asking her *out*? He hadn't even seemed that friendly. He looked away from her, out across towards the sea as if definitely expecting the next word he heard to be a firm 'no'. But on the contrary, the idea of lunch with him made her feel quite thrilled. All the same, he wasn't getting off lightly with an immediate acceptance.

'Er . . . Well, I'm not sure. You've surprised me. Do you really want to be seen with someone who's such a "disgrace"?'

He looked puzzled and a bit hurt. 'I wasn't serious. Just teasing, you know?'

Of course she knew. He used to tease her about being scared of crab claws, about being too posh to be any good at drinking straight from the bottle: 'I should bring a crystal wine glass for you,' he'd said, laughing at her one day on the beach as she'd managed to pour half a bottle of fizzy cider down her front.

'I was teasing too.' She smiled. 'And yes, thank you. I'd love to go to St Ives.'

She felt like a fluttery teenager again as they exchanged phone numbers. It was only lunch, and she was a long way from sixteen, but all the same her hands were shaky as she clicked his number into her iPhone.

After he'd gone Miranda turned her attention back to the email that had so freaked her out. This was going to be a problem. The hotel people wanted to move the meeting – to the middle of the next week. It would mean returning to London and coming back on either the next night or the early morning after. It was a pain but it could be done. Clare would understand – she'd run a business of her own till recently. And if Harriet stayed on for a while as a bit of grown-up company for Clare it would definitely work. It would have to – this was one deal she really couldn't afford to lose.

Clare was out walking the cliff path to the next village and back. She knew the others were holding back from nagging her about Jack's ashes and she felt she should at least go and look out to sea, think about making a decision about just where she wanted them to go. The boat issue still needed to be sorted but something would work out. Things mostly did. Not all things, of course, otherwise Jack would be walking along beside her instead of the cocker spaniel that belonged to the couple several hundred yards in front who, holding hands and leaning close in to each other, seemed oblivious of their left-behind pet. She tried not to envy them, tried to feel glad for them, to wish them a long and happy life together, but there was an inevitable brief, deep ache of her loss. She reached down and patted the black and white dog, told him to catch his people up, but he seemed content to trot along at her heels. Maybe she'd get a puppy when she went home. Or perhaps a rescue dog, something ready trained. She'd never had a dog before. A puppy might be too much like dealing with a toddler, all demands and incontinence, and she'd be wanting a creature to love, not to feel cross about.

Her flat back at home seemed a distant reality at the

moment. Considering the as yet non-existent dog, she really had to think hard about where in her bedroom she'd be able to put its basket. What was between the blue velvet chair and the chest of drawers? Was there a good-sized space or was it where she kept the laundry basket? She and Jack had lived there for four years; there was no excuse to start feeling vague about its details after only a few days away. But, strangely, she was beginning to feel as if she was never going to live any- where but here. Down here in Chapel Creek she was existing in a fuzzy, comfortable, unnaturally sunny bubble. Only a few days away from home and she'd almost stopped feeling constant spikes of panic about the future and of heart-stopping, tear sparking agony of loss. They were still there – she'd had one only moments before – but blunted and over faster. Late in the afternoon, after a walk such as this or lunch across the estuary, she'd lie on the lounger by the pool, doing her crossword and thinking about nothing at all except how blissful it was to have this kind of sun in England in August. Given the awful summers of recent years it felt as if they were specially blessed. The absence of Jack was never completely out of her mind – later today, no doubt, she would look across to the adjacent lounger and for a moment wonder why it was Harriet or Miranda lying there with a book and not her husband, but instead of the future of bleak loneliness she would manage to focus on something good to remember. She

thought of weekends they'd had in Venice and
Barcelona, of the trips to France, to Castillon-la-Bataille
where Jack had taught a residential masterclass in land-
scape painting, not far from where their daughter Amy
lived. That had probably been the last time he'd seemed
completely well.

The coast path was just how she remembered it, with
a few repairs and gaps and scars from rock falls here and
there. Pinky-purple thrift frothed out of clefts in the
stone. Vivid orange montbretia bloomed defiantly,
waving above the scrubland. Below in the sunlight, tiny
near-inaccessible beaches appeared almost Caribbean
with the sea all gleaming shades of turquoise where the
rocks parted and the seabed was a lemony drift of sand.

'We've had the same idea. Solitary escape. I saw you
from across the stile. I just came from the top of the hill
for a look-see at the ocean.' Eliot's voice startled her.

'Hello, Eliot. You needed to escape?'

He smiled. 'Well, with a stroppy teenager in the
house, you know . . . It's a long time since I lived with
one of those. Lola's in a sulk because Jess won't let her
take her boat across to St Piran in the dark. There's some
music thing on at the pub over there on Saturday that
she says *everyone* is going to.'

'What time does the ferry run till?' Clare asked.

'Oh, plenty late enough for a fifteen-year-old. But
you know what they can be like. May I walk with you
awhile?'

'Please do. I'd like the company.'

'One hell of a view, isn't it?' Eliot stopped and leaned on a rock and looked out at the sea. 'And when I say view, I mean just . . . the nothing of it. The unfathomable vastness of endless water. Have you been to Australia?'

'I haven't.'

'You can look out at the ocean there and the air is so thin and clear you can make out the curve of the earth on the horizon. And everything out there is strong, brilliant blue. Distant sea here goes hazy grey but there it's blue all the way out, darker further away but it doesn't fade away to that dreary English colourlessness for as far as you can see.'

She turned away from the water and looked at him. He was still gazing out at the sea and seemed miles away, somewhere far off in his own head. Was it the view he was so lyrical about or had there been something else? She was surprised by her own curiosity.

'When were you there?' she asked.

He laughed. 'Oh, years ago. Sometime after Liz upped and divorced me. Book publicity tours, that kind of thing. I got to like travelling. It was easier than being lonely at home. Not,' he suddenly looked at her, 'that I missed Liz that much, between you and me. Can't think how or why we ever got together in the first place.'

Clare smiled. How inappropriate would it be to parody the old Mrs Merton line and tease, 'So tell me,

Liz, what first attracted you to filthy rich, hugely success-ful author Eliot Lynch?' Better not, she thought. It was too much of a toss-up whether he'd find it funny or a bit insulting. All the years she hadn't seen him and now she was wary of losing his new-found friendship.

'. . . except for our mutual exploitation,' he said, answering the question for both of them, chortling deeply in the way she remembered he so often did, years ago. Maybe it wouldn't have been such a gamble to have said it after all, Clare realized as they set off again along the path together. The spaniel gave her one last lingering look and trotted off fast in pursuit of its owners, either disappointed by Clare's preference for a human companion or pleased to have found someone to hand her over to.

Many of the little beaches far below them were accessible only from the sea. A few were only reachable by paths that would have any vertigo-sufferer clinging to the gorse in wet-palmed panic. They were approaching one of these tracks now, where it turned off from the main path and led down to a beach Clare remembered well.

'Did you ever go down this one?' she asked Eliot, pointing to a barely discernible track that seemed to vanish over a sheer edge.

'Ha, yes! I think that's the one with the rope for the last ten feet or so? Am I right?'

'That's the one. I can't believe we used to cart a ton of

picnic stuff down there. Oh, the days of being young, fit and adventurous.'

Eliot looked over the edge to where the path zigzagged down. He looked back at her, his eyes gleaming with challenge. 'Do you think we can still make it down there?'

Clare laughed, 'Of course we can! Do you want to give it a go?'

'I'm up for it if you are.'

She didn't hesitate. What was the worst that could happen? That she went plummeting to a messy death on the rocks below? That would be one fast way to find out for sure whether you got reunited with your beloved in some kind of blissed-up afterlife. But all the splattered bits of body would be horrendous for the rescue people to collect up. She'd make sure she was very careful.

'OK, let's do it. It's not as if it's slippery from recent rain or anything. And no doubt the health and safety brigade would have closed it down if it were truly dangerous.'

Eliot went ahead on the narrow track and she followed, picking her way carefully on the uneven ground and daring herself every now and then to look down. She felt exhilarated by the danger and the concentration on where her feet should go. No one else was around. It wasn't one of the better surf beaches so no young board-carriers came scampering past in the terrifying way they so often did round here, sure footed as cats.

'Nearly there,' Eliot said after a surprisingly short while. He stopped at a point where the path petered right out and a tatty piece of old rope dangled down a near-vertical drop to the shore. 'I seem to remember it's a matter of half abseiling and half an ungainly scramble. What do you think? Shall we? There's always the danger we won't make it back up the same way, but I'm willing to risk it.'

Clare looked at the deserted stretch of glittering sand beneath them. It reminded her of a beach on the Isles of Scilly, all silvery as if someone had stirred crystals into the sand for fun.

'Well, we've got this far. Can't bail out now, can we? It'll be fine,' she said. 'Who's going first?'

'I will. Then I can catch you if it all goes horribly wrong.' Eliot took hold of the rope and grinned at her as he started the short but awkward descent. 'I'm not so good at this,' he said, looking down to find a foothold. 'If God had picked me to do his work instead of St Patrick, Ireland would still be overrun with snakes.' But within a few seconds he was down and Clare took the rope and made it down to the sand, stumbling slightly as she landed. Eliot caught hold of her and for a second she leaned against him, laughing.

The two of them kicked their shoes off and padded down to the water's edge. The sand was warm underfoot, crunching and brittle between toes. There wasn't a soul in sight.

'Bliss, isn't it?' Eliot said as they stood in the shallows, the sea lapping at their feet. Shoals of tiny shrimps could be seen in the clear water.

'It is,' Clare agreed. 'How could we have never been back to this for all those years? I suppose the rest of life and being in other places just got in the way.' They turned and walked back up the beach and sat together in the sun, leaning against a warm rock.

'Jack and I came down here and skinny-dipped once,' she said, remembering also what they'd done when they came out of the sea. Jack had always liked outdoor sex. Would she ever have sex again? Possibly not, realistically thinking. It was the first time she'd thought of it; something else to miss, in time.

'Did you now?' Eliot gave her a look, eyebrows raised.

'Yes. And yes, actually,' she said, replying to the unspoken question, turning away a little to flick a tear from her cheek.

'So you have a good memory of here to keep. That's lucky,' he said, then laughed. 'My only one of this beach is hauling a bloody heavy barbecue down here and Liz burning her toe on a spat-out hot coal on the sand. She shrieked like a banshee and said she'd be scarred for life. Oh, and the twins needed to be carried up that rope, like baby monkeys, one at a time on my back. Liz said never again.' He chuckled. 'She said that about a lot of things.'

The sun started to move away to the west and shadows fell over the shore. Eliot and Clare waited till the shade covered their rock and Clare reluctantly put her shoes back on.

'Now for the long climb back to the top,' she said. 'Everything ends.'

'Ah, now don't be thinking like that. Treasure the moment. It was a good one,' he said as he handed her the rope.

'It was. And thank you.'

'For what? This was a pleasure. I always liked you, you know.'

He steadied her as she made the first step up and clambered towards the path. When she got there and handed the rope back she smiled down at him. 'And I always liked you too, Eliot.'

TWELVE

'Ooh er . . . look at Miranda all dressed up for her date!'
Harriet danced round the pool terrace, waving her mug
of coffee dangerously. Miranda ducked out of the way,
not keen to risk spillage on to the long white top she
was wearing over old jeans and a little skimpy vest that
she hoped wasn't tight enough to show any midriff lard
bulges. It had looked all right in the mirror but you
could never tell – the light might just have been lucky.
The top was a mad, thin cotton asymmetric thing,
which would have been hugely expensive if she hadn't
found it on eBay, with a hem that looped up here and
there with ties. She'd spent ages fixing it so it looked as
if it was randomly put together with no thought at all.
It reminded her of Dolly Parton's adage that it took a lot
of money to look this cheap. In Miranda's case it had
taken a lot of effort to look this casual.

'It's not a *date*, Harriet. It's just, y'know . . . lunch.'

'Ha – there's no such thing as "just, y'know, lunch",' Harriet said, looking gleeful. 'I bet you don't get back here tonight. I bet you *anything*.'

'Ew, please, not in front of us.' Silva pulled a face and put her hands over her ears. 'That's like my *mum* you're talking about?'

'Of course I'll be back, don't be ridiculous,' Miranda said. Feeling flustered and nervous made her more snappy than she meant to be. 'Harriet's just being . . .'

'Jealous. I'll admit it. I'm jealous,' Harriet cut in. 'I'm the one in need of a man, not you. I'm in massive need of a mercy fu . . . sorry, I mean a mercy snog. Or something. That bastard Pablo has drained all my confidence away.'

'Not so's you'd notice,' Clare said, glancing up from her book. 'You seem pretty sparky to me.'

'I'm hiding my pain,' Harriet said, pouting. 'I won't feel better till I know he's left the county. He's *still* at that hotel.'

'Calling you every minute. Romantic,' Silva said, doing exaggerated sighing.

Harriet gave her a sharp look. 'He is,' she said, glancing at her phone as she habitually did every few minutes. 'Well . . . he was. He was texting, anyway. And there are press people hanging about at the hotel too.' She sat on the diving board, looking a bit thoughtful. Miranda and Clare exchanged glances. They both knew Harriet's phone had been silent for a good twenty-four hours, give or take the odd call from girlfriends who were treated to ever more fanciful reports about Pablo's dramatic arrival at the house. Of Pablo himself there'd been no sign, apart from overheard gossip in the harbour that 'the druggy footballer' had been seen whizzing round the country lanes far too fast in a scarlet Ferrari. Harriet made sure she was always wearing full-scale make-up, swearing she always did, but Miranda suspected it was in the hope that the press she'd claimed she dreaded would catch her 'unawares' and any photos would remind her TV bosses that she was way too pretty and talented to be dropped permanently from the network.

'OK – I'll be off in a sec,' Miranda said, looking at her watch for about the twentieth time in as many minutes. 'Are you sure you don't mind me going out and abandoning you all like this? Will you be all right?'

Clare took off her sunglasses. 'Miranda, for heaven's sake just go. You're on holiday. Go and have a good time. Of course we can fend for ourselves. Don't be so ridiculous.'

'That's you told.' Harriet giggled at her sister. 'But she's right.'

'Me and Bo are going down to Lola's. We're making a raft for the village regatta, with Freddie as well. That's OK, isn't it?' Silva said.

'Of course it is.' Miranda gave her a quick goodbye kiss before Silva could duck out of range. 'Jess and her brother Milo and Andrew and I used to make rafts too but we never won the raft race – that was always the locals. We thought they probably practised all year. Jess will be able to give you tips on flotation, if she can remember what we used to do. I seem to think it involved old oil drums, but I doubt you can get those now. I suppose huge plastic water containers might work.' On the lane just past the gate a car horn tooted gently.

'Ha – that'll be Steve,' Harriet said. 'It's definitely not Pablo. He'd have made sure the whole village could hear him. Off you go and have a good time, you lucky cow.'

'Thanks, Harrie. Bye, all. I'll see you later.' Miranda fluffed her fingers through her hair and took a quick look all down her long white top, not quite trusting it to be free from sudden seagull poo attack or a juicily squashed fat insect she'd managed to sit on. All seemed well and she went up the steps towards the gate where Steve was waiting for her. What was the etiquette regarding a hello kiss, she wondered, but he stepped back to hold the car door open as she approached so she decided the kiss wasn't expected. Maybe it wasn't a Cornwall thing, unlike London where everyone seemed only a heartbeat away from kissing the postman if he did your round more than twice. Steve looked – well, strangely breathtaking, if she was honest. What was it about a sky blue shirt against tanned skin? She wished she felt less jittery inside. A couple of drops of Rescue Remedy would have been useful, if she'd only thought of it sooner. But then, she hadn't expected to feel like this. It must be the power of that first-love thing, maybe. A certain consciousness, unmentioned elephant-in-the-room style, that they'd seen an awful lot of each other, quite literally. But heavens, realistically this was only a few hours out with an old friend – what did she expect to happen? The worst would be running out of things to say, but as they had twenty years to cover that shouldn't really be a problem, unless it ended up as kind of a list, like a CV.

'Nice car,' Miranda said, cursing herself for such a feeble comment as she settled into the little black Mercedes. The roof was down and she wondered if it would look prissy to scrabble about in her bag and find a scrunchie to tie back her hair. She decided not to bother. A bit of wind-blown mussing up wouldn't do it any harm.

'You like it?' Steve sounded surprised, 'Cheryl says it's a hairdresser's car and I should get something a bit more blokey.'

So. 'Cheryl says'. Miranda wasn't sure how to react to that but it did jolt her a bit. It seemed yet another confirmation that Cheryl was a hugely important part of Steve's life – maybe he'd wanted to get that little piece of information in early, just in case she had ideas. Which she didn't. Plus, of course, it wasn't any of her business. And not that it mattered. Not that she should care. But even so, they were barely out of the village and she was suddenly feeling bizarrely disappointed and wanting to turn back. Too late now.

'Not that it's anything to do with her,' he went on, giving Miranda the distinct impression that he was back-pedalling, 'but she does like to have an opinion on everything.'

'She doesn't hold back, that's for sure,' Miranda said crisply, recalling Cheryl's instant decision in the village shop that Miranda *had* to be a shoplifter. She glanced at Steve and asked the question that had to be asked. 'So Cheryl's a bit special to you then?'

He laughed. 'Yes, of course! I've known her for years,' he said, which didn't really do as much explaining about their relationship as Miranda had hoped. It had been the perfect moment to explain that Cheryl was married to his best friend or was actually his cousin or something but instead he was concentrating on the road, which, once past Helston, had become winding and narrow. She was surprised to realize she wasn't gripping the sides of the seat in terror as she tended to do when being driven in small cars by others. But then she remembered how all those years ago Steve had made her feel completely safe in a small boat too, even at the mouth of the estuary where the real waves of the sea met the more gentle flow of the river and it all became alarmingly choppy. He'd handled the boat with such calm skill – very much in the way, now she thought about it, he'd handled her nervously inexperienced body.

'I thought we'd park at Lelant and take the train,' he said. 'Is that all right with you? You get a stunning view of the beaches and coastline that you can't see from anywhere else.'

'Oh, yes. Great. The only times we went to St Ives before we went by car and parked miles away up a hill and had to walk up a million steps to get back to it later. Amy and Harriet cried with exhaustion and Jack had to carry them, in turns. God, that was years ago. I think it was just before the Tate gallery opened there. Jack – that was my stepfather – talked about going to it the next year but we'd sold the cottage by then.'

'Did you want to go there today?' he asked. 'I mean, I guess we could, later.' He was now driving past the mud-flats of the Hayle estuary where the tide was out and thousands of birds picked at the shore, watched by twitchers gathered along the shoreline with telescopes. Miranda had fleeting long-term memories of this scene from when she was a child, remembering wondering what they were looking at and Jack pulling in at the pub car park to point out curlews and pochards and oystercatchers.

'Oh no, it's OK. You've got a meeting or something, haven't you? And I was sort of saving it for later in our trip, somewhere to take the children and Mum if it rains.'

'That'll be next week– wet weather is due by then. You'll get plenty of chance to do the indoor visits.'

'Oh, the joy of Cornish rain – something to look forward to, then,' she said, thinking ahead to the children draping themselves moodily over the sofas and arguing about the TV remote.

'I feel really sorry for the holidaymakers in the rain. It can all get horribly expensive, entertaining the children. Or so I'm told, anyway. When I had the ferry I was forever being complained to if it rained, as if being a local I'd somehow switched the rain on on purpose to spite the visitors.'

'You should have blamed us lot instead, for bringing nasty up-country clouds.'

'Oh I did, believe me, I did. We locals blamed you for just about everything.'

They turned off the road close to the railway line, parked in the field behind the tiny Lelant station and bought tickets from a man in a garden shed-style hut. Steve wouldn't let Miranda pay, although she offered. The platform was already crowded with people waiting for the St Ives train and Miranda had her usual mild feeling of panic seeing small children running free, too close to the platform edge. By some primeval instinct, her hand shot out and gripped Steve's wrist as a little boy chased his sister between two oblivious parents who were each texting furiously.

'Sorry!' she said, letting go abruptly and feeling madly embarrassed. 'I just have this urge to grab small children and keep them away from the edge.'

'So I'm a small child?' He was laughing at her. Again.

'No! So sorry. It's just a ridiculous mother-type reflex. I still do it to Bo, even at road crossings, and it embarrasses him hugely because he's a hulking great fourteen and embarrassment is his default setting. On streets he walks about five paces away from me so I can't reach him.'

'Control freak!' he teased, but she could see him keeping an eye on the running children as the train pulled in. He got it, she realized, he got it, however much he mocked.

'What did you bring that horrible thing for?' Lola pointed to the pink inflatable crocodile that Silva had carried down to Creek Cottage.

Silva looked at her for a moment before she replied, searching out possible hostility signs: the tone of the voice, whether Lola had a sneer on her face and was likely to say something cutting; but she actually seemed genuinely curious and was smiling at her, which was either encouraging or a warning, the way you saw chimpanzees baring their teeth on wildlife programmes. She was wary of Lola. She could be snappy, a bit like a crocodile herself.

'I thought it might come in useful, you know, for making the raft. I mean, it does, like, float,' she told her, laying the croc down on the square of grass between herself and Lola, who was sitting astride the creek wall. It was only partly true. She'd become fond of the ridiculous toy, and found it weird yet slightly fascinating – in a slightly analytical way – that she still had that much of her child-self in her. It was, she'd thought last night, a bit of a shame the house didn't have a selection of leftover My Little Ponies in the guests' toy-box (which was full of worthy wooden baby puzzles and eco-friendly shape sorters). She'd probably have had to hide them away in her room to comb and plait their manes in secret, but at least down here none of her too-cool friends were around to catch her doing it. She could imagine Willow with that twisted-confusion face on saying, 'Are you like, *playing*? With *toys*?' Come to think of it, how many of her friends would also think constructing a raft was like *well* boring? Most of them, probably; all her classmates with their flicky hair and so much exaggerated attitude to the wrong clothes. Their loss, she decided, feeling quite excited about this communal project.

'Yeah, it could be.' Freddie nodded slowly. 'Good thinking, that girl,' he said, smiling at Silva. She liked Freddie, she decided. Though he was very shy.

'Mmm . . . maybe,' Lola conceded. 'At least the thing floats.' She prodded it with her foot.

194

'We'd need another one, though, I was thinking. There wouldn't be enough room on just this, not if all four of us are going to be on it,' Silva said, feeling a surge of enthusiasm. At least they weren't actually laughing at her. Bo had said no way he'd be pratting about on the water on anything pink so she'd ruled him out of the whole plan from the start, but he'd mooched down the lane after her and was now sitting on the grass, leaning against the wall close to Lola's long brown leg and looking pretty alert, for him. The power of girls, she thought, wondering if she'd ever get that Jules boy to look at her the way Bo looked at Lola. Probably not. At least, not till she was a few years older. Perhaps a couple of summers on from now she'd come back here and have become madly gorgeous, ugly duckling to swan style, and he'd fall crazy in love with her. She'd seen him on the beach after her surf lesson that morning with a mate, collecting driftwood. He'd waved and shouted 'Hello Kitty' at her and blown her a kiss. She'd blown one back and flutteringly half hoped he'd come rushing over and give her a real one but that was the stuff of fantasy and a life far more like Willow's perfect one than her own. Also, to be honest, it would have been a bit scary being grabbed without any lead-up. She wouldn't know what to do and then he'd know for sure she hadn't a clue when it came to boys. Would he be able to tell she was still a My Little Pony girl, deep down? Possibly.

'Good plan. If we got another, and put some planks or something in between, lashed on with rope, it would look kind of, y'know, different.' To Silva's surprise it was Bo who said it, looking up at Lola for approval. Maybe she shouldn't be surprised, she realized.

Jessica came out just then with cans of drinks. 'You'll need a theme, you know, not just a raft,' she told them, as she handed out Cokes. 'You're supposed to dress up for this.'

Freddie groaned. 'Do we *have* to?' Silva looked at him. He seemed to be blushing at the very thought. She hadn't really known boys got that shy. If Bo did too, she couldn't really tell – he was just *Bo*. Or maybe that was what the thing with hunching into a hoodie with his whole hands up the sleeves was about. Just shy-hiding.

'Course!' Jess told him. 'You don't think they just judge on the actual raft, do you? It's the whole package! You need to keep it simple because whatever you wear is going to get wet so you need to be able to swim in it. So nothing too drapy. Miranda and I went as mermaids one year and that got a bit dangerous. My brother had to jump in and haul us out because our legs were lashed together with green fabric and we couldn't swim properly.'

'Rules out a ballgown then,' Lola said, 'but I suppose we'd be OK with a jungle theme to go with the croc. Me and Silva in bikinis with fronds of greenery and stuff.

Pity the croc is such a naff colour. Can't we paint it? Spray it, maybe? Why didn't you get a green one, Silv? And where do we get another one that's about the same size?'

'It isn't hers. It came with the house,' Bo told her.

'Trago Mills?' Jessica suggested. 'There's not much you can't get in there. Or look on the internet?' She left them with the drinks and a pack of Jaffa cakes and headed back to the house, saying, 'I'll have a quick look now for you. About two metres long, isn't it?'

'Thanks, Mum!' Lola called after her. Silva was surprised to see that her eyes looked wet.

'That's kind of her,' she said. 'Not sure ours would bother.'

'She's a freakin' star, my mum,' Lola said quietly, then rallied, giving her nose a quick wipe with the back of her hand. 'OK – wood. What sort and where to get?'

'I saw Jules collecting a load of driftwood on the beach this morning,' Silva said, savouring saying his name.

'*Jules?* You actually talk to him?' Lola glared at her.

'Who's Jules?' Bo asked, looking puzzled.

'He surfs. Streaky yellow hair, earrings. Loud, cocky bastard,' Lola said. 'Not someone you'd want your sister to hang with, Bo. He's a total arse.' She glared at Silva, who felt thoroughly warned off and very pleased about it too. It meant she hadn't imagined it at the barbecue –

Lola must think of her as rival material. Talking of which . . .

'They might have been collecting it for a raft of their own.'

'They could, that's true. They won last year.' Lola looked round at them all and raised her Coke can like a toast. 'But they won't this time. *This* is war.'

'Wow, Steve, this is just stunning. It couldn't be better.' They'd just ordered and Miranda handed her menu to the waitress, leaned back in her chair and sniffed at the salt-laden shoreline air, feeling as content as Toby the cat in a patch of sunlight. They were alongside the broad stretch of perfect sand on the outside deck of the Porthminster Beach Café, beneath a sunshade. They had salted olives and oil and bread and a gorgeous lunch ordered. She sipped her wine, looking out across the beach to where children and families were digging in the sand, playing beach cricket and paddling in the shallows, jumping waves. 'What a fabulous setting this is. I'm sure the English seaside never used to have restaurants as lush as this. It all used to be greasy little caffs or chippies.'

'Up there with your fancy London gaffs, is it? I bet you go to them all: The Wolseley, Soho House, The Ivy, all those.' He was mocking her again. This was becoming a pattern. She didn't much mind, but he couldn't have it all his own way.

'Gosh, so you've actually heard of them, then, down here on the primitive tail end of the nation?' she asked, leaning forward towards him, feigning raised-brow surprise. She could see the reflection of the sea in his eyes, glinting silvery-grey.

He shrugged, 'Well, you know, sometimes we Cornish are given a day pass over the Tamar. Just now and then, so we can remind weselves which soide is the betterrr one,' he said in a comedy Mummerset accent. 'Not too often, though; they wouldn't want us to get used to those evil up-country ways. But as it happens,' he said, sounding like himself again, 'I do spend quite a bit of time in London these days. I pay a mate a kind of retainer on a teeny room to crash in at his flat in Shepherd's Bush. It's not big enough for him to rent out for someone to live in properly but it's doable for the odd night.'

Miranda took an olive from the dish and dunked it in the oil and balsamic vinegar mix. It was a bit big for putting straight into her mouth so she chewed round the edges of it, conscious that Steve was watching her intently. Shepherd's Bush was only a couple of miles from her own home. Funny to think he must have been, at times, only down the road. Maybe they'd even crossed on the pavement at some point.

'So what do you do in London? Is it a work thing?' she asked, at last popping the gnawed-down olive into her mouth and sucking the tender flesh from the stone.

'I do some of the stock deliveries, just to keep the contact going. My view is it's like being an organic farm supplier – when it's a specialized business, people expect the personal touch to go along with the goods.'

'Sounds like a top enterprise you've got going on here. It bought you the best house in Chapel Creek.'

He smiled. 'It's done fine. Better than I ever expected, but I was in at the right time when the sushi thing took off. You won't ever catch me eating the stuff, though.'

The waitress arrived with their food. Steve had ordered steak, Miranda the crab linguine. 'You don't eat your own products?'

'No. When you handle it all day it's the last thing you want. And I wouldn't say it to my customers, but I also have a sneaky old-fashioned feeling that fish should be cooked, not raw.'

Miranda wound a careful forkful of the linguine and wished she'd chosen something with a lower potential for making a horrible mess of her white shirt. Too late now, and anyway, she realized as she started to eat it, it was completely delicious – it would be well worth a few splatters.

'I completely get what you mean,' she told him. 'I work with colour and pattern, designing kitchenware – mugs and plates and fabric kind of stuff. And somehow, without me even being that conscious of the decisions when I bought them, every last plate and cup in our house is either plain white or blue. But that's easy – this is . . .' she waved her fork over her plate, 'this is *food* choices. Do you really never give the goods a road test?'

'Not since I gave up the lobsters. There was a day when I found out something about them and I couldn't take another from the sea ever again. But anyway, tell me about you. You have beautiful children. Do they come with a . . . y'know . . . a father?'

'Um . . . well, yes. Obviously. It's the usual . . . Oh, I see what you mean. No – well, they see Dan, of course, but we're not together any more. We were too young.' She could feel herself blushing and concentrated on her food for a few moments.

'Not too young for children, though?' he persisted. 'Sorry – none of my business. I was just curious. The last time I saw you, you weren't much older than your daughter. She looks a lot like you did then. It just seems . . . odd. Gives you a jolt about time passing. What did you do after you left school? How come you had children so young? If you don't mind my asking. It's unusual these days. Unless you live round here, that is, where loads of them are pushing prams by eighteen.'

'I did a degree in design and ceramics at Goldsmiths,' Miranda said, feeling the words coming out very fast, as if they were something to get over saying so they could move on. 'And somehow suddenly I seemed to have had a mad tiny wedding and got pregnant. And then again only weeks after Bo was born – there's less than a year between the two of them. I was exhausted and Dan was useless. He had this idea that because they were small and didn't take up a lot of space they wouldn't take up any time either. Turned out he was wrong, and although we plodded on together for a while it was never the same.' She gave a brittle laugh. 'Dan didn't exactly get the hang of feminism, although he thought he did. He'd been the one who most encouraged me to set up my design business and loved that it took off right from the start, but as for the domestic side of things . . . Sorry. You don't want to know all that. You must be well bored.'

'Not at all. I'm loving that you're filling in the time gap.'

'Yes, but that's just me. What about you?' Miranda asked. She'd finished the linguine and was picking at the rocket salad. She felt slightly nervous, suddenly convinced that Steve was about to tell her about his amazing girlfriend (please, *not* Cheryl) and their plans for a fabulous future. She couldn't grudge him that, she told herself. She would make sure she sounded *very, very* pleased about it.

'Not a lot to tell,' he said softly, looking out at the sea. The cries of seagulls mixed with shrieks from children jumping the waves at the sea's edge. 'I owned the ferry and the right to run it and managed to sell it to a bidder who came knocking with a ridiculous offer. Which is how I bought the house you're staying in. And the fish thing, well, like I said, right time for the sushi boom.'

'But . . . what about the other stuff?'

'Am I married and so on?' He smiled. 'No, not any more. Just for a couple of years, early on. It's what you do down here – all your mates are getting married so you sort of just do it. She wanted children.'

'You didn't?'

'Oh, I did. I do, even. But not that young, no. And I'd got it wrong. I realized in time for her to go and be with someone else that it wasn't going to work. She just . . . she wasn't my lobster.'

Miranda looked at him, wondering if she'd heard right. 'Your *lobster*?'

'That's right. My lobster. A lot of people think they mate for life. I now know they actually don't but I believed it for a long time. Ridiculous, no? You'd think I'd know better.'

There was silence for a few moments and Miranda watched a toddler pick up a beach ball that was almost as tall as herself and throw it to a proud-looking father.

'Is that why you don't catch them any more?' she asked.

Steve laughed. 'Don't go telling anyone what a soft old romantic I am, please! I'd never hear the last of it in the village. But yes, it's partly why. Once I'd heard about the for-life thing, I just couldn't lift a lobster out of a pot without thinking of its soul mate all alone in the ocean. And by the time I found out it wasn't exactly true it was too late. The idea was stuck in my brain. But hey, I might not eat lobsters but I do eat apple tart. They do a fabulous one here. Do you fancy it?'

Miranda looked at him and thought, yes, actually, I do. Very, very much. And some apple tart would go down well too.

THIRTEEN

If he opened his bedroom window and leaned out a little bit, Andrew could see most of Jessica's creekside garden. Years ago when it had been the Miller family who'd stayed there he hadn't bothered to do much staring out at them apart from when Clare had hung out a load of underwear on the washing line. He'd liked Miranda but she'd been a dreamy sort, drifting about in wispy vintage clothes and reminding him of an upright (and of course dry) version of Millais's painting of the drowning Ophelia. Jessica, though, she'd been earthier: sporty and curvy, with so much energy that although he'd desperately wanted to find himself (magically) in bed with her, he was quite scared that the reality would damage him. She could have bounced him to death. The one time he'd actually thought (wrongly, as it turned out) that he might be in with a chance of seducing her, he'd had to go to Helston library to research just how much alcohol it would take to get her to a state of languid calm. But the information had been confusing and the maths had been tricky and he'd given up, deciding it was a fine line between getting her mellow and making her comatose or sick.

Andrew sat on the window seat, looking out across the creek and down to the main estuary, checking out the boats. Or that's what he would say if anyone caught him and asked questions. Really he was hoping to catch a glimpse of Jess who, although now very slender and quite fragile-looking with her strange spiky hair hidden under scarves, still had her stunning smile and a look of potential naughtiness about her. He felt seventeen again, furtively spying on his quarry, feeling the old guilty excitement. He almost leapt out of the window when his bedroom door suddenly opened and for a terrible second he was whisked back to the time his mother had walked in and nearly caught him enjoying a moment of private sexual delight.

'So what's this insanitary dump worth? Have you come up with a figure?' Geraldine plonked herself heavily down on his old single bed. He turned to her and watched as a cloud of dust motes wafted up from the ancient floral eiderdown like tiny flying insects in a beam of sunlight. She was wearing khaki shorts that were surely big enough to make a tent for six boy scouts and had broad Birkenstocks on her strangely yellowish feet. He wondered if she'd heard that women tend to shave their legs in summer. Still, each to her own.

'Not yet,' he said. 'Water frontage always carries a top premium but the second homes market is depressed these days.'

Geraldine sniffed and took a look round his room. 'It could do with some work. Needs a thorough update, not to mention a scrub. I suspect mice, too. But then buyers often like a project, don't they?'

Andrew had once told her that very fact but was surprised to find himself wanting to argue the opposite when it came to his own family's house. 'Depends. If it's for full-time living in, then yes, they want to put their own mark on it. But if it's a holiday home, they don't usually want to spend a load of money on something they'll only be in for a few months of the year. They want a lock and go situation.'

She gave him a look, the same one she'd treated him to when she'd been moving to Esher and he'd told her one house she was viewing was 'deceptively spacious'. 'If you mean poky, just bloody well say so, Andrew,' she'd said. He couldn't blame her. Sometimes even he felt irritated by his own jargon, and he'd once wanted to leave a room and come back to start afresh after hearing himself telling a client they weren't only buying a flat but a 'lifestyle option', just because the block had a concierge and a basement swimming pool.

An idea was trickling its slow way into his head and he wasn't going to keep it to himself. Geraldine could approve or not, whatever she liked. This wasn't her house and never would be, so consulting her wasn't an issue. He'd got London friends and his little flat in Wandsworth but it didn't feel like *home* the way this cottage did. He glanced out of the window again and saw Jessica, Eliot and Lola come into the garden with oars and a basket. He watched as they went through the little gate in the wall and down the steps into a rowing boat, untied the rope and set off down the creek.

'Actually, I'm thinking of buying it myself,' he said, the decision suddenly made. Geraldine sprang up from the bed, disturbing the dust cloud all over again. He flinched. For a scared moment he thought she was going to attack him.

'Best idea you've had in your life,' she boomed, which almost floored him. He'd once thought it a good idea to accept his father's offer to pay to send Freddie to Andrew's old school (but she'd put her foot down, and when he thought about it, she was right. He'd hated it), and to let him go with his mates to Glastonbury (she'd won that as well) and to get him a drum kit (no argument, just NO). This had to be a one-off.

'You think so?' he said, suspecting she was going to come up close and bark 'Of *course* not, you imbecile' as she'd been known to do in the past (the time he'd suggested Freddie might prefer a puppy to a pony).

'Yes, of course. A bit of paint and a new kitchen and bathroom and this could be a little gold mine. *Then* you can sell it and make a nice fat profit. Freddie's going to need a lot of funding for university in a couple of years. Good thinking, for once, Andrew. I'll get some paint charts. You won't have a clue on colour, obviously.'

Obviously. Andrew looked out of the window again, across at the thousand shades of green on the hillside trees, at the ever-changing grey-brown ripples on the creek, at the delicate pinks and creams of the roses in his father's flower beds. She could get all the paint charts she liked, he thought to himself, but, somehow and whatever it took, this was going to be *his* project, and his (and Freddie's whenever he wanted) home.

Miranda wasn't sure this was a good idea but Harriet insisted she needed an urgent bikini wax and her nails, according to her, were 'beyond dire'. So the two of them were in Miranda's car, driving round the headland to Tremorwell and the Pengarret hotel where Pablo the errant footballer might or might not still be in residence. It was a risky venture, Miranda thought. Was Harriet softening towards Pablo, now that, although he was still in the area, he didn't seem to be so passionately pursuing her? Or was she planning to run into him 'accidentally'? She hoped not. From what she'd seen of him, the man was little more than an overgrown yob. Harriet could do much better than that. Miranda could only hope he, and the reputed cohort of press, had chosen this day to leave.

'We could go to Truro, you know,' Miranda said as they went up the lane and out of the village, 'Or to the spa at that hotel across the water. It's won awards. *And* they've got a lovely pool and you can get a cream tea. I could call them right now if you like.'

'We've got a lovely pool here at the house. And a cream tea will make me all swolled up. Anyway, this is nearer.' Harriet had her determined face on. 'I wouldn't want you to drive miles just for *moi*.'

'Very considerate of you,' Miranda said, trying not to sound as sardonic as she felt. 'So do you know whether he's still actually there or not?'

'Who?' Harriet asked, her eyes wide and faux-innocent. 'Oh, you mean Pablo? I have *no* idea. I expect he's gone back up to Manchester for training or whatever they do.'

'I thought he was banned for a while.'

Harriet shrugged. 'Yes, but he has to keep in shape. But anyway, it's nothing to do with me. I don't give a flying one, frankly.'

Miranda drove in through the ornate gates of the hotel and took a quick look at Harriet. For a woman who didn't give a flying one she'd certainly pulled out all the don't-care stops and was wearing a silky little white wrap dress that showed off both her tan and her cleavage, and a pair of sky-high pink platform shoes. Car-to-bar shoes, Miranda had thought earlier as she'd watched Harriet totter down the house steps and pick her careful way to the car. She'd also piled up her hair into a messy but sexy bed-hair arrangement and curly tendrils of it wafted prettily around her face.

'It's just as well you're not here for a facial,' Miranda commented as she parked. 'It would take half the appointment time to get your make-up off before they even started on you.'

'*What* make-up? Harriet said, looking mightily affronted. 'I'm not wearing any. Hardly.'

'Whatever you say, darling, and you know I was only joking. You always look fabulous, make-up or not,' Miranda said as they went in. Harriet hesitated on the front steps of the building. The place was a popular local wedding venue and Miranda couldn't help thinking that Harriet, looking around in a quite nervous way, resembled a jilted bride with her white dress and anxious face. There was no scarlet Ferrari among the parked cars and no sign of any photographers. Miranda felt suddenly sorry for her. Where *was* she going to live when these few weeks were over? Did she really have nowhere to go? It wasn't that long since she'd left her girly Manchester flat-share; her old room was probably occupied by someone else but it could be worth checking, in case the new person hadn't worked out. So far she'd refused to discuss it beyond some hints that she 'might try London', job wise. That would probably mean the end of Miranda's spare room in Chiswick but it would be a pretty dreadful woman who refused to accommodate her homeless, unemployed (see also untidy, fractious, demanding . . .) sister.

Harriet spoke to the receptionist and vanished down a corridor in the direction of the spa. Miranda hadn't booked any treatments for herself. She didn't want some masseuse's hands on her body at the moment. Like a teenager who's had her arm signed by her favourite rock star, she could still feel the touch of Steve's fingers as he kissed her goodbye after their lunch. It was only a small kiss, nothing that suggested anything more than that he'd enjoyed her company, but something about his touch had felt it was setting her clothes alight and the heat went right through to her skin. Ridiculous, she told herself now as she went out into the hotel's garden with a copy of *Vogue* borrowed from Reception, to order herself some tea and cake and sit in the sunshine taking in the gorgeous view across the water to Falmouth. Steve hadn't said anything about seeing her again. But something had crossed her mind. When he'd originally invited her for the lunch he'd said he had to go to St Ives anyway, for some kind of meeting. But he hadn't mentioned it again and he hadn't so much as made a call to any possible client or colleague on the day. When she was feeling positive, she told herself that he'd only said the thing about the meeting to make it sound less of a date. When her confidence wavered, she decided that whoever it was must have either cancelled or changed the arrangements.

'May I join you?' Miranda, on the point of tucking into the chocolate cake the waitress had brought her, looked up at a man who was standing by her table.

'Er . . . well, I'm not sure. I don't know you, do I? Or do I?' He looked slightly familiar, but she couldn't immediately remember where from.

'I was at your place with Pablo. You know, the other day?' He looked embarrassed. 'Name's Duncan.' He held out his hand, but as Miranda had a piece of cake in hers she had to offer him her left one to shake and the two of them ended up looking awkwardly as if they were about to go and dance. Duncan laughed. 'Sorry, didn't see the cake. Look, I'll go. Sorry, this was a bad idea.' He had a soft Scottish accent. Miranda remembered he'd had the good manners to apologize for gatecrashing their barbecue. Unlike Pablo.

'No, it's fine. Sit down, please. We can get more tea. The cake's good.' She looked across at the waitress, who nodded and went back into the hotel.

He pulled out a chair and sat across the table from her. 'You haven't tried it yet. It might be dreck.'

She took a small bite. 'No, it's divine. I promise.'

'I'm more of a shortbread man myself,' he said. She wondered what he wanted.

'Pablo's a git,' he announced abruptly, startling her. 'He treats women like shit but he did really like Harriet.

She's the only one he's ever actually let move into his place. Not that it stopped him . . .'

'Right. But if he liked her, why not make more effort to keep her?'

'Because he's an idiot. You've got to understand, he's living the dream. All that clubbing and stuff. He's like a kid in a sweetshop.'

'I heard the sweetshop's closed down, for him,' Miranda pointed out. 'Surely you can't do world class sport and serious partying at the same time?'

'No, well, when your role model is the legend of George Best . . . But I think he's learned. For now. It's just . . .' the waitress came back, bringing tea and scones for Duncan. 'They read your mind here,' he said, laughing. 'Well, almost.'

'It's just what?' Miranda prompted him, hoping he wasn't going to plead Pablo's case for another chance with Harriet.

'Well, I heard she's been suspended from her job because of the bad publicity, and that's all wrong. What her boyfriend does isn't her fault.'

'Well, we all know that. And I think – I hope – it's *ex*-boyfriend,' Miranda said, starting to feel irritated. 'But there's not a lot we can do about it.'

'I know some people at the network,' he said. 'I could put in a word.'

'Oh could you?' Miranda could feel irritation building. What did this have to do with him? They didn't even know him, though of course maybe Harriet did. 'So why aren't you having this conversation with Harriet? She is a grown-up.'

'Well, that's my point. Pablo isn't. He's still hanging around here, talking about making some grand gesture, waiting to come up with some big scheme that will get her running back to him, but in private he's first to admit it's really all about trying to claw back some kudos from the management. If the press see a reformed character – and he's aiming straight at the glossy gossip mags – he's halfway to getting back in favour and sponsored for some big girl's blouse of an advertising deal like aftershave and sunglasses and so on. That's where all the big money is. But he's no use for an adult woman yet. He's been a footballer since he was fourteen; had to be the good boy through the years when most kids get to let off all their steam so right now he's got to get stuff out of his system, and if he doesn't come through it and get back into the team – which he should because he's got a genius left foot – I don't want to see him taking your sister down with him.'

Some cogs started turning in Miranda's brain. 'It's very sweet of you to worry about her.'

He shrugged and looked a bit pink. 'Aye, well. She's a lovely lassie and she's good at her job. We get a lot of free afternoons so I've seen her on the box. And off it too. Footballers go out in crowds, you know. I was at most places she and Pablo went.'

'So you're another player?' Miranda didn't know much about football but he seemed older than others she'd seen Bo watching on TV. She couldn't help noticing he had a lovely athletic shape though – strong wide shoulders, glimpses of serious muscle power under the short sleeves of his white T-shirt.

'Goalkeeper.' He grinned at her. 'We're rare beasts so they tend to hang on to us. We peak later than the kids who do all the running around so with luck we get a longer career.'

'You like Harriet.' She didn't mean it to sound like an accusation and wouldn't have been surprised if his re-action had been to deny it.

He looked her straight in the eyes for a long moment, then took a deep breath. 'I do,' he said. 'And I'll be honest, it cut me up to see her coming in here today. I know she's not with Pablo now because he's gone off out in the car some place. Was she here wanting to see him?'

'She was here wanting a manicure,' Miranda told him. The bikini wax would be too much information.

'Oh, right!' He smiled so dazzlingly that she worried she'd actually told him he was in with a chance. But then behind him, emerging from the comparative gloom of the hotel interior, Harriet could be seen pick-ing her careful way through to the garden, with her hands held up and fingers stretched out.

'Manda – look at this colour! Isn't it divine? Oh!

Duncan!' She stopped both talking and walking and stood framed beneath an arch of roses, looking at Duncan, who got up and gave her a brief kiss on the cheek. She kept her fingers well out of range.

'Hello, Harriet. How are you?'

'Er, fine. Lovely to see you. So you're still here then?' Miranda could see Harriet's eyes flickering past him, scanning all around.

'Yes, I'm still here, babysitting the idiot.'

'He so *is* an idiot,' she said, sitting down in the chair Duncan had pulled out for her and managing to break off and eat a chunk of Miranda's cake using her index finger and thumb like pincers.

'They match your eyes,' Duncan commented, pointing to her greeny-blue iridescent nails.

'You like?' she asked, posing with her fingers resting just beneath her mouth.

'I do like,' he told her softly, leaning forward towards her. Miranda, feeling suddenly like a gooseberry, gathered up her bag and her magazine and decided to make herself scarce.

'I'll .. er . . . maybe just go to the loo,' she told Harriet. 'Or, tell you what, if you want to stay here for a bit and talk, I expect . . .' She thought vaguely of taxis, the unlikelihood that there'd be one within a twenty-mile radius. And yet here was this lovely man who clearly liked Harriet *a lot*. She'd drive back herself and fetch her if necessary.

'I can drop Harriet back,' Duncan told her. 'I've rented a hire car from Truro.'

'You don't mind, do you, Manda? Duncan and I can have a bit of a catch-up.'

'No – I don't mind at all,' Miranda said. 'Would you like to come over for supper, Duncan?' She glanced at Harriet, wondering if she'd gone too far. But Duncan looked at Harriet for the right answer and she was smiling encouragingly

'Er – that's kind of you, thanks. I'd love to,' he said. Miranda left them to it. She just hoped a great fit hulk like Duncan could survive a cobbled-together pasta dish and some salad. He had the look of someone who devoured the best part of a large animal on a daily basis.

Clare felt guiltily sure this was something she shouldn't be doing, but it had been nagging at her since the undertaker, with his professionally unctuous face on, had handed over the urn. She had to have a look inside, see what the final manifestation of Jack actually was before she consigned him to the sea. This would be the last ever contact with something that was still physically *him*, however remote from the reality of alive-Jack. She'd never seen human ashes before. Her father had been buried in a churchyard full of gloomy yew trees and her mother was alive and well and playing bridge on a daily basis up in Stockton-on-Tees.

She took the urn out of the wardrobe and put it on

the table beside her bed. The whole thing was quite heavy, which had surprised her the first time she'd held it as Jack had faded almost to a shadow in his last months. What must the ashes of a big overweight giant of a man weigh? She knew they had urns of different sizes depending on body weight, but even then, did they only give you enough of what they cringingly called your Loved One to fill the pot, leaving traces of them in the ashy oven to mingle with those of others from the same day? It was hard enough to sweep out every bit from a domestic fireplace, let alone an industrial-size furnace.

No one was home or Clare wouldn't have felt able to do this. She didn't want any of the children (of either generation) walking in and finding her investigating the contents of the urn, even though really there was no reason why she shouldn't open it. They'd think she'd gone mad. Perhaps she had.

Carefully, she turned the lid, half expecting it to prove impossible to shift, like the top on a new jar of marmalade. If it did stick, you could hardly jam it in a doorframe and give it a twist. Nor did she fancy running a boiling kettle of water over it to loosen it. If the water got in you could end up with a clayish mud that would have to be prised out with a knife. The thought made her feel quite sick. Poor Jack. This was no way to be thinking about him.

The lid loosened easily enough but Clare hesitated

before taking it completely off, slightly scared about what was in there. Crazy, she thought; after all, she'd be scattering Jack on the sea in less than ten days' time. She'd certainly be seeing the ashes then, so why not now? She didn't immediately look as she took the lid off and put it on the table beside the urn. Then she took a deep breath, leaned forward and peered inside, her eyes half closed. Just ash. Powdery, pale grey ash, as if he'd been no more than a log fire. She felt a bit disappointed at the sight of it. Jack had hated the colour grey, whether it was clothing or sky. On a gloomy day he'd once looked at the miserably pallid clouds and asked her why God had so little imagination as to make them such a watery, nothing colour.

The sound of a car whizzing up the gravel startled Clare. In a heart-pounding rush to get the lid back on, she knocked the urn and it tipped over, the contents spilling all over the wooden floor.

'Nooo!' she wailed, hesitating to scoop up the mess with her fingers. She ran to the door in a panic, hurtling down the stairs and colliding with Miranda who was just coming in.

'Mum! What's the matter?'

Clare was shaking, running to the utility room and searching for a dustpan, howling, 'He's on the floor! He's all over the place!'

'Who is? What?' Miranda hauled her back into the kitchen and sat her in a chair. 'Tell me what's happened.'

'I was just looking. Just looking . . . I don't know why. I just had to,' Clare gasped. 'And now he's spilled! I've done . . . damage! It's got to be a thousand years' bad luck at the very least.'

Miranda switched the kettle on, took mugs and tea bags from the cupboard and said, 'Look, whatever it is it can't be that terrible. Where is . . . whatever it is?'

Clare pointed upwards. 'Jack.'

'I'll go and look,' Miranda said.

Clare said in a shaky voice, 'Some of him has gone down the floorboards, in the cracks. He'll be here for ever. In the house. He didn't want to be in a house.'

Miranda poured the boiling water into the mugs and, grasping at last what Clare meant, quietly went into the utility room and fetched the dustpan and brush she now realized Clare had been looking for.

'You will sort it, Miranda, won't you?' Clare put her face in her palms.

'Yes. I'll sort it. I'm sure it'll be fine.' And it would be, though she felt a bit sick.

'Thank you. I'm so lucky I can always rely on you,' Clare said.

Miranda crept up the stairs feeling the weight of her mother's recently acquired dependence. But oh, how sad for Clare, she thought as she tiptoed nervously into the bedroom and saw the upturned urn and the swath of ash across the floor. Tenderly she swept it into the dustpan, wishing she'd washed it first in honour of her much-loved stepfather. And yet . . . she felt a strange compulsion to laugh. Jack would have found this funny. If he could only come back right now he'd be the first, after a drink or two, to be sitting at a social supper telling this story against himself. 'All over the bloody floor,' he'd say, giggling with a schoolboy's hilarity. 'Like the cat's upended litter tray.'

With enormous care, Miranda managed to get the ashes back into the urn. There was still a pale smudge across the wood, as if someone had dropped grubby talcum powder. She went into the bathroom and looked for something to wipe it clean as she didn't want any traces left visible to upset Clare. She couldn't use a flannel – it would have to be loo paper. She ripped a few sheets off and moistened them, then went and wiped the remains of powdery Jack from the floor. But a couple of steps back towards the bathroom she stopped, the paper soggy and greyish in her hand. She couldn't flush him down the toilet like a dead goldfish; it would just be too wrong. She sat on the bed for a moment, wondering what to do. It was weird; she felt she'd gone through this before. And of course she had. She'd had the same dilemma twenty years before, hiding clotted blood in her mum's little pink soap box and wondering what on earth to do with it that didn't involve the insult of being consigned to the rubbish bin. In the end, she and Jessica had sent the soap box's contents out to sea, sellotaped into a clam shell. She'd cried then, watching the shell drifting on the shoreline. And she found she was crying now as she took tissues from the box beside the bed and wrapped them round the gritty piece of loo paper. She would bury this tiny powdery trace of Jack, she decided, tears falling down her face, bury it in the garden, by herself and with no fuss.

FOURTEEN

Miranda hadn't heard anything from Steve and was a bit stunned by how much she minded this. She was more than a tad out of practice at this fancying someone lark, and also it seemed mad when less than two weeks ago she'd given him just those occasional summertime thoughts over all the years. But there it was. She'd got a big fat crush on him all over again. It was probably to do with the lobster thing. Who couldn't love (OK, deeply fancy) a man who'd not only *believed* that stuff but actually let it make a difference to how he worked? She now found she was picking up her phone and putting it down again like an obsessed teenager and minded that too – she should be more grown up than this. She'd sent a text and thanked him for the St Ives lunch and he'd replied saying it had been a pleasure but had said nothing about meeting up again. Not even a hint. But then why would he?

She couldn't expect to waltz back into the village and be the centre of his world all over again. Maybe that one meeting was all there would be to it: curiosity on both sides satisfied, and in not much more than another week she'd be on her way back to London and he'd continue his life with (she presumed) Cheryl and forget about her for another twenty years. Or for ever, even. The thought that she might not see him again, possibly ever, made her feel more unhappy than she'd have thought possible, but as it had fallen on her to be family cheerleader she kept her thoughts hidden and her face brightly smiling. Having Harriet beaming like a cream-filled cat over breakfast didn't exactly help and when everyone else was out of the kitchen in the morning she intended to tackle her about Duncan. The two of them hadn't turned up for supper the night before after all. Harriet had called at the last minute and said there'd been a change of plan, adding vaguely that she'd be 'late' and not to wait for her.

'I suppose we should be amazed she phoned at all,' Clare pointed out when Miranda was looking crossly at easily twice the amount of cooked spaghetti as their diminished party was likely to eat. 'She's never been known for her consideration, that one. She's not reliable like you.'

Oh, that reliability thing again. Every mention of it made Miranda want to fly out of the house and run away to be reckless. Just let the chance come up, she thought, just let it.

'So, Harrie, did you stay at the Pengarret for dinner?' Miranda asked after breakfast the minute the children had gone off to the beach. She so hoped that wherever she'd been, it was with Duncan and not the awful Pablo. The worst case would have been him running into the pair of them and charming Harriet away from Duncan, back into his Ferrari, his bed and his life. Please not.

Harriet smiled sleepily. 'No. Much better than that. Duncan hired a water taxi and we went way up the river to the most cute little restaurant. *So* gorgeous, Mands, you'd love it. We had supper out on a high-up terrace overlooking the water. They give you a blanket to snuggle into when it gets cold. Total bliss.' She gazed out of the open doors and looked dreamy. 'And they have rooms. It would be a fabulous place to spend a couple of romantic nights.'

Miranda gave her a sharp look. 'With . . . ?'

'Not with Pablo,' she said. 'Definitely not. Duncan is *so* not like him. He knows how to treat a woman, you know, like holding chairs and stuff. It made me realize what a slob Pablo was. When we went out I used to make excuses for him in my head and think, well, maybe it was cos he was still a bit young that he held his knife and fork as if they were daggers. Duncan doesn't. But he's just a friend, you know, and he drove me back here without even, you know . . . suggesting anything. Unusual, that.' She looked surprised and Miranda felt defensive for her. Why shouldn't she have someone who didn't immediately expect to sleep with her? Someone who would relish the chance to get to know her properly first?

'Maybe he didn't fancy me,' Harriet said, looking thoughtful.

'Of course he did!' Miranda reassured her. 'Any fool could see that. Any fool like me, yesterday. He couldn't take his eyes off you. Maybe he's just not the type to rush into stuff.'

'Really?' Harriet looked puzzled, 'I've never had one of those before. It's kind of . . . prehistoric? Nice though. And like I said, he's just a friend.'

A bit of reticence *was* a change, Miranda had to agree, and yet. She was gradually realizing she'd give a lot for Steve to want to rush her into bed. Here was the usually impulsive Harriet contemplating something on a slow burn that might turn out to be long-term while Miranda was aching for the excitement and heat of quick-fire desire. One lucky sister out of two wouldn't be bad, so good luck to Harriet.

'But hey, you haven't said much about your lunch with Steve. Tell me all.' Harriet pointed her perfect blue-grey fingernail at Miranda. 'I might not be having a sex life but I can hear about yours.'

Miranda got up and went to open the doors wider.

Sun was streaming in and she sniffed at the warm morning air. There was a change to it and it felt slightly charged, as if soon the heat was going to turn menacing rather than simply comfortably hot. 'There's nothing to tell. We went to St Ives, had lunch, talked about what we'd been doing since we last met and that was it, really.'

Harriet wasn't having that. 'Oh, come on, Manda, you came back grinning like a goofy puppy. Did he snog you? He did, didn't he?'

'No, he didn't.' Miranda started putting mugs in the dishwasher, not wanting Harriet to see her face. She was sure everything she was thinking would be clearly evident on it.

'But did you want him to?' Harriet's voice was so softly sympathetic that Miranda almost felt like crying. Again. This had to stop – she just wasn't a cryer. Which reminded her, she still had to deal with the ash-mopped tissues which were hidden in the underwear drawer in her room. She'd got an idea about that, for later.

She turned to Harriet. 'Yes, OK, I did. I do. But there's no point thinking about it. He's with someone else, I'm pretty sure.'

'If he didn't actually say he was, in like *actual words* when you were out with him, then you don't know. Fuck's sake, just text him, invite him for a drink. We haven't got long down here, Mands, so get on with it if you want to. And don't go saying this is three hundred miles too many from home for a relationship. Everything's doable if you want it to be. Go for it, babes.'

Miranda envied her younger sister's simple optimism, and tried the idea on for size in her head. Some of it worked. After all, why *not* ask him? He'd taken her all that way and bought her that gorgeous lunch – it was only good manners at least to offer a return match, even if it was only a drink at the village pub.

'Y'know, you're right, Harrie. I'll do that. Just as soon as I've been down to the shop for the paper and some supplies. Do you want me to pick up the rubbish press for you or are you past all that?'

Harriet laughed. 'Hell, no thanks! I'm not interested in Pablo's exploits any more. Time to get on with my life. Anyway, I haven't got time to read the papers. I'm meeting Duncan at eleven. We're going to do a bit of the tourist thing and have a look at St Michael's Mount.' She gave Miranda a cheeky smirk. 'Just as friends, obviously.'

Miranda walked down to the harbour with Clare, who was going across to the gallery in St Piran, and had a look at the boats moored up around the sailing club as they walked down the pontoon to the ferry. Steve had said in St Ives that one of them was his, but not which. It could be anything from the biggest gin palace out there to the smallest rowing boat.

'Your old friend Steve has a boat here, doesn't he?'

Clare said, breaking into Miranda's thoughts in quite an alarming way. Were mothers supposed to be able to tell what you were thinking? She didn't have much idea what went on in Silva's head and wondered if she'd failed there. Was Silva's lack of communication on all things personal a matter of privacy, secrecy or simply having not a lot to say at this particular teenage moment?

'He does, but I don't know which,' Miranda said. She had the screwed-up ball of ashy tissues in her handbag. Could Clare also see through the leather to the sad little trace of Jack? God, she hoped not.

'If it's a boat that's big enough,' Clare started hesitantly, 'do you think . . . would it be too much to ask him if he'd take us out on the water to, you know . . . do the ceremony? I mean, I know I didn't want strangers driving us but he's not one really, is he? And I don't know who else we'd get. Eliot and Andrew, they're more sailing boat sorts.'

'Andrew could do it – he's done the relevant tests – but he'd have to find something to borrow. He really just sails dinghies – he keeps one down here full time. But he did know Jack, so he might be better.'

The ferry was approaching from St Piran. Miranda had a bit of a flashback from when she and Jess used to go across the estuary with Steve at the helm. He always stood to drive the boat, holding the tiller and balancing in a rather cocky way, showing off. They'd sit at the back close to him, their faces at his crotch-level, trying not to giggle. Such silly, smutty little girls they'd been, she thought; if seeing her again had jogged those kinds of memories in Steve, it was no surprise he'd be reluctant to see her again.

'No. Andrew's very welcome to come along, and Jessica too, but I'd rather it was Steve. He must know the water out there like the back of his hand. He'd know exactly the right place.'

She'd have to see him again now to ask him, Miranda thought. How could she not? You could hardly send a quick text saying, 'Hi Steve, would you like to come out with me to bury my stepdad?' Tempting? Not really.

'I'll see you later, darling,' Clare said as the waiting ferry started to load passengers. 'Have a lovely morning. What are you planning? Anything nice?'

'I'm going to call in on Jessica. Other than that, I might do some drawing back at the house. All those agapanthus in the garden have given me an idea for a design. Good luck at the gallery.'

'Thanks. I'm going to make that woman take a dozen of Jack's Cornish paintings, whether she likes it or not,' Clare said, looking steely and determined. 'Though there is a bit of an issue about how to get them here from Richmond. We'll have to sort something out with transport. I expect you'll come up with an idea.'

Ah – another problem to work on. Miranda already

had her rail tickets for London in a few days' time but maybe she should have thought it through and taken the car so as to bring the paintings for Clare. But she'd wanted to leave the Passat for the others to use. Wrong again, then, in spite of good intentions. Damn.

She waited a while on the pontoon till the ferry raced away with its full load of trippers. They were a mixed bunch: sporty sorts with bikes and Lycra, others in full-scale hiking gear, families with dogs and small children and the usual British collection of complicated beach kit, and surfboard-toting teenagers including the good-looking streak-haired boy with the earring whom she sometimes caught Silva looking at. Maybe she *could* read Silva's thoughts a bit after all, she thought as she turned back towards the centre of the village to go to the shop.

The shop was busy – customers were whizzing in and out like wasps from a nest and Miranda sat for a while on the wall outside thinking she'd wait till it was a bit quieter and take the opportunity to send Steve a text. Amazingly – for the service was patchy in the village – there was a mobile signal and she sat looking at the phone screen wondering what to say that didn't look cravenly needy. Eventually she simply asked if he fancied a drink at a pub of his choice that evening. They could sort the where and what time details when (if) he replied.

A family of six emerged from the shop, squabbling over who had ordered what kind of pasty, so she reckoned there'd now be room to move inside.

'Hello! How are you? Having a lovely holiday?' Miranda was almost knocked over by the unexpected warmth of Cheryl's greeting. The girl was absolutely glowing with well-being. Someone's had a good night, she thought, feeling more than a bit envious.

'Hi. Yes, great, thanks. You look happy,' Miranda said, smiling. Cheryl was thoroughly radiant and looked a hundred times prettier than when she was scowling and cross. Miranda took a *Guardian* from the rack and put a loaf of sourdough bread in one of the fancy wire baskets.

'That's because I *am* happy!' Cheryl told her as she put on her gloves to prepare a sandwich for a customer whom Miranda recognized as the dour northern lady from her first day, the one who'd been so outraged by the shop's prices. Now here she was buying fancy focaccia and handmade hummus and not quibbling. 'Absolutely bloody *ecstatic*,' Cheryl went on.

The other customer sighed and turned to Miranda. 'I think we're supposed to ask why,' she said. She didn't fool Miranda – that was sheer nosiness and Miranda smiled and sympathized and took her cue because, frankly, she wanted to know too.

'OK, why?' she asked. 'Has the lottery fairy called?'

'No, nothing like that. I've got a *well* hot date tonight,

is all.' Cheryl was blushing prettily as she scooped garlic-stuffed olives into a polystyrene tub.

'Lucky you. I expect they're few and far between in these remote parts,' the other customer said, but even that rather caustic remark didn't shift the happy grin from Cheryl's face. The text alert on Miranda's phone pinged in her bag but she didn't look. She had a horrible feeling she didn't need to. The northern lady paid for her goods and left the shop and Miranda added half a dozen pasties and some organic local rocket and courgettes to her basket and took them to Cheryl at the check-out.

'Isn't life great sometimes?' Cheryl gushed as she rang up the total. 'You know what it's like, you hope something's going to work out your way for once and suddenly, when you least expect it, it just *does*.'

Miranda had a feeling she actually *didn't* know what it was like. Cheryl was *that* close to dancing on the spot and squealing 'eeeeek' with excitement. Oh, the envy, Miranda thought, wondering if she'd ever feel like that again.

'And maybe it'll happen for you some time,' Cheryl said to Miranda by way of a parting shot, her eyes glittering in a not entirely friendly way as if she'd just remembered she wasn't supposed to like her. Miranda thanked her and told her she hoped so and did her best to look as if she was taking this at face value, but once she got outside and looked at her phone it was no surprise to find a reply from Steve to say thanks but no, he was going out somewhere else tonight but he'd be in touch.

Yeah right, Miranda thought, fighting back a tear that even she thought ridiculous in the circumstances; perhaps they'd meet again in another twenty years.

Silva looked at Willow's Facebook page and groaned out loud. How did she do this? How come she was so freakin' cool? It was a classic shot, a pyramid in a swimming pool with three *totes* fit boys at the bottom, two girls standing on their shoulders and, of course, star of the show Willow balancing right at the top, her long yellow hair blowing about in the breeze. There were champagne bottles and glasses on a table beside the pool. The other girls looked a bit older than Willow, all post-braces perfect American teeth and tiny bikinis full of well-grown breasts. Perhaps they saw slender Willow as the baby of the group, the no-threat cute English girl who could be allowed at the top of the pyramid like some kind of harmless mascot. How wrong they were, Silva thought, looking closely at the photo and seeing the eyes of one of the boys staring upwards between Willow's tanned and parted thighs. He didn't look as if he was just checking she was safely balanced. Silva clicked 'Like' under the photo but didn't leave a comment. What was there to say? 'I'm well jel' would about cover it but she wasn't going to give Willow the satisfaction.

She closed down the computer and went outside to the terrace, sat on the steps and looked down at the pool shimmering turquoise below. Actually, thinking about it, she felt OK about the Florida photos. She was actually happy right where she was, and who wouldn't be? How spoiled would you be to complain? She might have felt out of her depth on Willow's holiday. Willow could cope with those older, muscle-bound sporty boys – the sort arty Bo would dismiss as 'jocks' – but Silva would probably feel uncomfortable and that near-year between her and Willow would be really showing. Here in this Cornish village she was now feeling quite contented. She didn't mind the odd dig from Lola. Lola was just *born* spiky. It didn't mean anything. And she had a sweet side to her as well. And also there was that Jules boy. He kept turning up everywhere. Freddie had a theory that he was really identical triplets but Silva didn't care – she just liked the way he always smiled at her, asked her how her surf lessons were going, treated her like a girl he was almost (only almost, she didn't have *that* much confidence) interested in.

A City Link van pulled up outside the gate. You didn't see many of those round here, she thought idly, picturing home streets full of red buses, ambulances with sirens blaring and the general dusty kerfuffle of town life. A man walked into the garden clutching a parcel. 'Anderson?' he asked, holding out the package. 'Can you sign here, my lover?' Silva giggled and signed and took the parcel into the house. It was addressed to her. She ripped it open and out fell a crumpled, folded lump of plastic. 'Whee – another crocodile!' she squealed, looking at the picture on the packaging. 'And purple!' Lola's lovely mum – huge thanks to her for knowing *she* would be the one who'd actually *want* this! She set to work immediately, puffing herself out inflating the pool toy. She went and got the crocodile from the utility room and laid the two of them out on the floor side by side. Almost the same size and not so rounded that their project wouldn't work. All they had to do was work out how to attach some wood (and Freddie had found an old pallet in his dad's shed that they could take apart) and the raft would be sorted.

Poor Willow, Silva thought as she lined up her two childish toys against the utility room wall; when it came down to the deep down old-school fun of being like a little kid again, she might actually be *missing out*.

'I'm so glad you're here,' Jess said to Miranda as they sat on the wall dangling their legs over the creek as they used to when they were teenagers. 'I'll miss you when you go back. You'll come again, won't you?'

'I hope so – I don't see why not,' Miranda said. 'Now we've rediscovered the place I can't imagine never coming here again. Though maybe I wouldn't stay in Steve's house next time.'

'You can always stay here,' Jessica offered. 'There're only two of us here so there're two spare bedrooms since I had the attic done. Come any time.'

'Where's Lola's dad?' Miranda came straight out with the question she'd been wanting to ask.

'Australia,' Jess said. 'I met him in France. He thought we were a holiday thing and I thought it was more than that and when I got pregnant he flew off back to the homeland so fast I don't think Qantas were even involved.' She laughed. 'There've been a few others since but nothing that lasted very long. With all of them I ended up thinking I just preferred it as me and Lola, on our own. I wouldn't mind hooking up with someone, though; I want Lola to be able to go off to university or travelling or whatever she wants and not feel she's got to be kind of responsible for me for the rest of my life, especially since the cancer. But I'm not sure there are many men who'd be too keen on this.' She patted her front.

'Would you want one who *couldn't* cope with it, though?' Miranda asked. 'I mean, look at most men – the older they get the more worn round the edges they are. They should be so lucky as to get you, frankly.'

Jess hugged her. 'Thank you! But honestly, I'm fine. Though . . .' she glanced across towards the house next door, 'it's funny having Andrew around again. I kind . . .

of . . .' she looked down at the river and Miranda could see her face going pink, 'I sort of like him, you know? I didn't think about it seriously but last night, really late, I was out watering the pots and there was Geraldine having a cigarette in the garden.' Jess looked across towards Andrew's cottage. 'I can't believe she smokes so much when she's always going on about healthy stuff. Is she totally mad?'

'She likes to fuss over Freddie, I suppose. A case of do as I say, not as I do. But go on – tell me about last night.'

'Ah yes, well, Andrew leaned out of the window and asked her to move because the smoke was going into his room. It was his old room, that one with the single bed in it. And I thought, oh good, he really definitely isn't sleeping with her. I sort of surprised myself with the thought.'

'Andrew, though?' The words were out before Miranda could stop herself. 'Sorry – I didn't mean it to sound like that. He's sweet, it's true. And he looks far better now than you'd have thought he would back then.'

'I know. He's kind of grown into his geeky look. I like that. And I like it that he's still quite an innocent-seeming sort and you don't get many like that. I don't think there's a bad bone in him. But anyway, you said you had something you wanted to do here. Tell me – I'm intrigued.'

Miranda reached down into the bag behind the wall

and pulled out the wodge of tissues she'd been carrying around.

'We have to bury this. In this garden,' she said.

Jess looked at the scrumpled paper in Miranda's hand. 'Twenty years I don't see you, back when we did the funeral on the beach, and you tell me we're doing *another* one?' She was almost exploding with pent-up laughter. 'Sorry! It's not funny, but I can't help it. And the other one wasn't even remotely funny. Sorry.' The laughter escaped and pealed so loud across the creek that it echoed back at them. 'But what *is* this?' The hilarity vanished as suddenly as it had come, 'Oh, God, you haven't lost . . . ?'

'No, no! Nothing like before.' She told Jess about the spilt ashes and about mopping up the last of them. 'So I just couldn't bin him, could I?'

'No. I guess not.' Jess started laughing again. 'Sorry, but I'm picturing you on all fours wiping up the ash and apologizing to it at the same time. It's really not funny. Not even a bit.' She was shaking with laughter and by now so was Miranda, but eventually Jess managed to speak. 'And you want to bury him here?'

'Well, he loved this house. Loads of the plants in this garden were put in by him and Mum. I thought, maybe under that white camellia? If that's OK? It's one he bought for her. It was at the flower and produce show in Helston. I remember trailing around the exhibits in the tent, bored witless and probably moaning about it, the way Silva would now. At thirteen you're too old to make gardens on a plate but too young to appreciate giant marrows.'

'I'll get a spade from the shed.' Jessica climbed off the wall and gave Miranda another hug. 'And we'll make it pretty deep. When Lola was small and we were in London, we buried her dead guinea pig, wrapped in a bit of pink blanket. The next morning when I got back from taking her to school I could see the foxes had been. There was the blanket, trailed across the lawn, and no sign of poor Gilbert the piggy.'

'Oh, awful. But didn't you worry he hadn't been dead in the first place? I would have.'

'No, he was dead all right.' Jess mimed feet in the air and eyes shut tight, which made Miranda giggle. 'Still, I suppose it's a form of recycling, isn't it?'

The ground was tougher than they'd thought it would be. 'All these roots plus no rain,' Miranda said, leaning on the spade.

'Also doing it in flip-flops. Come on, give me a go.' Jess reached out for the spade.

'No, I'm stronger than you.' Miranda held on. 'Plus you're feebled from chemo. I don't want you to strain something.'

'Hello. Are you two doing gardening?' And there was Andrew, climbing nimbly over the fence from next door.

Miranda glanced at Jessica, who was smiling at him, all sparkly-eyed.

'Just digging a hole,' she told him. 'But the earth's like concrete.'

'Give me the spade,' he said. 'How deep do you want it? And is it OK if I make it big enough to put Geraldine in?'

'That bad?' Jessica said. 'Is she staying all summer?'

'That wasn't the plan. She said a few days. She's terrifying. And I very much mind being lectured about the dangers of soft cheese through a haze of poisonous smoke,' he told her. Jessica was beaming. Miranda felt like creeping away and vanishing, just as she had when Harriet had joined her and Duncan at the hotel. Always the gooseberry, she thought, but this time she thought it in a happy way. Quickly, she explained about the ashes, and Andrew, appreciating the situation and not even thinking of suggesting the kitchen bin, bless him, easily got the hole to a good eighteen inches deep. Miranda, feeling slightly awkward, put the tissues in and covered them over with earth.

'We've done this before,' Andrew said, looking puzzled, as if his own memory had quite startled him.

'We have. But at sea that time. Thanks for the digging, Andrew,' Miranda said, giving him a quick hug. He didn't flinch, which was something, but he did look surprised.

'Yes, thanks,' Jess added, also hugging him. Miranda

noticed that with her he actually put an arm round her and squeezed her to him. Good, she thought. Time to make her excuses and leave them to it. Who knew? Maybe they would make a lovely and happy couple. Another one.

FIFTEEN

Where were Steve and Cheryl going that evening and what would they be doing? As if she couldn't guess. Cheryl wouldn't have been so hyper if they were going to quiz night at the village pub. Miranda tried not to think about them as she slowly stirred stock into the risotto on the stove. The stove in Steve's own house, she thought, stroking its glossy black surface. She was feeling almost self-indulgently maudlin and wondering if he'd chosen all the fittings or if someone else had had a hand in it. She imagined him driving back from London in his fish van, having loaded the empty storage space with this set of pans from John Lewis that she was using and boxes of the cutlery that was laid out on the table. Apart from his two brief visits to this house, she'd never seen him in any domestic setting. Years ago he hadn't set foot in Creek Cottage and she'd never visited him at his parents' house. She didn't get the impression he'd be a lazy sort like Dan, one who would pile up dirty plates in the sink 'to soak' and imagine the washing-up fairy would deal with them. But you could never tell. Maybe it was just as well that she'd never know. She was beginning to look forward to going home and feeling normal again. This crush business was very wearing.

'When's food? I'm starving.' Bo wandered in and collapsed in his usual drama-boy way on to one of the Ghost chairs, then tipped it backwards so it was only on its back two legs.

'Bo, please don't do that. We have to pay for break-ages,' she snapped at him. Steve would not be happy if his carefully chosen furniture got broken.

'Won't break it. Not stupid,' he grunted, but he did put it back down on its four feet then got up and wandered over to the cooker, peering into the pan. 'What is it?'

'You know what it is. It's a risotto. There'll be prawns, baby beans and peas and herbs in it. You've had it before.'

'Prawns,' he said. 'It's not, like, meat.'

Miranda, feeling criticized, flung the spoon down in the pan, splashing herself with the newly poured stock. 'Shit.' She wiped at her front with a tea towel.

'No, it's not *like* meat, Bo,' she said, feeling so wound up that if she went outside she'd surely spin through the air all the way down to the harbour. 'You don't need meat every damn day.'

'You're in a mood,' he said, putting his hands in his pockets and shuffling backwards out of her way.

'Well done, Sherlock,' she said, then felt guilty. It wasn't his fault. Nothing about her dark blue mood was his fault, her beautiful, sweet, ever-hungry, ever-growing boy. She took a moment to shut her eyes and imagine taking a photo of Steve and Cheryl with a loved-up glow you could light a room with holding hands as they walked into a gorgeous restaurant; then she pressed a kind of mental delete button and opened her eyes again, determined that that was the last bit of attention they'd get that night. 'Sorry, Bo. I'm just a bit tired.'

''S OK,' he said. 'But it was only about meat, not the Gaza strip. I don't mind prawns. Prawns is cool.'

Miranda's text alert pinged and her heart did a couple of massive thumps as she grabbed the phone. Jessica, inviting her for a drink at the pub. 'Andrew's coming too,' she said. Miranda wondered if she should leave them to it, just the two of them, but then decided that a short break with them would be good. She didn't have to stay long. She replied and went back to stirring the risotto.

Clare bustled in, bringing a heap of dry towels and swimsuits from the line. They were stiff from sun-blast and even above the scent of the risotto Miranda could smell the warm outside air still on them. You didn't get that in Chiswick, she thought, where even though they were a good way from the Heathrow flight path there was still the hint of aircraft fuel in the air and the ever present dust from the nearby tube line. And now she found herself, after briefly thinking that home would be a good option, wondering about what it would be like living down here full time. Would the children like it? Probably not. They were used to being able to walk out of the house and find fast easy transport as close to the doorstep as you could get, to anywhere they wanted to be. They had their circles of friends – shrieky ones in Silva's case, watchful and taciturn in Bo's – and there was school, though she knew from when she was sixteen and Clare and Jack had followed up a whim to move to Totnes that change was possible and quite exciting. New friends could be made, adjustments, changes; all of it was doable. People did it all the time.

'Any sign of Harriet?' she asked Clare.

'Oh, sorry, I should have said. She called and said not to wait up again. Key to be left out under the flower pot like last night.'

'Lucky girl,' Miranda said, mentally ripping up the Steve–Cheryl picture as it threatened to return.

'Oh, dear. Are you feeling a bit of envy? You could do with some love interest in your life.' Clare came close and Miranda felt her body stiffen. She didn't want to be swamped by pitying sympathy. All was fine. Really it was. All she'd got was an inconvenient crush, probably caused by hot weather and too much sun. It would go away when some of the rain that the weather reports promised fell. And it wouldn't do to moan about the lack of a love life when her mother was mourning a more final end to hers than Miranda could even begin to imagine.

'Supper's ready,' she said, briskly moving to the fridge to get out the salad she'd already made. 'Can somebody shout for Silva? I think she's Facebooking with Willow again.'

Bo sloped out of the room and Clare closed the door after him. 'You know, Miranda, you could always try internet dating,' she said in a hushed whisper. 'There's no shame in it. Not these days.'

Miranda laughed. 'Mum, I tried that about two years ago. But after I got a guy who told me on day one that he liked to dress up like a toddler and another who stared at my feet all the time and then said he wanted to lick them, I kind of gave up. And before you say anything, no I haven't been tempted to repeat the exercise.'

Clare opened her mouth as if she were about to speak, then changed her mind. She adjusted a couple of forks on the table instead and then fetched the plates. Miranda took the dish of risotto to the table and looked at her mother's thoughtful face. She'd been about to say, Miranda was sure, that none of them were getting any younger. And even if she hadn't, the thought was criss-crossing Miranda's own mind like idiots playing chicken on a busy A-road.

'By the way, I'm going to the pub for an hour with Jess

and Andrew later. Would you like to come too?' She could have worded that better; it sounded insultingly after-thoughtish. She hadn't meant it to.

'No thank you, darling, you go.' Clare smiled, looking a bit watery around the eyes. 'There's a programme about Vivienne Westwood on TV and I'd really like to see it. Have a good time.'

Andrew felt too much like his seventeen-year-old self, and he tried to keep a lid on his excitement as he ate the seared tuna with pink fir apple potatoes that Geraldine had cooked for the three of them. He didn't want her to quash his happiness. 'Proper healthy food, nothing mucked about,' she'd said as she plonked the plates firmly on the table. Why did she always sound as though she was handing out a telling off? How did Freddie put up with it, Andrew wondered. Not that she directed it Freddie's way. All discontent was aimed at Andrew, as if he couldn't possibly have managed to exist, feed, clothe and house himself perfectly adequately since that brief encounter at the long-ago wedding party. Still, it surely wasn't for long. She couldn't hang about with them for ever. But all the same, so much for 'just a few days, to make sure Freddie was settled'.

But tonight, later, Andrew would be out of the house without her. Jessica had agreed to go out with him for a drink at the pub. OK, Miranda was coming too and it wasn't like an actual date, but he was going to call next door like a proper escort, walk with Jess over the creek and through the village and be *out* with her. He couldn't wait. And she needed looking after. Sitting beside him on the bench in her garden with tea, she'd briefly told him about her illness and how happy she was to have her hair growing back. He liked it as it was, actually. It was starting to curl at the ends and reminded him of one of those pretty poodle-cross dogs. She didn't give a lot away, and certainly no surgical details, but one thing had made him feel for her, when she'd told him she no longer felt quite whole any more. How he'd longed to put his arms round her and gather her close to him. One day, he told himself. Maybe one day soon.

The night air was still and heavy and it was warm enough to sit at a table outside by the river. Miranda didn't intend to be out long because she wanted Jess and Andrew to stay on together without her. If she couldn't have a romance, she didn't want to get in the way of a possible one for somebody else. It was still just about light as she walked down the lane from the house, and she remembered the times she'd been in the village years ago around midsummer day and it had seemed as if it didn't quite get dark at all sometimes. Even at ten thirty at night there'd been a silvery glow in the sky on the horizon in late June, and she and Jess, with Milo, Andrew and the boys from the pub and the

boatyard, used to sit on the beach with beers and a driftwood fire, their eyes developing perfect night vision.
She stopped on the wooden bridge by the creek to
watch a pair of swans dipping their heads in and out of
the water into the reeds beneath. Now they really *did*
mate for life, she thought, remembering what Steve had
said about lobsters. Maybe these two were actually
descended from the ones that had cruised the creek so
scarily in the dark when she and Steve had been coming
back from the beach in his little boat.

She heard a car engine and looked up, just in time to
see a small black convertible turn off the road by the
shop and vanish up the hill. Two people were in it,
the passenger a blonde woman. Looked like she'd
guessed right then, Miranda thought as she walked off
the bridge, past the leering gnome in the phone box and
on towards the pub.

The other two were already there, sitting together on
the same side of a wooden bench at a table on the river-
side terrace. One quick drink, Miranda decided, then
she'd go. Because these two certainly looked like a
proper dating couple even though the chances were they
were only talking about something mundane like the
ever-escalating local council tax. Fairy lights were hanging between the four tall Cornish palms, and the air
smelled of the sea and of the night-scented stocks that
grew between the petunias in the hanging baskets.
Small children, out for a holiday supper treat with their

families, were starting to drift towards sleep, drooping on laps, leaning against dads and ignoring melting bowls of ice-cream which mothers, with the excuse that they hated to see it go to waste, would pick at delicately in tiny self-deceiving teaspoonfuls till it was all magically gone.

'Last time we were all here together we were too young to be served,' Miranda commented as she sat down opposite the other two.

'It never seemed to bother that Australian barmaid,' Jessica said. 'She never asked for ID.'

Andrew looked a bit fidgety and stood up, saying, 'On which, I'll get some drinks in. Do we want wine by the bottle or something else by glasses?'

'White wine?' Jess suggested, looking up at him. Miranda watched him gazing down at her, looking as if he'd forgotten what the question was. He'd always liked Jess, she remembered. How funny that these things from what was pretty much childhood still lurked. If she'd have been kinder to Steve back then perhaps he'd have wanted to see her again now. Just stop it, she told her brain. It's just summertime randiness. It will pass.

Andrew went up the steps to the bar and Jess turned to Miranda. 'I shouldn't have mentioned the barmaid,' she whispered, giggling. 'Do you remember? He had sex with her at that party after the regatta, up against a tree by the sailing club.'

'God, yes. The fireworks started and everybody saw.

Jeez! What a lot of mad old secrets we have in this place.'

Jess looked at her closely. 'What's up, Miranda? You look a bit miz. Is it the Jack thing? When are you going to scatter the ashes?'

'No, it's not that. Though we have to get on with sorting it. We just need to borrow a big enough boat. I'd quite like it to be one big enough to have a bit of a celebration on. Some champagne and cake, to make it a good send-off.'

'You should ask Steve. He's got exactly the boat. Thirty-seven-foot six-berth cruiser. Well, six at a push.' She pointed across the water. 'See that one with the blue stripe? That's his.'

'Wow, nice. Also, you're right: perfect. But, you know . . . it's Steve.'

'What about him? You're OK with him, aren't you? Have you seen him since your lunch in St Ives?'

'No. He's – well, he's out somewhere. With someone. Tonight.'

'Oh. Are you sure? He might be out on deliveries or something.'

'No, I think he's gone somewhere with Cheryl.'

'*Cheryl?*' Jessica said, 'Are you sure? Cheryl from the shop?'

'I think so.' Miranda wavered. 'I mean, I think I just saw them in his car when I was on my way down. Also, I saw her earlier and she was very excited about some date she'd got tonight. I put two and two together, is all.'

Jess laughed. 'I'm only guessing, but I'd say your maths might be a bit out. I mean, I know they're old friends and that, but . . .' At that moment Andrew came back with wine and glasses. Behind him, puffing a bit from the effort of having walked round from the house, was Geraldine, clutching a pint of lager. Andrew mouthed 'sorry' at them as he approached and looked mightily put out.

'I could see you all from the house so I thought I'd join you. Budge up,' Geraldine demanded, glaring at Miranda. 'Make room for a small one.' Jessica spluttered into her wine.

'Try to sip it slowly, dear,' Geraldine told her. 'Cheap wine can give you terrible heartburn.'

'It wasn't that cheap,' Andrew said.

'There's nothing at any price on a country pub wine list that could count as "not cheap",' Geraldine told him. 'Now, Andrew, while Freddie's not with us, what are we going to do about this regatta malarkey? What's all this about building a raft for a race?'

'Village tradition,' Jessica told her. 'It's fancy dress and it's just a fun thing. It's the last event in the regatta and everyone tends to fall in.'

'Well, quite. That's precisely what we don't want. Not with his chest. Andrew, you'll have to tell him not to do it.'

'Why me? And anyway, no, I'm not going to do that,' Andrew said. 'How do you think he'd feel? He's not a baby.'

'How do you think he'll feel with pneumonia and . . . and dysentery?' Geraldine countered.

'But he goes sailing and surfing and he swims in the sea,' Miranda pointed out.

'Yes, but he's good at sailing and he doesn't fall in. And the sea is different. It's . . . moving about all the time, keeping itself fresh. But up here by the creek,' Geraldine waved an arm in the general direction of the water, 'it's not healthy. It's *captive water*. It's sure to be full of sewage and . . . stuff. I mean, please don't tell me the outfall from the toilets here doesn't end up *out there*.'

'They have a septic tank,' Jessica told her. 'Like all the houses here.'

Geraldine shuddered, actually shaking all over like a wet dog, and Miranda watched fascinated as her breasts wobbled like a half-set pudding. 'You don't get that kind of thing in Esher,' she said, 'thank goodness. I'll have to think very carefully about letting Freddie come here again, now I know what there is just yards away from the back door. Honestly, Andrew, does everyone down here live like something from Dickensian times?'

'Yes.' Andrew and Jess said it at the same time and turned to each other, laughing. Miranda felt delighted at the sight of them bonding together against the dreaded Geraldine. She really was a nightmare, and yet between the two of them, albeit separately, she and Andrew had somehow raised the very lovely Freddie.

'Freddie likes it here,' Andrew said firmly. 'And

anyway, maybe we can have this conversation another time?'

Even Geraldine went quiet at that. The silence was filled with the sound of distant music and revelry from further along the coast.

'Kids partying on the beach again,' Jessica said, looking across the water. 'They come out with the dark like bats and hang about in the dunes with vodka.'

Geraldine frowned again. 'That's something else you don't get in . . .'

'I bet you do, apart from the dunes, obviously,' Miranda said. 'Teens always congregate together everywhere for fun. It's natural. But anyway,' she finished her glass of wine and stood up, 'I'd better get back to my two, make sure they're not trashing the place. Er, Geraldine, why don't you walk back with me?'

Geraldine looked up, surprised. 'What for? You're not scared of the dark, are you?'

'No, of course not. I just wanted to ask you about . . . er . . . allergies?'

Geraldine was up off the bench faster than Miranda would have thought possible. 'Really? Right, well there's not much I can't tell you. Come along then, chop chop . . .' she said, gathering up her bag and walking away from the table without a backward glance at the other two. 'What did you want to know?'

Miranda looked back at the others and waved. 'See you tomorrow, maybe?'

'Definitely,' Jess said. 'And,' she hissed loudly after her, 'thank you!'

By the morning the wind had got up and rain was threatening. Miranda remembered that Steve had said there was stormy weather on the way. Was it too fanciful to imagine he had some mystical seafarer's instinct for reading the weather, or did he simply look at the forecast on his iPhone like everyone else? Her own phone app prophesied thunder and lightning for the next day when she was off to London. The paper and the radio said gales. She called the local cab company and booked a taxi to take her to Redruth station in time to get the nine fifteen train and started thinking about what to take with her and what to wear to the meeting, which was to be at one of the airport hotels. It would feel odd to wear something madly smart and proper heels after all this time of drifting around the village in flip-flops, shorts and T-shirts. And she'd have to flip her mind into work mode as well as her clothes. What she really needed was Harriet, who was a clothes genius, having had all the practice of putting together the perfect smart-yet-not-overdone outfits for her TV show for the last two years.

Thinking now would be a good moment, before the children came back from their surf lesson and started whining about the weather and about what they should do with their day, Miranda went up to Harriet's room

and knocked on the door. She realized almost immediately that there'd be no reply. Funny, she thought,
how you could pretty much tell when there was someone there or not without having to look. It was like the
afternoons back at home when she'd go into the house
from her studio workroom in the garden and call up the
stairs to see if Silva and Bo were back from school yet.
Often she'd shout a name but know perfectly well at the
moment she did that there'd be no reply. Was it something to do with disturbed air, maybe? Did the
atmospheric molecules settle to stillness when no one
was there to break through them? She turned the handle
of Harriet's door and went in. 'Are you here, Harrie?'
she called softly, but the bed was still made. Wow, she
thought. So much for Duncan taking things slowly. And
then her next thought, the one she'd already had the
day before: please let it be Duncan.

Back downstairs again, Miranda cleared clean crockery from the dishwasher and switched the kettle on just
as Clare came into the kitchen, fresh from her early
swim in the sea, hair tangled and salty and her face
glowing from the exercise. 'It's getting quite a swell out
there and the orange flags are up,' she said. 'I didn't dare
go out as far as the island. But the surfers are loving it.
The children's lesson was cancelled, though.'

'Really? So are they just hanging about on the beach
still?' Miranda noticed that Clare always looked much
less troubled after she'd been swimming. There must be

something incredibly soothing for her about being in the water. Maybe she should try it herself, but she still had a bit of fear of what was under the surface in the sea. She didn't trust it not to turn nasty on her.

'Bo's on his way back up here but Silva's talking to the boy with the streaky hair.' Clare laughed. 'She looks a bit star-struck, bless her. Are you making coffee? I think I might have toast.'

As Clare went to the larder to find bread, Miranda caught sight of Harriet outside on the terrace, still in last night's cute lilac shift dress and half hiding behind the big hibiscus. She must be freezing, Miranda thought, going to let her in. But Harriet peeped round the plant and waved, putting her finger to her lips in a plea for secrecy. Miranda nodded to her and pointed towards the larder, indicating to her to wait. Harriet gave her a grin and went back behind the shrub.

'The bunting's going up in the village,' Clare said, putting the loaf on the board and hunting in a drawer for the right knife. 'It's tatty old stuff and I bet it's the same as when we were here last. I wouldn't be surprised. I mean, who buys new bunting?'

'Oh, I don't know, what about for the Jubilee? Royal weddings?' Miranda suggested as she poured boiling water into the cafetière, conscious of Harriet shivering behind the hibiscus.

'But it's probably a parish council matter and they'd discuss it till they all got bored to buggery and then not make a decision and all go home with nothing sorted. Imagine being a councillor. Also, you can feel the season turning. By the middle of August the flowers have all started to go over. The gardens are looking tatty. I think people forget that England really peaks in May and June, not the main school holiday. Everyone should get plenty of time off when the colours are at their clearest and the plants are at their most flourishing. Then there'd be time to stand back and appreciate it all in its full glory.'

It was just starting to rain. Miranda thought of Harriet in her silky dress, out there in the wet. She'd do better to go down and shelter in the pool hut. She glanced out through the terrace doors but Harriet was still there, a tiny bit of lilac fabric visible through the leaves.

'Tell you what, Mum, why don't you go and have a shower and get dressed and I'll do the toast for you?'

'Oh – well, that's kind. Are you sure?'

'Yes, yes – you must be feeling cold.'

'Well, I am a bit. And Miranda? Will you talk to Steve later? About the boat? When this bit of horrible weather's over we could, you know, do the thing for Jack?'

'OK, I will, I will. Now go, or the toast will be done and cold before you're back.'

As soon as she'd gone, Miranda opened the door and let her sister in. 'So, the walk of shame,' she said, laughing. Harriet's hair was a bit wild and she was carrying her shoes. Miranda didn't blame her; they weren't exactly built for walking. 'Are you going to tell me where you've been all night?'

'Hang on. I'm dying for the loo.' Harriet peered round the kitchen door into the hallway. 'Where's Mum?'

'Upstairs having a shower. But you're not a kid; I think she'd agree you're allowed out. She'd probably congratulate you.' Lucky girl, Miranda thought, feeling envious but pleased for Harriet, who was looking disgracefully radiant.

'I know, I know. Just give me a minute.' Harriet bolted up the stairs and was back in what seemed like seconds, in denim shorts and a pale blue cashmere jumper. She hugged her arms round her body and shivered. 'Bloody cold out there, Manda. Like *winter*.'

'Hot night, though?' Miranda asked as she stuffed more bread in the toaster, then went to look in the fridge. 'Bacon sandwich for you, or have you had a leisurely breakfast in bed?'

Harriet giggled. 'I could murder a sarnie, thanks, and no, I didn't. I had time for a shower then just coffee and a teeny choccy croissant. I was too excited to eat. Ooh, Manda, he is just . . .' Harriet sighed like someone from an old movie romance. 'He's, you know . . . he's just *gorgeous*. I think I'm in love. I am. Definitely.'

She started twirling round the kitchen. Miranda watched her, loving how excited and sparkly she was.

She couldn't remember the last time she herself had felt like that.

'You've got a big case of POG.' Miranda laughed. 'You should see yourself!'

'What's POG?' Harriet stopped twirling and looked puzzled.

'Post Orgasmic Glow,' Miranda said. 'Haven't you heard that one before?'

'No, I haven't – but,' and she looked prettily bashful for a moment, 'I can't say you're not right. Wow, very right. I'm so *happy*. Squee!' She hugged Miranda and then said, 'Oh, and I forgot to say . . . I saw your Steve last night.'

'Not *my* Steve. Did you? Where?'

'At the Pengarret hotel, quite early on. He asked if you'd be around tomorrow but I told him you had a meeting in London and would be off on the train in the morning and away for a couple of days.'

'Oh, right. Thanks.' So at least he hadn't completely put her out of his mind, Miranda thought, her spirits rising a bit, unless he was just making conversation with Harriet out of politeness.

'He had that Cheryl girl from the shop with him,' Harriet said. 'And I have to admit, she might be a total cow but she scrubs up pretty good.'

Miranda reached into the oven to get the bacon out from the grill and managed to burn her hand.

'Ouch!' she squealed, going straight to the tap and running cold water over it.

'What have you done?' Harriet came over to look and gave Miranda a hug. 'Oh, poor you! That's going to sting.' She passed Miranda a sheet of kitchen roll. 'Here, wipe your tears with that. I always cry as well when I hurt myself. It must be a family thing, cos it's not as if it's *that* painful. I expect it's just the shock.'

'I expect you're right,' Miranda said, blowing her nose on the paper. 'I'm sure that's all it is.'

SIXTEEN

'Do I *have* to?' Bo hunched so far into his hoodie that Miranda wouldn't have been surprised if he'd furled his body up into a ball and vanished inside the fabric. His hands went up into the sleeves and his head drooped.

It actually wasn't an unreasonable question, in Miranda's opinion, but it wasn't about her or about him. In the middle of the drizzly morning, when Harriet had given in to lack of sleep and taken herself off to bed and Bo and Silva were starting to argue and muttering about wanting to watch mindless television, Clare had taken a look at the rain and the wind-blown trees and brightly suggested a trip out 'as a family'. That she'd managed to say this without also welling up at the poignant thought of the one who was missing made Miranda feel that yes, whatever the children thought about it they were to be dragged along, and they'd bloody well enjoy it even if she had to bribe them. She quite liked the idea, herself, thinking how good it would be to get out of this house of Steve's and inhale some invigorating fresh air miles out of the village. She'd have preferred a long, tough walk on the coast path but this would do perfectly well instead and had the advantage that she could call in at the supermarket after and stock up on food for the rest of them while she was in London. Clare might argue that she didn't need to but Miranda was feeling childishly cross about the idea of putting money into Cheryl's greedy till. In a spirit of envy that she knew was totally unjustifiable yet satisfying, she'd have the whole village boycott her if she could. Not kind.

'Sorry, but I think you do. It'll make your gran happy and hey, it's only half a day; a few hours out of your life. Be nice, please?'

'S'pose. But it's for, like *kids*,' he groaned. 'I mean, a *seal* sanctuary. Big floppy seals that don't like *do* anything except swim and smell.'

'There are otters too. And some penguins, I think. Or at least there were when I was your age.' How long did a penguin live, Miranda wondered. If there were some there still, they couldn't be the same ones, surely?

'Oh, well, that makes a massive difference. Not.' But there was a hint of a smile and Bo's hands started to emerge from his chewed cuffs like the head of a shy tortoise tempted from its shell by the promise of a strawberry. At least Silva was happy about the outing and Miranda felt grateful that she hadn't so much as pulled a face. She could already be moody when she felt like it and by this time next year she'd probably go into a gigantic mega-sulk at the very idea of anything as uncool as being seen in public with her mum and her gran.

Just as they were leaving, Clare surprised Miranda by saying, 'Er, I hope you don't mind, but Eliot called me and he says he'd like to come too and bring Lola. Is that all right? I said we'd meet them there.'

'Fine by me,' Miranda said, but she looked at the children and noted their contrasting reactions. Bo seemed in danger of looking positively cheerful, but Silva was now the one with her hands huddled away in her jumper and a face like the rainclouds that were gathering over the village. 'Do they *have* to come?' she whispered to Miranda as soon as Clare had got into the car and shut the door. 'Lola's like, y'know . . .'

'I thought you two got on OK?' Miranda said.

'Mostly. But you never know what mood she's in. Bo likes her.'

Miranda hugged her, feeling Silva's slender body stiffen in protest as she held her. 'Gerroff, Mum. It's OK.' But her face promised that it wasn't acceptable at all. They could do without this.

'Yes. It *is* OK and it had better stay that way. As I said to Bo, it's just a few hours. How much can it hurt?'

As she said it she felt a twist of pain inside herself, pushing at the ridiculous nagging ache that had been there since Harriet so casually mentioned that she'd seen Steve with Cheryl. But if she could put a brave happy face on, and if Clare could manage it in the middle of all her grief, then the children would just have to as well. She stroked the soft ginger head of Toby the cat, who was sitting in his usual place on the stone wall watching the seagulls, and got in the car and switched on the engine, mentally telling the ache to go away and leave her alone and let her enjoy the moment. She'd be halfway back to London this time tomorrow, and frankly she could hardly wait. Surely she'd slough off this idiotic unrequited teenage-crush feeling the moment the train crossed the glorious Brunel bridge at Plymouth. Even now, driving out of the village made her feel she could breathe a bit more easily. What she needed was a girly evening out in London, with plenty of white wine. Bring it on. Unless, and knowing her luck just now it's how it would be, all her mates would be off on their own holidays somewhere.

Eliot and Lola had got there first and were waiting outside the Gweek Seal Sanctuary. Lola was looking as moody as Silva had been, gazing at her shoes in a glowering adolescent way. Eliot was reading a poster on the wall and looking quite cheerful.

He came over to the car, opened the door on the passenger side and gave his hand to Clare, who smiled up at him as she took it. Neither seemed in a hurry to let go of each other, Miranda noticed with something of a shock as she locked the car. Clare looking that way at someone who wasn't Jack? She must be imagining it, she thought. It had only been six months. Getting involved with someone else would be the last thing on her mind. It was just a happy rekindling of a long-ago friendship and she was just projecting how *she'd* been feeling. She had that jolt again, like being lightly but menacingly punched. There'd be this trip to London, then back for the last week here and she could go back to real life and never think about Steve again. Maybe.

'I've already got tickets for us all,' Eliot said, then chuckled. 'I always get a kick out of being a concession, even though it's a swings and roundabouts thing, isn't it?' He looked fondly at Clare. 'Not that you'll know about that for many years yet.'

'Ha, not that many,' she said.

'Ah, well for sure you'll need to carry ID with you at all times. They'll be thinking you're an ol' liar, claiming to be over the age for the discount, so they will.'

Clare went pink and giggled briefly like a young girl. Bo looked at Miranda and muttered, '*Wha'?*' at her.

Miranda shook her head and whispered, 'Shh! He's always been an old charmer.' But she knew as she said it that this, for Bo, wasn't the point.

'But . . . *old.*' Silva caught up and joined in, looking confused.

'Shush! And hey, listen you two, you can feel just the same at seventy as you do at seventeen. Don't ever forget that.' They didn't believe her and both burst into a chorus of the inevitable 'eeuw' and 'yuck' that they always came out with when faced with any unappealing fact about anyone more than ten years older than themselves, as if the teen years were the only valid age range on the planet.

Signs at the entrance warned that it was a long walk down to the seal tanks, but all Miranda's party rejected the idea of an easy ride in the little train that was on offer. Bo, Silva and Lola ran off ahead down the path and soon were out of sight. Clare and Eliot walked together, talking, but with people coming up in the opposite direction and so many of them pushing prams there really wasn't room for three abreast so Miranda dropped back and let them go ahead. The path was enclosed by trees and bushes, but glimpses through the foliage to the trees blowing wildly on the far side of the river told her that the day was getting more stormy by the hour, and when she reached the seal enclosures and emerged from the shelter of the surrounding shrubbery she felt the full force of the high wind and her hair whipped harshly against her face. The air was strangely hot, which seemed all wrong in the strong wind, and it felt heavily charged too. The forecast thunder surely couldn't be far away.

Miranda caught up with the others by the largest

enclosure where the seals were waiting for feeding time and the humans had gathered to watch them being fed. The seals honked and shuffled, keenly anticipating their food on the poolside, and children wailed about the strong fishy smell and whinged for ice-cream.

'No, Tarquin and Emilia, we can *not* go to the shop. This is educational.' The brisk, clipped voice of the kind of whip-thin pushy London mother that Miranda remembered all too well from her primary-school-gate days rang out as she addressed her pair of bored children, who were not remotely interested in these floppy, grey, ungainly creatures. 'You will write about this for your holiday project.'

'I can't get a signal,' Lola grouched as she leaned against the glass, fiddling with her mobile phone and holding it up and waving it. 'Mum might have called.' She sounded concerned.

Eliot came over to her. 'She'll be fine, Lo-lo, don't you worry. Let's just watch the seals being fed and then I'll take you home if you want.'

Silva was standing beside Lola, looking puzzled. 'Is she not well?'

'She's well,' Eliot told her. 'She wasn't, but she is now. OK, Lola?'

Lola nodded, put her phone away and turned to look at the pool as the volume of seal-honk increased and a keeper arrived with buckets of fish. Children cheered and the girl with the fish called for volunteers from the audience. Silva nudged Lola. 'Shall we?'

'Are you *mad*?' Lola said, glaring. 'We'll get fish-hands and all stinky.'

'So? Oh, come on, just for a giggle?' She grabbed Lola and pushed her forward in front of her. Lola started to laugh and the two girls joined a selection of much smaller children in the enclosure. Bo whistled and whooped at them.

'Go Silva!' he shouted.

'She's a sweetie, your girl. I can see how it is between them – a bit unsure of each other – and that was very kind of her,' Eliot said to Miranda. 'It's not been fun for Lola, you know, her mum being so ill when there's only the two of them, and it's left her snappy and scared. There was plenty of family help, but in the end it's just Lo and Jessica.' He looked sad. 'And everyone needs a special someone, don't they?' he added, glancing across to Clare who was taking photos of the two girls, who were now shrieking with laughter as they threw mackerel into the water and the great creatures tumbled about splashing them thoroughly.

'They do,' Miranda agreed, sending up a little prayer for Andrew and Jessica to be lucky. And not just them, she thought, looking quickly at Clare before turning back to Eliot with a smile. 'They definitely do.'

It was a vile night. The thunder and lightning raged over

the village as if this place alone out of the whole nation deserved a huge celestial telling off from on high. The thunder had rumbled away to terrorize someone else by the small hours but the wind became more and more demonic as time passed and whirled round the house making howling noises and sending twigs and small branches hurtling to the ground. The rain was pounding down at a tropical rate and Miranda, after some fitful sleeping, was properly woken up not long after five in the morning by the branches of a mimosa sapling outside her room whipping against her window. Unable to sleep any longer and feeling hot and sticky because the poor cat, soaking wet from a brief foray into the garden and scared by the weather, had climbed on to the duvet and was trying to snuggle against her, she got out of bed and went downstairs to the kitchen to make a cup of tea. The rain was streaking down the windows so she opened the terrace doors to watch the low purple and black clouds, looking rather like giant prunes, scudding across the sky against a background of murky grey-yellow. The colours were amazing, she realized, thinking immediately in terms of a bold abstract design for a fabric, and she went to her work bag in the sitting room and fetched her coloured pencils and sketch books and sat at the table drawing till daylight started creeping in and she'd covered four pages with lavish patterns in lurid bad-weather shades that she was completely thrilled with. When she got back she'd scan them into her computer and play with them a bit more, adjusting it to achieve the boldness of colour that you couldn't get with the pencils.

It was now nearly seven and there was no time to get any more sleep. I'll doze on the train, Miranda decided, stretching her stiffened body and yawning.

'Bloody 'ell, you're up early.' Harriet came into the kitchen, plonked herself down on the chair opposite and started looking through Miranda's work. 'Wow, these are good. I'd wear this if it was material and you made me a dress.'

'Would you really? Well, it's a thought. I haven't done a clothing fabric line.' Miranda considered. 'Not an easy field to get into, but worth looking at. I think I'll get some sample lengths made up and take them to the big fabric shows. I mean, obviously I do that anyway, but only for the cushions and stuff for my own business, not to sell on. But it could be another outlet.'

'I'm talking about like for a clothes designer so you can supply limited amounts. Not general market-stall rolls, you know?' Harriet yawned. 'God, what a horrible night. I hardly slept.' She giggled. 'That makes two in a row.' Miranda gave her a look. 'Sorry,' Harriet said. 'I shouldn't flaunt my gorgeous new sex life when you haven't got one.'

'Thanks for reminding me.' Miranda snapped shut the box of pencils. 'Do you know, just for the last few hours it hadn't even crossed my mind for a minute.' She'd meant it as a joke, but actually it was true. Maybe if she just concentrated on working really, really hard for absolutely every minute of the day she'd never think about the neglected – almost cobwebbed, like Miss Havisham's boudoir – area in her life where Steve had inconveniently (and, to be fair, accidentally) reminded her the passion department should be. Also, she'd have every chance of being a mega-rich tycoon. Every cloud . . .

'What time's your train?' Harriet asked. 'And are you going to leave earlier in case there are trees down? The night was a bit damn wild.'

'Oh lordy, don't even think it!' Miranda said. 'I *have* to be at that meeting tomorrow morning if I have to walk there.'

'Oh, you'll get there. You've got ages. You're not like me – I'd have left it till tonight and got the sleeper and left myself no leeway for anything going wrong and then I'd panic and cry. Don't worry. More tea?' She went to switch the kettle on and the moment she touched the switch all the lights went off. 'Aaagh – power's gone. Was it something I did?' She prodded the kettle switch but nothing happened.

'Oh, great,' Miranda said. 'I can't leave you all here with no power. Maybe I should go this afternoon, or on the sleeper like you.'

'Don't be ridiculous,' Harriet said. 'It'll be back on in no time. Just go! Have you packed? And you are going to wear that cobalt blue shift dress for the meeting, aren't you?'

'I've packed, and yes I'll wear it. Thanks for the help and for the loan of that mad silver necklace. It's perfect.' Miranda put her cup in the dishwasher and went off to get dressed. Halfway up the stairs she could hear her phone ringing in her bedroom and she raced to answer it, her heart no longer doing the swift rate increase it had twenty-four hours ago as she was sure it wouldn't be Steve. And it wasn't, it was the cab company telling her that, oh the joy, there were no trains to London as the torrential rain had caused a landslip on the line at Dawlish and did she want to cancel the taxi or still see if she could get a train as far as Plymouth?

She'd have to take the Passat after all, she realized, thanking the bearer of the bad news and cancelling the cab. She just hoped the others wouldn't mind.

'Don't be ridiculous, Miranda, of course it's all right,' Clare said when she told them. 'You'll be back on Friday – we can easily manage a couple of days without a car. It's not as if there isn't a shop if we need anything, and you bought loads of food yesterday. And if the weather doesn't clear up I'll get the children out to do some proper walking, like we used to do.' She looked quite pleased at the prospect.

'Hmm – good luck with that.' Harriet giggled. 'I can just see them stomping round the fields in their fancy

London trainers. Can you imagine Silva risking getting cow crap on her Converses?'

Why is nothing simple, Miranda thought later as she shoved her bags in the car and prepared to drive down the lane. She hugged everyone goodbye and they wished her a ton of luck with the meeting and off she went, only to find after less than a hundred yards that the end of the lane was blocked by a fallen oak tree. No way could she drive past it and it would take a crane or someone with industrial-strength chainsaws to clear a path. She climbed out of the car and, ridiculously, went up close to the tree as if by getting near to it and possibly asking it nicely it might just get up and move out of her way.

'Damn and arse!' she said, kicking at the massive trunk. She could cry with frustration. Why did nothing she wanted to happen seem meant to happen? Was it karma? Could the fates in this place really still be holding against her the fact that she wasn't the best of girlfriends at sixteen? For heaven's sake, who was?

She kicked the tree again, which this time hurt her foot. 'Oh *fuck*,' she yelled, sitting on the tree trunk and trying not to burst into tears, this time with pain as well as frustration.

There was the sound of a vehicle squealing to a halt below her on the main village road. Maybe this *was* the magical man with a chainsaw and salvation but she quickly saw that it wasn't. Just a white van . . . in fact

Steve's white van with the curly fish on the side. And there he was, climbing out, and there *she* was trying not to cry and clutching her painful foot.

'You've no chance of getting past that,' he said.

'Oh, really?' she said, not amused. 'And there I was waiting for the tree elves to push it aside for me.'

He had the grace to smile, which she didn't deserve. 'Sorry, yes, the school of the bleedin' obvious. Why don't you take the car back and then come and get in the van? I'll give you a lift.'

Miranda thought for a second. 'OK, but where to? I was going to . . .'

'London. Yes, I know. So am I.'

Clare wished she could ask Jack, just ask him if it was OK. Would it be too soon to have any feelings that were even the tiniest bit more than basic friendship? Yes, of course it would. Even ten years on would be too soon, she imagined, when you've lost your life partner. And yet . . . She sat on the floor of her bedroom looking at the urn there among her shoes on the bottom shelf of the wardrobe and actually contemplated talking out loud to Jack. That way madness lay, she thought. She didn't even believe in any form of life after death, though in the last months she'd wished she could. Jack had joked about it, in a grim kind of way, pointing out that if he didn't qualify for heaven at least in hell he'd be in the company of all the fun people. She'd remembered that when she and Miranda had been at the florist, discussing funeral flowers. One arrangement they'd been offered by the meticulously serious shop manager which had had them almost on the floor with crazy hysterical laughter had been something called 'The Gates of Heaven' which was an arrangement on wire of a sort of floral archway sitting on a cloud of flowers with a little pair of metallic gates, half open. They'd reminded Clare of a house up the road in Richmond where the owner was mightily proud of his curly metal gates, which opened with a remote control. She hadn't been able to look at them since without thinking how well they'd look surrounded by chrysanthemums and topped with a little white harp.

'Why isn't there a "Gates of Hell"?' Miranda had said as they'd fled, still weeping with excess hilarity, from the poor bemused florist. 'You could have shades of brilliant orange flowers and a tiny pitchfork and some horns on the top of the gate.' That was the trouble with death, and especially with funerals, Clare thought now as she sat on the floor, leaning down to each foot in turn to do some yoga stretches: everything, from coffins depicting the Last Supper to matching keepsake urns for putting on the ends of a mantelpiece, was so kitsch that you could tip over into unsuitable hysterics at every turn. And the laughter went over so easily into tears and so damn often. Clare was quite aware that she'd been like a leaky tap for months now. Jack wouldn't approve of that – he gave tears short shrift during life. She doubted he'd be any different after death.

'So, maybe if . . .' she whispered to him, in the general direction of the wardrobe, 'I mean it's not very likely, is it, not when Eliot's been used to women of glamour, but just say *if*. It wouldn't be too terrible, would it? Just a . . . you know? Well, not sex probably . . .' She broke off and thought for a minute. Was she really never, ever going to have sex again? This thought had come up before and at the time she'd been sure she'd never want to. But now the rest of her life as a lone celibate woman seemed like an awfully long, passionless time.

'Mum? Who are you talking to?' Harriet put her head round the door and looked at Clare. 'What on earth are you doing down there?'

'Stretches. Keeping myself fit. No swimming this morning – even the pool doesn't look too inviting in this wind and it's full of leaves so I'm doing a bit of yoga instead.'

'Well, a woman needs her exercise,' Harriet said, a massive grin splitting her face almost in half.

'Yes. A woman does,' Clare agreed, kicking the wardrobe door shut with her foot. 'Make sure you don't let those muscles go, Harrie – you know what they say about using it or losing it.'

'Don't worry, Mum,' Harriet said. 'Believe me, I'm already keeping it in mind.'

SEVENTEEN

'Oh yes! Oh wow, that was the best, best *ever*.' Miranda sat back and sighed and wiped the back of her mouth on the back of her hand. 'God, that was *so* good.'

'That's quite a reaction to a simple fried egg sandwich. I'd love to see you on steak and chips.' Steve was laughing at her. Miranda sighed.

'Well hey, I was hungry. No breakfast, been up since five.' She wrapped her hands round the café's thick white mug and sipped her tea, feeling that contentment really was a trucker's café just off the A30 with strong tea and the tabloids to skim through.

'Bad night then? I hope it wasn't an uncomfortable bed. I haven't had any complaints before.'

Miranda gave him a sharp look. 'No, well, I suppose you wouldn't.'

'I meant from the rental punters.'

'So did I,' Miranda said, trying to look innocent.

They'd only got as far as Okehampton and if this was going to be the level of innuendo, Miranda could hardly think how it would be by the time they hit the M3. She went off to the loo and scrubbed bits of egg and melted butter from her fingers and face. She'd been so hungry she'd gone at the sandwich a bit like a ravenous wolf. Not what you'd call ladylike, she thought, but then it didn't matter. She'd made a decision about Steve now that she was out of the village. He was to be Just A Friend. Everything was easier all round that way and she could get back to being a normal, capable woman again, especially as there wasn't much more than a week to go of living in his house. If her mother had her down as the Reliable One, well so be it. There was a lot to be said for being sensible. Probably. She applied a bit of perfume to dispel the fried-egg scent, rinsed her mouth from a miniature bottle of breath freshener and put on a bit of minty flavoured lip gloss. A woman's faux-diet trick, she thought – there was something about tasting mint flavour that made you feel the several hundred calories just ingested had actually vanished into thin air.

'Not too whiffy for you, is it, all the fish in the back?' Steve asked as they got back into the van. 'You smell all fresh like a toothpaste ad.'

'I can't smell anything. You've got a really good aircon system going on here.' It was true – there was a faint overall scent of fresh fish but nothing that Miranda found anything but mildly appetising, or would if she hadn't just stuffed a doorstep of bread and egg. Besides, they weren't in the same compartment as the actual fish – there was a barrier between the seats and the refrigerated freight area.

'Well, when you drive the stuff about as much as I do, you really wouldn't want it to be all-pervasive. I don't really notice it any more, but I remember my father always carried the scent, sort of Eau de Haddock. That's the kind of memory that means I spend half my life in the shower.'

She had a moment of imagining him naked and soapy after a fishy day's work but quickly deleted the thought from her head. She must concentrate on thinking about the next day's meeting. She must *not* feel that awful zing from being only inches away from him for hours on end yet not allowed to touch him, not even accidentally. And she mustn't think about him with that shrew Cheryl. Though, in fact, perhaps it kind of helped if she did. Because after all, if he was dating her, what kind of taste in women did that tell her he had?

The miles were flying by and Miranda felt hugely grateful for this unexpected lift.

'It's so lucky you were passing,' she said as they approached Stonehenge. 'That tree will probably be there for weeks and I hadn't a hope of getting out. I hope it doesn't keep the rest of my lot trapped in the garden for too long. They were hoping to get out in the car and maybe do that St Ives Tate visit. Bo wanted to go to Newquay too.'

Steve laughed. 'Are you serious? This is Cornwall. There'll have been people all over it like vultures on a dead dog by eight and by ten o'clock it'll have been reduced to neat piles of logs all stacked in village woodpiles. All there'll be left to show it was ever there will be the remains of the stump and a scattering of sawdust.'

Miranda felt nervous as the van approached Chiswick. She wanted to think of a way to thank Steve but wasn't sure how. There was no food in the house, not so much as a pint of milk; she'd go out later to Waitrose on the High Road for some basic supplies. For now, though, she couldn't even offer him a cup of tea.

'Er . . . it's left here,' she said. 'And do you want to come in for . . . well, it would have to be black coffee or tea? Sorry. It's about all there is till I go out later.'

'No, I won't actually, but thanks for the offer,' Steve said, then laughed. 'Such as it was. I've got to get this stuff delivered. Will you be OK? You've got a key and everything?'

'Please – you sound like my mum!' she said, yet suddenly feeling mildly panic-stricken and starting to search through her handbag. Phew, yes, the door key was there. She knew she'd remembered to take it off her key ring when she handed the car keys over to Clare but there was always a remote chance it had got dropped somewhere. If bad luck couldn't get you one way, like the tree and the landslide, then it often tried to get you another.

'Actually, I suppose you're staying at your friend's flat tonight?' she asked tentatively as he pulled up outside her house. He gave her a wide-eyed look. Was it alarm?

'I just wondered, I mean I don't want to get a load of food in and cook as I'll only be here a night, but I was thinking, you know, if you're not doing anything . . .' she was waffling on, she realized, wishing she could just get the words out. OK, so there was a risk of a big fat NO, but as it was only a friends thing that really wouldn't matter. At all.

'I'm not doing anything,' he said, looking at her, waiting for the rest of her request.

'I just wanted to thank you for this. For the lift. If you hadn't happened to be passing, you know . . . all that. So, I wondered, could I buy you supper tonight? There's a nice little place just round the corner here – I go there a lot. I'll be going there later anyway but it's more fun if you're not on your own. Um, you'd be doing me a favour. Another one.'

'Yes,' he said, smiling at her.

'Yes? Yes you will?'

'Of course. I can't let a lady go to a restaurant by herself. It's too sad. And horrible men will hit on you.'

'I doubt it,' she said. 'I've been there several times on

my own and only the waitress talks to me. It's always full of older men with their wives who've believed the fashion pundits who say it's fine to wear leather trousers when you're over forty.' She shouldn't have said that, she realized; it sounded bitchy and he might hate her for that, which she didn't want, even if she had absolutely no interest in attracting him. But he laughed anyway.

'Toying with an oil-free salad?'

'That's the kind of thing,' she agreed. 'So I'll see you later?' She didn't quite believe it. She hadn't wanted to ask about Cheryl while they were in the van as it could be an awkward conversation to deal with if you still had a hundred miles to go in close proximity, but later she'd find out, over a glass or two of wine. Even though in a way she didn't want to know, she sort of *had* to. Any woman with the normal amount of inborn curiosity would feel the same.

'I'll come and knock on your door at seven thirty and ask you out to play,' he said, climbing out of the van to help her with her bags. He carried them to the purple front door and hesitated. 'Till tonight then,' he said eventually.

'Tonight. And thanks again, so very much, Steve.'

'You can thank me properly later,' he said. 'Dinner, I mean.'

'Sure,' she said, putting the key in the lock and thinking, yes, just dinner.

*

'Thank goodness for Sea Scouts. Not something I ever thought I'd say.' Lola was laughing as she looked at the one hopeless bulging and useless knot she'd tied compared with the many brilliantly tight and firm ones that Freddie, who'd learned dozens of them in his Thames-side troop, had managed.

'I only joined for the uniform,' he said, looking serious. 'A proper old-school circular sailor hat. Can't beat that.'

Lola and Silva stopped trying to tie their knots and looked at him. Did he mean it? He couldn't keep the expression up and started laughing. 'No really, it's great for learning boat things. You get to do dragon boat racing and powerboat skills and shooting and trekking and loads of really good stuff. But actually, the big love for the hat: not so much. I used to carry mine to the meetings hidden in a Sainsbury's bag in case I got beaten up.'

The raft was done. It was two inflatable crocodiles and a double rack of wooden planks so expertly tied together that even with the four of them balanced on board it would take a whale to sink it. Lola now thought it needed painting. 'If we paint say the top ones pink and the bottom ones purple, it'll match the crocs.'

'Or alternate planks pink and purple? Because you won't see the bottom ones, they'll be under water,' Silva suggested.

'I expect the whole thing will end up under water,' Bo said, looking a bit gloomy. Silva prodded him, hard.

'Don't be so negative,' she told him. 'It's got to work. It'll be my birthday so it's got to work and we've got to win. But . . .'

'But?' Freddie asked.

'Maybe we should have painted the planks before we tied them on.'

'Hmm.' Lola considered. 'Or maybe flagpoles with the right coloured fabric, like streamers, instead? Mum's got loads of scarves. There're bound to be some the right colours. We're going to need to take it for a test drive, too.'

'Not on the creek though, surely?' Bo said. 'We don't want any opposition people to see it. How about the pool up at the house?'

'Good idea,' Lola agreed. 'Mum's been painting in the house and there are loads of dust sheets. We can put a couple over it so no one sees.'

Silva felt ridiculously happy. Any residual envy of Willow's high-pressure boy-fest in Florida had completely vanished. School was, she realized, divided into those who were so stuck into cool that they couldn't actually ever buy a T-shirt unless everyone knew it was from Hollister and others who were more adaptable and could just fit anywhere, cool or uncool, like this, where they'd all, even Bo, reverted to being like they were nine again. She imagined if Willow were here right now. She'd be sitting on the wall a bit detached, watching and bored and asking every few minutes when they were going over to St Piran to sit outside the wine bar and look at fit boys. She'd have spent an hour that morning bigging up her hair and putting on nail varnish and picking out the right earrings. If she could be persuaded to join them on their raft, she'd want to go and buy a glitzy new bikini to be seen in and probably have to go to the Pengarret spa for a tan top-up. And then – and this is where a small cloud came into the picture – that Jules boy would be all over her and she, Silva, would be consigned back to the role of Little Girl. That was the trouble with having the friend who was the pretty one. You only got a chance at shining if you were on your own. She had a little waver of confidence. Jules always talked to her. But he talked to her like a young sister or something. How many years would it be before she got to be treated like a proper teen, the sort boys fancied?

She was twiddling with a bit of leftover twine, and when she looked up from her thinking, there was Freddie looking at her. She smiled and he smiled back then went back to concentrating on the last of the knots.

'Anybody fancy a sail a bit later? The wind's gone down quite a lot so you probably won't fall in.' He'd asked them all but he was looking at Silva. 'I can't promise, though.'

'I'd like to,' she said. 'And I don't mind falling in.' She liked Freddie, probably in the same way that Jules liked her. But maybe Freddie liked *her* the same way she liked Jules. That was fine. It didn't hurt to be nice to him.

The house looked a bit odd, as if the time away meant she could see it, for once, from a stranger's perspective. Miranda felt conscious that from getting here to the point where she and Steve went out, she wouldn't be able to settle to anything useful without feeling madly jittery. She left her bags at the bottom of the stairs and wandered through the cool, rather dark rooms, opening the plantation shutters and letting light pour into the long knocked-through sitting room with its soft creamy sofas and palest turquoise walls hung with a mixture of Jack's paintings and the naïve Caribbean art that she loved. It felt as if, although she hadn't been gone that long, the place minded that she'd been away and wasn't going to let her have back her usual easy familiarity with it as easily as she'd expected. Or maybe, she thought, wondering if she was actually slightly loopy, the house had plans of its own for these weeks and wasn't pleased that she'd sneaked back early.

She opened the kitchen's French doors and went out into the garden. The house might be immaculate, thanks to Nadja the cleaner, but in the short time she'd been gone, the garden had already started to get out of control. She drifted along the side flower bed, picking the dead heads off the cornflowers and cosmos, fetching her kitchen scissors and snipping the tatty browned seed stalks from the lupins and foxgloves. She thought of what her mother had said about gardens being at their best in June and realized she'd been right. Here, looking around at what felt like the dry hot high point of summer, she could see autumn sneaking up. If she'd been here to tend it, she could have forced some of the plants that had rampantly gone to seed to carry on blooming for longer, but she'd missed the moment with most, though the hollyhocks next to her studio were flourishing. A bit of her wondered if it was the same with people. Or, strangely, a bit the opposite. All the young women who were forever moaning in magazines that they were about to hit thirty, maybe they should stop and think, hey, this is the best bit, appreciate it and look after it.

Miranda unlocked her studio and went in to collect the samples she'd need for the meeting the next day. The place felt dusty and hot and there were dead flies all over the floor. It would need a good clear-out before she could start work again, but that was all right. There was something about September that would – and even Clare at her age still felt the same – be for ever the ever-hopeful start of term, like school. Carefully, she wrapped the crockery in coloured tissue paper and took the fabrics into the kitchen for a final ironing before packing them away too. Then, after a brief foray down the High Road to get milk, croissants and fruit for the morning, she turned her thoughts to the evening.

What to wear? The eternal question. She stared into her wardrobe at what was mostly a winter collection of clothes, way too hot for the sultry town evening that it was going to be here. She didn't want to wear tomorrow's blue dress because for absolutely certain sure she'd spill red wine down it. In the end she picked up her keys and bag and left the house. What was the point of having a high street full of lovely shops only a few steps away if you didn't go out and take advantage of the sales? All that was missing was Harriet to tell her that no, that goldy colour did nothing for her.

She was trying on a strappy black linen dress in Whistles when her phone rang. Her heart lurched a bit as she had a sudden horrible fear that it would be Steve, cancelling, but instead it was Dan.

'I spoke to Silva. She said you're back in Chiswick for a day or two,' he said, his ever-smooth tones purring down the phone at her. If an old-fashioned patrician voice was ever a useful thing to add to a CV then he'd have had plenty of lucrative work over the years.

'Only for a meeting tomorrow. Is there a problem?'

'Well, I could have gone down and taken over the childcare and had a few days by the sea if I'd known.'

'Dan, they don't need childcare. And besides, it's for

less than forty-eight hours. I'm going back tomorrow, plus Mum and Harriet are with them and they've got friends to hang out with. They're fine.'

She was overdoing it, she realized. She sat on the little gilt chair in the changing room and wondered about a cardigan to put over the dress. It wouldn't be so warm later, but there were several in her drawer. She couldn't justify buying something else, not really.

'Oh well, as you're here, do you still have my old Black and Decker stuff? Mother wants some shelves up and seems to think I can do them. I did tell her that just because I'm a man it doesn't mean I'm automatically good with power tools but she said something weird about not being born with an iron in her hand. Most odd.' He sounded as if he truly didn't understand.

Miranda laughed. 'Wow, she's discovering her inner feminist at last. There's a thing. Good on her! And yes, the drill thing and all its bits are in the shed. When do you want them?' This could be awkward; she hoped he wasn't going to say 'Right now'.

'In the morning? I could stop by around ten?'

'OK, but please make it earlier if you can, or if not then between two and five. I have to be at a meeting at twelve, and in the morning I'll need some time to get ready and rev up for it and everything.'

'Do your hair and file your nails, you mean,' he said, sounding grumpily pompous.

'What I do pays the mortgage,' she said, sadly aware

that he wouldn't get the implied irony of the missing words, which were 'which is more than you ever did'.

'Whatever you say. Right then, ya? See you anon. Will let you know re actual time, probably p.m. though.'

Silva and Bo were staying at Lola's for supper and Clare was all set to have a sandwich in front of the television, for once able to watch her choice of programmes without someone else coming in and either asking to change channels or plonking themselves on the sofa with a huge discontented sigh if there was something on they didn't like. But there was a knock on the door and Clare found Eliot on the doorstep.

'Have you eaten yet and if not do you think you'd do an old man a favour and come out with him?' The evening was chilly and still windy and his hair blew about round his face as he stood waiting for her answer.

'Hello, Eliot. Come on in, and no I haven't. I wasn't going to bother with much, but well, yes, it would be lovely.' Was he asking her out? He seemed to be. Clare felt rather delighted. This was like being young again. Or was it? Maybe it was just two people at a bit of a loose end, needing a little free time away from the exuberant young.

'It's fine. I just thought it would be fun, you know. And Jess's house is full of *da yoof* and they're not exactly a quiet bunch. I thought we could escape by ourselves, get a bit of peace. Is the sailing club bar OK for you? Do you think they still do chicken in a basket in those baskets that were really just polystyrene? Or is that too hideous a thought?'

'Sailing club is fine. Come in and hang on in the kitchen for me while I tidy myself up a bit.'

'You look fine as you are to me,' Eliot said, following her into the house.

'Yes, but not to me,' she told him. 'I'll come back down probably looking exactly the same but feeling different. Just give me a minute.'

Clare went up to her room and whizzed around the bathroom, brushing teeth, applying scent and some eyeshadow and then coming out and changing her top for her pink cashmere jumper. She looked at her face in the mirror as she brushed her hair and remembered how she used to feel so sexy in Eliot's presence, all those years ago. He'd been one of those men who really *looked* at a woman and had been quite openly appreciative of curvy breasts and bottoms without being pushy or offensive. He was just . . . natural. She was thinner now, curves gone sharp. Grief had taken her appetite and she'd eaten only the tiniest portions of any meal for months, feeling mildly queasy at the thought of a plate full of food. But now, tonight, she actually felt properly hungry for once. She went back down the stairs and Eliot, hearing her, came out to meet her in the hallway.

'Come on, let's go. And let's sneak past Jess's house so they don't see us running away,' he whispered, taking her hand. 'We don't want them trailing after us and asking what we're up to.'

She laughed, enjoying the feel of his rough skin on her fingers as he kept hold of her all the way down the lane and past the big heap of sawdust where the poor tree had been cut up. When they got to the hedge beside Creek Cottage he drew her into the shadows, and with a feeling of both terror and excitement she thought for a moment he was going to kiss her, just as he'd twice so thrillingly done in the past. She was surprised by how much she'd like that to happen again. Maybe Jack was up there after all, giving his blessing.

'Shh,' he said, his eyes sparkling. 'We have to scurry past like the SAS so they don't see us. They'll only want to tag along.' So no kiss then, but that was fine. Eliot pulled her along fast until they were actually running past the cottage before they slowed, seeing the sailing club just up ahead, beyond Andrew's cottage.

'So where are you two scuttling off to?' boomed the voice of Geraldine from an upstairs window. Smoke from a cigarette billowed out beside her head and Clare thought she looked weirdly like a badly placed gargoyle. Unfair really, as she had rather a pretty, round face, but in the half-light and with the smoke it was all a bit surreal.

'We're eloping,' Eliot called up cheerfully. 'Don't try to follow us – you'll never catch up.'

'Good God, man, at your age?'

'It's the very best time to do it,' Eliot called back. 'You wait. You don't know what you're missing.' He squeezed Clare's hand and pulled her to him. 'She's only jealous. And if she's not, she should be.' He chuckled. 'I mean, come on now, chicken in the basket – who *wouldn't* be jealous?'

EIGHTEEN

'They know you here,' Steve said as the maître d' gave him and Miranda a corner table by the window and several of the waiting staff said a cheery hello to Miranda. 'Guess you're a regular, then. You and yer fancy London ways,' he added, going back to his mock Cornish accent.

'Only because it's just round the corner. My local. And top food.'

'Hey, you don't have to justify yourself to me,' he said, laughing at her.

'Good,' she said. 'So don't you tease me or I'll tell you that you smell of your fish van and you won't know if I mean it or not.'

'God, I hope I don't,' he said, sniffing at the cuff of his white linen shirt. 'I ran the flat shower almost dry, I was in there so long.'

In honour of this date, Miranda wondered, or did he

do that every time he delivered fish? The second was the more likely option.

'I shouldn't have brought the van tonight,' he said. 'The scent of mackerel has probably escaped. But there was nowhere to park near the flat and Gus has run out of visitor parking vouchers.'

'You don't have even the tiniest aroma of mackerel,' she reassured him, thinking how good it would feel to get close enough to make absolutely sure of that. 'And you can leave it outside my house for the night if you like and get a cab back, so you can have a drink,' she offered.

He looked at her in a rather speculative way and she felt a bit uncomfortable. It was only a bit of road space she was offering, nothing else, though that odd mild lust that in Cornwall she'd assumed was about hot weather was somewhere in the mix. Perhaps he could tell. Maybe some men really were attuned to the scent of hormones in women.

'OK, I'll leave the van,' he decided. 'Shall we look at the wine list or start with some champagne? Celebrate your new contract tomorrow.'

Miranda shook her head. 'No. That would be bad luck. I know it's all in the bag really,' she crossed her fingers and touched the wooden table in case, 'but I don't want to jinx it.'

'Let's have some anyway then, just to celebrate . . . I don't know, being here and meeting up again and all that. Being alive, even.'

'OK, then let's,' she agreed, catching his enthusiastic mood. He didn't seem to be pining for Cheryl, exactly. This wasn't looking like a duty date.

But as soon as they'd ordered both drink and food, Miranda had to ask him something. 'Steve, I need to ask a favour. And yes, I know, another one. Today you were a total hero and I hate to do this, but I need to ask for more help and this time it's not just for me.'

'If it's a lift home, I guess I could hang on for you tomorrow if you like,' he said, leaning forward and smiling.

'No, it's not that. It's . . . Oh look, the drinks.' The waitress arrived with a bottle of champagne and glasses and took her time opening the bottle, getting Steve to taste it and dealing with napkins and an ice bucket.

'Here's to you, for tomorrow.' Steve said, chinking his glass against Miranda's. 'Now what was it you wanted to ask?'

'It's about your boat.'

'The old Cornish crabber or the Moody?'

'Er, the white one with the blue stripe,' she said, feeling a bit ignorant.

'That'll be the Moody. What about it? Do you want to go out on it?'

'Well, yes. Look, say no if you want, but much of the reason we all rocked up in the village again is to scatter Jack's ashes on the estuary. He loved it here and he'd asked Mum to make sure that's what would happen. It's just – Mum really didn't want to rent some boat with a total stranger on board. She'd had this idea we could just hire something and take it out ourselves but it seems we can't these days.'

'No. Well . . . you can still *buy* a boat and drive it away as a total ignorant twat on the water, but not rent. So you'd like me to be the designated driver?'

Miranda felt uncomfortable. 'Um . . . well, if you have time, or . . . but say no if you'd prefer not to.'

'It's fine. I'll do it. But why me?'

'Oh, you know.' Miranda's discomfort increased. She didn't want to remind him of how uncaring she'd been back in the day. 'Because of your mother, really. She looked after our house for all that time and it kind of makes you . . . well, part of us, I suppose.' She ran out of steam a bit and gulped her champagne too fast and coughed.

'A bit like extended family? Or the ever useful hired hand?' Steve asked. She looked at him carefully, wondering if he was being sarcastic. His mother Jeannie had been their cleaner, probably underpaid and overworked.

'Just as a friend,' she said, taking a chance.

He considered for a moment, then smiled. 'I'm sorry. Yes, of course I'll do it. I feel rather honoured, to be truthful. It's a responsibility, isn't it? Carrying out someone's last wishes. And it's a lot more civilized than the old-fashioned local fishermen's funerals. Not that they do it nowadays.'

'What do you mean?'

Steve looked a bit shifty. 'Well, funerals cost a lot. Let's just say that use of an undertaker isn't enshrined in law and fishing people don't like to waste their cash.'

'So it can be a do-it-yourself thing? I've seen a programme about that. Bit gruesome, I thought, doing everything hands-on and just buying a coffin.'

'Not if you nail old Mr Fisherman into some heavy box you've cobbled together yourselves and take him out on the tide with the fleet,' he said. 'Illegal, obviously, but used to be the tradition.'

'They do things differently in Cornwall then,' she said, wondering if it was time to get on to something more cheery. 'But thanks so much for saying yes, Steve. Will you have time next week? Maybe Friday?'

'Wednesday would be better if that's OK with you all. They'll start moving boats around to get them out of the way for the regatta on Thursday.'

'OK, let's go for Wednesday then. I think Mum wants to make it a bit of a celebration, with cake and wine. Is that all right too?'

'Only if you let me have some,' he said.

She found she'd somehow reached across and taken his hand. 'You're part of it. You knew him. So I think that's a yes, don't you?' She let go, thinking perhaps she'd gone too far, and the food arrived. He hadn't exactly pulled his hand away, though. If she'd had anything other than just a fun evening and dinner in mind, Miranda might have felt mildly encouraged.

Andrew was in the garden, lurking behind the big camellia that his father had planted many years ago. They were unwieldy things if you let them get out of hand, he thought, working out how much it must have grown in inches per year and wondering if he really wanted to keep it. It would be criminal, he supposed, to cut it down, but it flowered too early, one of the first blooms of the year, and even down here by the water where it was mild a few rays of sun on near-freezing dew and the flowers became tinged with brown and spoiled so the effect ended up like tiny pink party dresses trodden through mud.

He felt a bit cold, though he was wearing a cashmere hoodie that his mother's girlfriend had sent him for his birthday. He liked the girlfriend – she had such an eager take on life and had transformed his mother Celia from a prim woman who would barely venture further than the library without getting in a tizz to someone who thought a European hotel with more than one star was for wimps. Good on her, he thought. She had, after all, become an inspiration.

Because the purpose of the lurking was to see when the brood from Jessica's took off, as they sometimes did, to hang about on the beach. They wouldn't be gone for long. Geraldine had no idea that Freddie had been to the beach at all at night and there'd be ructions if she found out, but Andrew was happy to keep his son's secret in the interests of the boy's having a normal life. Not only would she worry about the company he was keeping (mostly from the up-country top private schools, if she did but know it) but she'd worry about him slipping on a damp, weedy rock in the dark and breaking his neck, or putting an unwary hand on seagull crap and dying of psittacosis. He knew that Silva and Bo would be out only for a short while too, not staying till it all got raucous and the dope and vodka started up.

Eliot was out. Geraldine had seen him and Clare going up the road. She'd said they were holding hands and told her they were eloping, but he thought they were probably heading for the sailing club for a drink and a bag of nuts like most people who wandered past his house. Geraldine was given to fanciful statements like that, just to shock. Not that he would be shocked. Actually, it would be rather lovely if it were true. Even lovelier if it were he and Jessica running away together into the night instead.

He could smell Geraldine's foul cigarettes from his kitchen doorway, so this was the moment to make his move, while Geraldine was shrouded in smoke and concentrating on deep inhaling and the bliss of the tobacco hit. She tended to close her eyes for that, which was useful. He scuttled nimbly across to Jessica's fence and hopped over quickly, finding yet another camellia to hide in, the one where they'd buried that tiny bit of Jack the other day. What was it they'd had the funeral for, off the beach all those years ago? Jessica had said it was a baby bird but he'd doubted that even at the time. It was all right, though; if he wasn't meant to know then that was fine by him. Right now, he had something to give to Jess. Himself, he thought, if she'd ever consider it, which she probably wouldn't. For now, it was enough to think of himself as her friend. There was time. Or so he hoped. He sent a fervent prayer up that her cancer would never return. She'd said it almost certainly wouldn't. And when it came to it he might be the one to die first. He could drown, or just get run over by a bus. Anything . . .

He shivered a bit behind the camellia. Perhaps tonight the young ones were giving the beach a miss? The weather hadn't exactly been glorious, though it had recovered a lot after the stormy night. It wasn't that he minded all the children being there normally, but for this, just tonight, he needed to be alone with Jess.

At last he heard sounds of movement and the back door opened and then slammed shut again. Clumpy teen footsteps could be heard stamping round the side of the house in the direction of the road, and goodbyes and see-you-laters were being shouted.

Andrew took his chance and walked up the path to knock on Jess's door, hoping he wasn't about to make a complete idiot of himself.

*

'And you get fish *magazines*?' Miranda felt mildly drunk and incredibly happy. They'd talked about anything and everything (except Cheryl) and Steve had made her laugh so much about the absurdities of village politics that she was aching across her middle. She mustn't have any more wine, though – the next day was too important for her to rock up with a hangover.

'Trade mags, yes, of course. Don't you in your business?'

'Well yes, but then any of the soft-furnishing porn ones – not *actual* porn, obviously,' she said, not wanting to mislead, 'but anything with chairs and cushions in it like *Elle Decoration* and *Livingetc*, I suppose that's what I'd call my trade. So fish – what are they called? *Mackerel Monthly*? The *Haddock Gazette*?'

'The *Plaice Chronicle*?'

'No, really?' she said, leaning across her crème brûlée and in danger of dipping her necklace into it. He reached across and moved it slightly, out of range of the pudding.

'No, not really,' he said. 'But there is one called *Fry Monthly* for the chippie trade.'

'You can't help wondering about the journalists, can you? Is it a stepping stone to working on the *Guardian* or do they have to be *really keen* on seafood, do you think?'

Steve laughed. 'OK, let's picture the *Daily Cod* guy.

Nearly retired, smokes roll-ups, used to be ambitious but now has a bitter streak. Can't even look at a chip shop without his lip curling in disgust.'

'Also he has a gambling habit,' Miranda contributed. 'How about *Mackerel Monthly*? Posh boy work experience?'

'Yep, thick as a plank but the editor is a chum of Daddy's and hey, it's a step up. Next stop *Newsnight*.'

Miranda was enjoying herself a lot, enjoying being just plain silly. She was feeling rather hot and realized she was the only woman wearing a cardigan, though that had been because of the outside evening chill. She slid it off and hung it on the back of her chair.

'So, the *Plaice Chronicle*.' She smiled at Steve, who was looking a bit thoughtful after watching her take a layer off. 'I think she's in her thirties and she slept with the editor once because he promised her a column on beauty and fashion. But it never happened.'

'Ah, poor girl.' Steve said, doing a sad face. 'The way of the world.'

'It's a shame, because there's nothing she doesn't know about moisturizer.'

'Her day will come,' Steve said, pouring them the last of the wine.

'It will. She's writing a romantic comedy in her spare time.'

'That's all right then.'

'But she's thinking of getting a cat. Probably two.'

'Not so good.' Steve leaned forward and took her hand. 'Do you have cats, Miranda?'

She thought for a moment. There was Toby, but for her purposes right now she delegated him to the children's care. And in fact he had originally been Bo's pet.

'Bo has old ginger Toby but no, just as *me*, I don't,' she said, hoping Toby would forgive her.

'That's good.' There was a long moment of silence, then he said very quietly, 'Shall we get the bill?'

He didn't think she'd cry. It hadn't crossed his mind. He reckoned she'd be pleased, laugh even. He should have thought it through. Andrew handed Jess another handful of tissues and put his arm round her, hugging her close. She snuffled and sobbed into his chest and if he hadn't made her obviously unhappy he'd have been loving every minute of it. What would he have given to be this close to Jessica when she'd been sixteen? Still, better late, as Geraldine would probably bark at him.

'I'm so sorry. It was a huge mistake. I am a complete idiot.'

'No you're not,' she said, sitting up a bit and blowing her nose, looking pink and blotchy yet thoroughly appealing. 'It was such a sweet thought. And anyway,' she gave him a quick but wobbly blast of her lovely smile, 'it was me who was an idiot, I mean what a thing to do. I was horrible to you, sending you a topless photo of me like that as a massive tease. What was I thinking of?'

'Was it your idea? Not Miranda's?' He kind of needed to know.

'No, totally mine. I'm sorry. I was only playing.'

'Well, we were only young. And please don't be sorry.' He laughed and reached across to pour them both a bit more wine. 'I was seventeen years old, remember. To this day I *honestly* don't think I've ever had anything through the post that was more exciting. And that includes my five hundred pound premium bond win.'

'Really? But it's such a tiny photo, and in black and white, from the booth, I think, in the post office in Truro.'

'It must have taken some nerve,' Andrew said, conscious that although she'd stopped crying she hadn't moved away from him and was still lying with that lovely curly head against his body.

She giggled, sounding teenage again herself. 'I was pretty damn scared, I can tell you. Miranda was on guard but it was only that flimsy curtain between me and the shop. I wouldn't have minded being topless on a beach, but, you know, it's not really the done thing in the Truro post office.'

'I can imagine the curtain being flung back and the whole queue gawping at you.' Andrew laughed.

Jess looked serious again. 'Yes, well they wouldn't

now. I'm . . . you know, rebuilt, but it's not the same. Part of me's gone, as if it's died.'

'But that part wasn't well. Its time was up.' Andrew thought as soon as he said it that it was a risky line to take.

She frowned. 'It just makes me think, there's no after-life, is there? Because how much of your body do you have to have chopped off for it to kind of *go* somewhere and wait for you to die? Will I get to whatever "heaven" is and be reunited with all my old fingernails and my left breast? I don't think so.'

'Brain energy,' Andrew said. 'I suppose it's all down to that. That and, I don't know, some inner spark? Like a battery?'

Jessica laughed. 'It's a bit heavy, isn't it, for what started as a little photo of my naked tits? I remember Miranda's dad – well, stepdad – Jack. He once said something was a "heavy reality sandwich" and Eliot said that was a typical dippy old hippy thing to say – not in a bad way, he liked Jack – but it was so funny. They said things differently then.'

'They're doing him a big send-off on the river. Are you coming?'

'Yes. And I know it's selfish, but every minute I'll be thanking whatever's out there that it isn't me.'

'Me too,' Andrew said, looking down into her eyes. This was the moment. He leaned forward to kiss her but just as his mouth connected with hers there was a general slamming of doors and some shouting. 'Yo, Ma, I'm back!' yelled Lola.

Great, Andrew thought. Terrific. But at least he wasn't left thinking there'd be no other time.

Well, Miranda hadn't expected that. Or maybe deep down she had, actually, if she was honest. Well, more hoped than expected. Steve was still asleep beside her. The light through the shutters' louvres hadn't landed on his face yet but had woken her first and she had a chance to look at him, his eyes closed, the lashes brown and long against his tanned face. She'd never seen him asleep before. Sixteen-year-olds having sex don't usually get the opportunity actually to close their eyes and nod off. Rest after sex was a privilege for grown-ups only, unless, like the young, they only got to do it on beaches and in the backs of cars. Fall asleep where she and Steve used to go and the tide would get you.

It would soon be time to put a new parking permit in his van and she didn't want him to get a ticket from the over-eager wardens, so with great reluctance she slid out of bed, put her dressing gown on and went downstairs, found his keys on the hall table and went out quickly to put the voucher on the dashboard. Then she went into the kitchen and switched the kettle on and opened the garden doors. The day was a beautiful one, sunny and warm. It would probably end up too dry and dusty compared with Cornwall but for now it was just perfect.

She went out and did some more deadheading while the kettle boiled, and was almost singing to herself. When was sex last that good, she wondered. She was sure she must look like Harriet when she came back from that night at the hotel with goalkeeper Duncan, all glowy and glossy and with a smile as wide as the Thames estuary.

She went back inside and made two mugs of tea and took them upstairs.

'Morning, you,' she said to Steve, who was just waking. The sun through the shutter slats made stripes across the skin on his naked chest. She leaned down and kissed a pale one, then a dark one.

'Morning,' he said, smiling at her. Then, 'No regrets?'

'No! Of course not!' Strange question, she thought. Why would there be? Or . . . oh, right. Was this just a one-off, a follow-up to a fun night out? How little she knew him, really.

'I was your first, back in that summer, wasn't I?' he'd said the night before, as he took her hand outside the restaurant.

'Yes,' she'd told him.

'That means you're mine then. I can claim you.' And he'd kissed her, very thoroughly, right there on the street.

'Claiming sounds a bit . . . medieval,' she'd said, putting in a rather weak bid for feminism.

'It does, but sometimes the old ways are the best,

unless you're burying a fisherman, of course. But if you'd rather I went home right now, I can see a bus at the traffic lights a couple of hundred yards away.'

And that's when the decision was made. And it was never going to be just an invitation for coffee.

'No regrets here either,' he said now, kissing her shoulder. 'And maybe we could . . .'

There was a clattering sound downstairs and someone shouted, 'Shit!'

'Bloody hell, what's that?' Miranda said, pulling her robe around her and making for the stairs.

Steve, pulling on jeans, was right behind her. 'Wait, you don't know . . . let me.'

Miranda followed the repeated curses into the kitchen. There was Dan standing in front of the dresser holding an empty drawer whose former contents were all over the floor. Behind him on the table was his old drill in a box.

'What are you doing? And how did you get in?' Miranda demanded.

He smirked and pointed at the open doors to the garden. 'I was wandering down the alley, short cut from the station as per. You really shouldn't leave the doors open, Miranda. Anyone can get in.' He addressed the last sentence to Steve, who was putting his shirt on. 'And you are?' he asked, his tone imperious.

'You are such a knobhead, Dan,' Miranda said before Steve could reply. 'Don't ever think of just walking in here again. Ring the front door bell another time.'

'Sorry, sweetie. Just looking for a couple of missing drill bits. I've already burgled your shed for the Black and Decker. Your friend isn't saying much. I say friend; maybe plumber or something?'

Steve stepped forward and Miranda thought he was going to hit Dan, for which she honestly couldn't blame him, but Dan put his hand out. 'Lovely to meet you, old chap. I'm Dan. Miranda's husband.' Steve didn't take the hand and Dan stepped back a bit.

'*Ex*-husband,' Miranda hissed. 'Dan, will you just take what you need and go?'

'Sorry.' Dan pulled an exaggeratedly apologetic face and looked from one to the other of them. 'Have I spoiled the party? Big sorries.' He rummaged a bit more among the screws, batteries, string and various sorts of tape that he'd spilled all over the floor. 'Good to see you still keep a Man Drawer, Miranda. So useful knowing where all the working parts of a house are.'

'Like you'd know. You were never a working part of a sodding house.'

'Miranda, the language. Hardly in keeping with this genteel neighbourhood. Talking of which, have you seen? Some tradesman oik has parked a fish delivery van outside. Can you believe it? I thought you bought into a nice residential area when you abandoned me and took our children away. But now look. Some fast-buck fish fryer's obviously a new neighbour.' He picked out a couple of Allen keys and stood up, just in time to be grabbed by Steve and marched at great speed towards the open door.

'Steve . . .' Miranda said as Dan was hurled out to the garden, whoopingly cheerful in defeat. 'Honestly, we've been divorced for years.'

'I believe you,' he said. 'But – you know, if you don't mind I'll be on my way. It was great, you were . . . great. But.'

'But?'

'Fish fryer? Fuck him. Your ex is a total arse. But you know, deep down, nothing changes, does it? Good luck with your meeting. I'll call you.'

It must have taken Steve all of three minutes to gather the rest of his clothes, start the van and go. Miranda was left alone on the doorstep, all the glow of the night fading.

NINETEEN

She couldn't think about it now. She couldn't. She called Steve's phone but he wasn't replying. He couldn't claim lack of mobile signal in west London so she had to conclude it was his choice to ignore her and simply get on with her day.

There was too much to do to allow time for worry about her private life, too much at stake, and she didn't want to screw up the meeting. Everything else could be thought about later. Miranda very carefully took one step at a time and felt she was doing everything by numbers: showering, washing her hair, mechanically telling herself what came next so she'd stay focused. 'Spray on the Frizz-Ease, Miranda,' she found herself saying. 'Now plug in the straighteners' and so on.

At the last minute, after a final glass of water having brushed her teeth yet again, Miranda put her blue dress on. The cab driver had called to say he was outside. She added Harriet's silver necklace, took one last look at herself and decided that was *it*. She was ready to face the room full of suits, as she thought of them.

The meeting was at the big white Holiday Inn just by Heathrow airport. It seemed appropriate that it was a hotel, as that was where her products were destined for, but she'd have thought they'd choose a smaller one, something more like the boutique type that they already ran. In fact, one of theirs would have worked, somewhere over in France, perhaps. A day or two out of the country would have gone down well with her, shaken her horizons up and forced her to remember there was a lot of world out there, not just this bubble she felt she was currently in.

The cab pulled up at the hotel and she went in through revolving doors big enough to accommodate a ton of luggage. She didn't trust those kinds of doors, thinking there was too much scope for the whole thing to get stuck and leave the occupant trapped like a fish in a bowl, slowly gasping for air and crumpling to the floor.

She was met by a waif of a girl in a blue skirt and a jacket which looked too big for her, as if it needed pinning together at the back like one on a dummy in a shop window, although her shoes, as she click-clacked across to the lift, had the scarlet soles of Louboutin. Serious stuff, Miranda thought, taking a deep breath as, up a couple of floors in the lift, the girl showed her into a room where six men and two women sat round a boardroom table. Here we go, she thought, putting her bag of goodies down in front of them.

Silva felt slightly frightened. She woke up from difficult dreams about trying to swim through mud and remembered the night before with a bit of a shiver. She buried herself deep under the duvet for a couple more moments before gradually sliding back up the bed to face the daylight.

Jules. On the beach. Just as it was getting dark and when they were all about to head back home . . . he'd come up and sat beside her on the rock, so close that most of his body was snug against hers. Bo and Lola and Freddie were mucking about with seaweed and looking for stuff on the shoreline to decorate the raft. Seaweed wasn't going to work, she thought, because it might fall to bits and she didn't like the slimy feel of it, but they were collecting great bunches of the stuff and ramming it into a couple of supermarket bags that they'd found lying around.

'So after the regatta, you'll be coming down here for the party?' Jules asked her.

'I don't know. It'll be my birthday. There might be plans.'

'Would be a shame to miss it. Should be a good one.' He smelled slightly of beer. She didn't mind that too much. It was better than smoke, anyway, if she had to choose.

'Time to go, Silv.' She heard Bo calling to her and looked up. He was staring at her, giving her a look that meant something but she wasn't sure what. Freddie was already halfway up the hill and Lola was trailing a last piece of seaweed from the sea's edge. There was loads of the stuff, Silva was thinking, dumped by the storm.

'So I'll see you on Thursday then?' Jules went on. Behind him, further along the beach, Silva could see others lighting cigarettes, passing them round. They weren't just cigarettes, she realized. How cool was that? Or was it? And the number of bottles of vodka going round – it was all new to her.

'I . . . probably,' Silva said, getting up to follow Bo.

'Excellent.' He slid down from the rock, suddenly put an arm round her and kissed the edge of her mouth. 'Goodnight, Kitty,' he said.

Silva lay in bed now, touching the bit of her mouth that he'd kissed. There'd been a boy at her ninth birthday party who'd decided she was *definitely* his girlfriend and kissed her hard and made her cry, but apart from that she hadn't been kissed before. Also, if she were to tell Willow (and this wouldn't be going on Facebook) she couldn't even claim it as a snog, nowhere close. But it was . . . nice. Tingly. Slightly scary. But best of all, it looked like the beautiful Jules, the boy at the top of the local surf-tree, actually fancied *her*. Bring on next week. She couldn't wait to be fourteen.

*

318

Done, finished, sorted and worthy of massive celebration. All order details were confirmed, dates set and an income stream for at least a couple of years was in the bag. Miranda should have been up in the air with delight, but as the train pulled out of Paddington station late that afternoon all she could feel was a sad numbness and an ache where she was pretty sure her heart should be.

The train was crowded and everyone else seemed to be talking on the phone. She should have reserved a seat in the quiet carriage but she'd booked in a hurry and hadn't thought it through. All the grey-clad business people in first class were spreading out over the tables with their laptops and their so-important papers and were yacking about projects and spreadsheets down the phone as if what was left of the industrial and financial life of the nation depended on them.

She took her phone out and checked again for messages, just in case. Nothing. What had he meant, 'nothing changes'? She'd thought about that in the cab back to Chiswick from the Holiday Inn. She had a vague idea and it was about that old thing called class. Bloody Dan, kicking off about the van like that, how dare he? He was hardly the prime example of the Protestant work ethic himself, relying on family trusts, his saintly but skewed mother and old-school-tie gallery owner friends who occasionally, over the years, had let him exhibit his impenetrable abstracts on their walls. He'd once accused her of 'selling out', back when she'd sold her first set of chinaware to a major department store. She'd thrown one of the mugs at him then, in fury. 'It's called earning a living. Money for food,' she'd said, hoping the two small children upstairs wouldn't be woken by the crash of china on the chipped tile floor of their rented flat's tiny kitchen.

When they got to Exeter and the numbers in the carriage thinned out, Miranda called Harriet to tell her which train she was on, thankful she was on one at all after the disruption from the storm.

'Everything all right?' she asked. 'Are the children OK?'

'They're fine, everyone's OK. The kids are in the pool, testing their raft and trying to get all four of them on it. They keep falling in and shrieking and must be driving half the village nuts. I've done them all some supper. Eliot's here too. He and Mum keep giggling.'

'A party without me. Jealous,' Miranda said, not entirely joking. She had a sudden massive longing to be back with them all, getting a virtual hug in a cocoon of the family warmth. To think she'd rather dreaded Harriet's coming to stay – now she wondered how she'd cope without her. Harriet was now the grown-up and she the chucked adolescent.

'How's Duncan?'

Harriet giggled. 'Still brilliant. I think this is a keeper. Er . . . not in the goalie sense, you know. But proper. He likes me, Mand!'

'Well of course he does!'

'No, *really* likes. But there's one weird thing. Pablo is still around. I haven't seen him but his car's there. And he hasn't gone away and just left it here either; Jessica said she saw it zapping through the village. I don't know why he's still hanging around.'

'Perhaps he doesn't have the brain to find his way out of Cornwall without Duncan to guide him.'

'Miranda, he's dim but not *that* dim. And anyway, I bet people would be queuing up to program his sat-nav for him if he really wanted to leave. The Pengarret staff, for sure. I heard he's big on room service at three a.m. But tell me about Steve.'

Miranda sighed. What could she say? She looked out of the window as the Exmouth estuary approached. Soon there'd be no signal as the train went through the tunnels in the red Devon rock.

'When I get home, Harrie,' she said. 'Meet me at Redruth?'

'OK. But for someone who's had a brilliant day, you sound a bit dow . . .' The phone cut out and Miranda put it away in her bag and took out the newspaper. She'd give the cryptic crossword a go, she decided, realizing she was turning into her mother.

It was all the other way round for once. Harriet seemed to be looking after Miranda and the family and taking the domestic load off her. Who would have thought

Harriet could, after all, keep a kitchen clean and be a fussy mother hen when it came to teenagers trailing sand across a clean floor? Miranda, trying her best to keep her mood of misery to herself, set off for the shop on Monday morning to get a few supplies. Got to face the enemy some time, she thought, picturing the loved-up face of Cheryl.

'Maybe it could never have been more than a one-off,' she said to Jessica over coffee when she called in on the way. 'It just felt like so much more. You'd think at my age I could tell the difference between a one-nighter and something else. I set myself up for it, really. I was so sure about Cheryl.'

'I still think you're wrong. They've known each other for years – why would they suddenly be an item? They weren't before. It doesn't make sense.'

'What *does* make sense, Jess? Maybe he was just getting revenge for my treating him badly all those years ago.'

'That would be one long-held grudge. Listen, why don't you just call him up, and if that's the case tell him to get over it?'

Fortified with that advice, and knowing she'd be seeing him on Wednesday for Jack's ceremony (he had at least texted to confirm a time to pick them all up at the pontoon), she went off to the shop for bread, eggs and milk.

Cheryl was there, talking across the counter to

Geraldine as Miranda approached. 'Still all "loved-up" as you young ones say?' Geraldine was booming.

'Yeah, I *so* am!' Cheryl confirmed as she weighed out mushrooms. 'I won't be here much longer. I'll be moving away from this place very soon. And about time. All my mates have gone up-country years ago. Mind you, most of them came back.'

'God knows why,' Geraldine said, pocketing her change. 'There can't be any work. I suppose you all just have babies.' She stomped out, giving Miranda a brief hello, and receiving a V-sign from Cheryl as soon as her back was turned.

Miranda picked up a loaf, a dozen eggs, some apples and a couple of bottles of milk and took them to Cheryl at the till. 'Good luck with your move,' she said, trying her best to smile and be generous with her wishes.

Cheryl gave her a look. 'Well, coming from you, that's a surprise. After everything an' that.' In sulky silence she bagged up Miranda's goods and took her money. 'You'll be going home soon then,' she said, pretty much speeding her on her way.

'Saturday, yes.'

'Won't be seeing you again, then.'

'Probably not. Looks like it'll be me coming back to the village in the future rather than you, if you're off. I've got friends here still.'

'Well I've got me mum and me old mates. I won't lose

touch with my roots and go all big-time on them, if that's what you're thinking.'

Miranda wasn't thinking anything of the sort, but she wished her well and took her heavy shopping bag and even heavier heart out of the shop and up the lane back to the house. Steve's house.

It was time. Clare took the urn out of the wardrobe and carried it downstairs. She put it on the table in the hallway and stared at it for a few moments. Something was missing inside her – not love for Jack, that would never go – but the idea that he – or any essence of 'he' – was inside that container. All the same, the ceremony had to be got through. She hoped the girls wouldn't be horribly upset by it. And more than that, she hoped no one would get seasick. There was still quite a swell out there, left over from the storm

'You ready?' Miranda came out from the kitchen carrying bags of food and bottles of champagne.

'Ready,' Clare said. 'I need something to put this in.' She pointed at the urn. 'I don't want to carry it through the village like some sort of weird . . . thing.'

'Um . . . OK, hang on. I can put the fizz in a Sainsbury's bag and the urn in the basket?'

Clare waved her away. 'No, I'll use the Sainsbury's one. Jack wouldn't care,' she said. There was a noise outside and someone tapped on the door. 'Is that Eliot?' she asked, perking up.

'Aren't he and the others meeting us at the pontoon?' Miranda said, wondering why Eliot would trail up the hill just to walk all the way back down it again minutes later.

'He said he'd come up and give us a hand,' Clare said, opening the door. Eliot came in and kissed her, holding her tight for a few seconds. Miranda noticed and thought how kind he was.

Steve was waiting on the pontoon with the boat and Jessica and Andrew were there too, already aboard. He greeted the party warmly but only nodded briefly at Miranda, who felt hurt. How could he be like that after what they'd done and the evening they'd had and the laughs? But it wasn't about her, this trip, so she put on a bright enough face and climbed on board without accepting the helping hand he was offering to them all to steady them.

Steve drove the boat out of the creek and into the estuary, taking the route Clare was telling him to. Miranda sat at the back with Harriet and the children, thinking about how this would be the last event connected with Jack. From now on of course they'd talk about him, though presumably less and less as time passed. And he'd be remembered on anniversaries, preferably more on his birthday than on his death day, but essentially after today he would be in the past.

'Fancy a drink?' Harriet nudged Miranda. 'Time to open a bottle?'

'OK, let's.' Miranda could do with one, though she also knew quite well that, in the end, champagne can make you tearful and gloomy. Still, if they were having a funeral that wasn't such an unexpected thing, was it?

Below the deck, Miranda unloaded paper plates for the cake and opened a bottle of champagne, pouring it into cheap plastic glasses and hoping the spirit of Jack wouldn't mind such lack of class. He'd probably say something like 'I can see you really pushed the boat out for me, then' and wait, looking pleased with himself, for them to acknowledge the pun.

'Drinks, everyone.' The boat had slowed so Miranda felt steady enough to go back up the ladder with some of the glasses. 'Steve? One for you?'

'No thanks,' he said, looking at her only briefly before turning back to look where he was going. 'I like to keep a clear head on the water.'

At last Clare was happy with where they'd got to and asked Steve to slow right down. She took the urn of ashes out of the bag and Harriet fetched the bunch of flowers (agapanthus, lilies, cosmos, verbena) she'd picked from the garden that morning. Andrew had a bunch of roses from his own garden, the roses his father had grown. Miranda thought it poignant that Jack would have remembered those and she felt tears pricking in her eyes.

'It's the right place. You can see the headland,

Falmouth and across to St Mawes from here as well as right out to sea. Jack will start where he most loved to be and end up wherever the ocean takes him.'

Steve kept the boat steady and Clare unscrewed the urn, having first asked Andrew which side of the boat she should throw them from. Miranda was glad about that. She'd heard stories about ash mishaps; a friend of hers had tipped her late father off the end of Brighton pier only to have most of him fly back in her face. It wasn't on a par with the apocryphal tale of Keith Richards smoking some of his father's ashes but it was uncomfortably close.

In silence, Clare tipped the ashes over the side of the boat. Miranda watched as they floated out on the current, just a pale shadow going in and out of various shapes as she watched. She and Andrew dropped their flowers into the water, beside the spreading slick of grey. She stood close beside Clare, Harriet on the other side. 'Bye, Jack,' she and Clare murmured. Harriet was crying quietly. 'Bye, Dad,' she said, and they all raised their glasses and drank to his afterlife.

'I hear you're going away.' Miranda was last off the boat and had to say something to Steve. She couldn't just leave it like this, with this heavy and ridiculous silence between them. The others had gone ahead and this was her chance.

'Am I?' he said, looking startled. 'Yeah, well, I have

been thinking about it for a while. You don't always want to live and die in the same place.'

'I suppose not. Well, good luck. And thanks so much for today. And . . . for everything.'

'Look, Miranda . . .'

'Yes?'

'Sorry about dashing off back then, but . . . you know, that git of a husband of yours . . .'

'*Ex*-husband. Very long time ex,' she reminded him.

'It was what he said. Just reminded me, that's all, that we're not the same, you and me.'

'And reminded you I was a horrid, selfish little teenager back then? I didn't know any better. And if that's what you think I'm still like then it's your choice. But I really thought you'd seen a better side of me now I'm grown up. Be lucky and be happy.' She gave him a very quick kiss and turned and left, fast, before she could burst into tears. Up ahead on the path she could see Andrew and Jess walking together. He had his arm round her. Her spirits lifted at the sight. At least things would work out for someone, it looked like. For the absolutely best and most brilliantly right people too.

TWENTY

The regatta really marked the beginning of the rundown of the tourist season for the village, at least until the prices dropped in late September and the place refilled with older people down by coach for the off-peak prices and autumnal garden tours. After that small yet profitable surge, it would be an empty run for rentals and guest houses till the Turkey and Tinsel theme trips filled the place again, at a point way too early for any sensible person to be thinking about Christmas. After this bank holiday weekend the visitor numbers would crash to a sudden low as families – both renters and those with second homes – rushed back home to sort out school uniforms and get stuck into last-minute holiday homework.

Miranda, thinking about this, realized that neither Silva nor Bo had so much as opened a book since they'd got here.

'Um – I know I must usually be the least pushy mother on the planet, but is there something you two should have been doing for school while we've been away?'

Her children, about to get in the pool for one last practice go on their raft, looked at her blankly, as if she was talking in a strange and unfamiliar language.

'School?' Silva asked, looking puzzled. 'Do you have to mention school? On my *birthday*?'

'Yes, I'm sorry but I do. And school, well, it's a big building with lots of teachers in it. You go there to learn stuff so you can get some kind of job, maybe, later in life?'

'I like, know what it is, Mum. Chill,' Silva said, sliding off the diving board and into the water. Bo was saying nothing.

'So – was there something?'

'Bit of maths,' Bo said with a don't-know shrug, 'And like maybe a book.'

'*Maybe* as in definitely?'

'Yeah, but it's only a *book*. Plenty of time when we get home.'

'Which book?'

'*Wuthering Heights*,' he mumbled, pulling one of the raft's ropes a bit tighter. Miranda could see he didn't need to and was just avoiding looking at her. No knots of any son-of-Andrew would be loose.

'*Wuthering Heights*? It's quite long. And I know you'll

only read it in reluctant bits. If you'd brought it with you, we could all have read it and talked about it or something.'

'I did bring it with me,' he admitted, giving her a grin. 'Also, yeah, but I saw it on telly. Tom wossname, Hardy. He was thingy. Heathrow.'

'Heathcliff,' Miranda said.

'Not a nice bloke. Can't see how that can be what Miss Fenlon at school called a "romantic lead". He's not hero material, in my opinion.'

'No – well, you know, it takes all sorts,' she said, suddenly thinking of the moody look on Steve's face. He and Heathcliff, they could glower for Britain. Best to forget about both of them for now, maybe. She would, instead, be cheered up by the big chocolate cake Clare had made for Silva.

'I made costumes for you and Amy, for the fancy dress,' Clare was telling Harriet over a lunch on the kitchen terrace of bread with various hams, cheese and pickles and leftovers trawled from the fridge. It wasn't worth having a major stock-up, Miranda had decided, as they'd be going in a day or two. And they could fill up on cake for now. She wasn't looking forward to the Saturday traffic on one of the busiest turn-round days of the year but even sitting in a jam for hours could be endured.

'I vaguely remember,' Harriet was saying. 'Were we Romans?'

'Antony and Cleopatra. You looked wonderful, even if I say it myself. You didn't win, though. That would have broken the rules.'

'Rules?' Silva asked. 'What kind of rule says you can't win if you've gone in for it? That's not fair.'

'The kind of rule that says it has to be a local, full-time resident to get prizes, because the visitors are just *that*, backed up with a sub-clause that it mustn't be a child who has led a thieving spree at the village shop.'

Bo burst out laughing. 'Harriet? You *stole*?'

'Certainly not. What do you take me for? I just dared all the others to do it.'

'Hmm – that's not how it was seen at the time. But anyway, that was then. Let's hope Bo and Silva do better with their raft. It's certainly looking good.'

'Maybe we should whisper to the judges that it's Silva's birthday and see if that helps.'

'Silva wouldn't want an unfair advantage, would you, darling?' Clare said. Silva didn't look so sure about that and sat frowning, considering. 'I want to win. But it's a race so there's no way to cheat. Is there?' She looked hopeful.

'No cheating,' Miranda said. 'Jeez, what have I raised here?'

'Fourteen,' she said later to Jessica when she met her on the way to the regatta. 'Where did that go to? I don't remember how she went from being a tiny baby to, say, twelve.'

'We had them pretty young, compared with parents now. God, don't I sound old?' Jess giggled. 'But most of my friends are only just thinking about having their first babies. In our mothers' day they were all told their eggs had gone rotten by the time they got past thirty. You could start again,' she said as they walked across the footbridge to go and bag places on the pub terrace to watch their children. 'You could have a whole second family.'

'Ha, yeah, and that would be with . . . ?' She laughed. 'Nobody wants me.' Would it be a little lone afterthought if she *did* have one, she wondered. But her mother had had her first and then years later the two other girls. And Jess had little half-brothers much younger than her. It wasn't such an unfeasible idea.

'Steve did. I bet he still does,' Jessica said. 'He's just, you know, got too much stubborn pride.'

'He's got Cheryl, is what he's got.'

'No he hasn't. You've got to let go of that one.'

'But she said . . .'

'She didn't, you just think she did. Look, I know better than most that life's too friggin' short. If you want him, make an effort.'

'Why doesn't he? He's the one who took off the minute he'd shagged me. What does that tell you?'

'Well, there is that. But there's something else. And I've Cheryl to thank for the information.'

They were walking past the old phone box. Someone

had added another, smaller gnome to the hideous giant one. A gnome-baby.

'What is it?'

'Well – did you actually see any boxes of actual fish in the back of Steve's van last week?'

Miranda thought for a moment. 'Well no. But they were in the separate bit at the back.'

'Ah, but were they? Cheryl told me he never delivers to London on a Wednesday. Only Tuesdays and sometimes Fridays. And someone else had already done Monday.'

'And that means . . . ? An extra unexpected order? An event or something?'

'No, you idiot. He just took the opportunity to give you a lift. To *be* with you. Don't you get it?'

'But then why would he bolt?' Clouds were beginning to clear a bit. She wondered if it could possibly be true. But how did he know she was going that early and would be at the end of the lane right then? She could hardly accuse him of deliberately getting lightning to strike that tree.

'You see, I just think if you two got together on your own, for ten minutes, you could sort this right out.'

'Hmm . . . maybe.'

'No maybe, just do it. Give him a call and make him talk to you. Do it now.'

They were just passing the village shop. Cheryl was inside, squealing with laughter. Could Jessica be right?

If she didn't actually find out now, she'd go away wishing she had. Miranda took her mobile out and clicked it on. Nothing, no signal.

'Typical, isn't it?' she said. 'Just when you really need it.'

The pub was open all day and doing a massive trade in pasties and beer. The spectators crowded on to the terrace to watch the boats racing in the various categories. Freddie was out in Andrew's dinghy, showing a lot of skill against slightly miffed local sailing club stalwarts and winning two of his three races.

'Chip off the block, Andrew,' Clare said, pleased for him. Even Geraldine looked thrilled when Freddie did so well.

'It's hardly changed at all, has it, Miranda?' Clare went on as a line of small children in home-made fancy dress outfits (as well as one in a blatantly shop-bought Snow White frock) lined up on the terrace to wild applause from doting parents. 'I bet it'll still be the same when your own grandchildren are coming down here.'

Miranda felt unexpectedly tearful at that. What were the chances of that, after all? Unless Jess was still in the village (and with Andrew, it now looked pretty certain from the way they seemed hardly able to be more than a foot apart), she doubted she'd be back. Unless . . .

Bloody phone, Miranda thought, moving up to higher ground in search of a signal. Still nothing. Below on the river, the races continued. Rowing for the over-fifties, mixed pairs, parent and child, on they went till the last one of the day, the raft race.

Miranda watched as Silva and Lola, dressed in bikinis plus pink and purple sarongs and garlands of flowers and bracken on their heads, went down to the water with their raft still hidden under cloths. Bo and Freddie, who had come to the decision that speed was preferable to participation, were no longer going to be aboard as there simply wasn't the room, so they were on launch duty and there for the cheering on instead. There were about six other entrants, one of them including the streaky surf-boy that Silva talked to. Miranda saw him say something to Silva down on the shore and she moved closer to get a better view of the race, fnding herself standing next to Cheryl who was wearing the highest espadrilles Miranda had ever seen and tiny denim shorts with a pink glittery halter-neck top. It all seemed quite a get-up for a simple village event, but then, Miranda remembered, she was moving on. Probably to Essex, she caught herself thinking rather nastily.

The klaxon blared and the rafts were off, two of them immediately capsizing to encouraging cheers from the onlookers. Silva and Lola seemed to be just about keeping their balance and the pair of bright crocodiles were heading out to the halfway mark quite strongly, closely followed by the blond surfer and his friend on something made, it seemed, entirely of big plastic water containers.

It was going to be close. Miranda and Jess stood with the boys, cheering the girls on as they tottered on their fragile craft and the waves from the inexpertly wielded paddle on the next raft threatened to upend them. Then, just when it looked as though the surfer would overtake, he leaned too far forward and fell in, coming up laughing and spluttering. The girls, clearly delighted, made it back to the shore where they leapt into the water and danced around, hugging each other.

'Oh, sweet, they're all bonded!' Jessica said, tears in her eyes.

'Like us,' Miranda said, giving her a hug too.

Just then a small plane headed towards the village, swooping low. It carried a streamer, the sort that usually advertised things like the Flambards theme park. Everyone was gazing up at it and a bit of quiet descended as they read the message.

'Cripes, I wonder who that's for?'

Miranda squinted up. ' "Marry me?" Bloody hell, that must have cost a bit to fix. Wonder who it's for?' There was a squeal beside her and Cheryl was jumping up and down. 'Yes, yes, yes!' she screamed, waving at the plane. 'Oh God, yes!' She grabbed Miranda and hugged her. 'Lucky lucky me!' she squealed in her ear.

'Er . . . congratulations!' Miranda said. Well, what else could you do?

*

'Talk to me, Steve. And are congratulations in order?'
Miranda, back at the house, left a voicemail message for
him. She had less than twenty-four hours to make up
with him, whether this was going to be just a civilized
goodbye or some better kind of sorting out.

The children were going out to the beach. 'It's not
exactly a party, Mum, just, you know, an end of holidays
thing. And it *is* my birthday,' Silva said. Miranda noticed
she was doing that more grown-up look again.
Eyeshadow and blusher and lip gloss, though not a lot
of it. Not a London amount.

'No drink.'

'No drink. Promise.'

'And . . . just be careful, OK? Don't go in the sea in
the dark or anything silly.'

'We'll probably be back before dark,' Bo said. 'It's not
all that, a beach bash. And it gets cold.' He was huddling
into a hoodie again. Fragile boy, feeling the cold,
Miranda thought. Her phone beeped: text message.
'Sailing club at 8?' It was Steve and her heart rate leapt.

She texted back. 'OK.'

They were all older than her and Lola and Bo, and
possibly even than Freddie, Silva thought, eyeing the
others on the beach. And worse, they all seemed to
know each other. This was her birthday and she wanted
to feel that everything was about her, but really it looked

338

as if it was going to be about the ya-ya girls with the flicky hair and a really silly way of holding cigarettes. She and her friends sat on their usual rock with some beers and Cokes and looked at the ones who flirted and shrieked and passed vodka bottles and spliffs around. Freddie seemed to know some of them ('from school' he said, looking a bit embarrassed) and they seemed friendly enough, but Silva felt out of her depth. Jules was there but he wasn't looking her way, but then at last he saw her and came over, offering her something from an unmarked bottle.

'What is it?' she asked.

'Home brew.' He laughed. 'By which I don't mean, like literally, just a mix of stuff from actual home. Think there's gin and vodka and maybe some rum.'

'Looks like piss to me,' Bo said, looking grumpy. Silva wanted to kick him but he was too far away.

'Yeah, well I'm not asking *you* to drink it, am I?'

'You shouldn't be asking her,' Bo retaliated.

'Shu'up, Bo,' Silva warned him. 'I can look after myself.'

And she could, she decided as she wandered away from the others, down the beach with Jules. She glanced back. Freddie was watching her, not smiling, looking worried. She'd be OK. What could happen?

Old jeans, flip-flops and hardly any make-up. The hardly-any that takes ages to put on. Miranda grabbed a long blue cashmere cardie and her bag and shouted goodbye to Harriet, Duncan and Clare.

She raced down the track and up the lane towards the sailing club then slowed to catch her breath. She didn't want Steve to think she'd run all the way to meet him.

He was there, sitting at a table on the balcony. No sign of Cheryl. Not that she'd expected to see her, not after the sky-written sign that afternoon. Steve had a sense of humour but she couldn't see him spending an absolute bomb to ask a question that could so much more easily be done in private and for free. It seemed, frankly, a rather tacky and dumb thing to do.

'Miranda. I thought you might change your mind. Drink?' He didn't kiss her. She sat down, said a spritzer might be nice and waited, looking out over the harbour and part of the beach, while he went to the bar.

'Could we go further away? There are too many people up here,' he suggested when he returned with the drinks. There was a small terrace garden beyond the doors and they went through and found no one else there. They sat together on an old rusty metal bench. Miranda took a small sip of her drink then put it on the table, waiting for him to say something, but as he seemed to be finding that difficult she asked the question Jess had told her she needed to know.

'Were there any fish in the van?'

'No,' he said. 'How did you know?'

'Jessica, by way of Cheryl. I didn't believe her.'

'Believe her.' He took her hand. 'I just wanted to be useful.' He smiled. 'No, that's not true. I wanted to spend time with you.'

'But we could have just gone out for dinner here, or sat on the beach or something.'

'Or gone out in the boat. I know. It's just, when I heard the early morning news about the trains being cancelled, I saw the chance and took it.'

'You nearly missed me.'

'No I didn't. You'd never have got past that tree.'

'This is true. But . . . I don't understand. Why did you just race off after . . . you know?'

'After that fabulous night? God, I don't know. I just thought back, suddenly, when that bloody *husband* of yours . . .'

'Ex.'

'Ex. Arrogant prick. He reminded me of when we were young and you and your mates, you were so . . . you know, *exclusive*? Do you know what I mean? There'd been you and me and all that we did and I really, *really* liked you, but when they all turned up it was like, bye-bye yokel Steve, these are my real mates.'

Miranda took a sip of her drink. 'Oh God, was that how we were?'

'Yes, I'm afraid you were.'

'It wasn't an easy summer for me, that one.'

'Oh, really?' He laughed, not without a touch of bitterness. 'I used to watch you having a "not easy"

341

summer. All privilege and indulgence and not seeming to care for anyone outside your own circle. I don't know, some bits of us don't grow up as well as they should. You're not like that now.'

'I didn't think I was like that then. Maybe we just didn't know each other that well.'

He laughed. 'Oh, I don't know.'

'Hey, you wait till you have children of your own . . . see how they change, how they grow, and you think you know them but then they slide through your fingers.'

'I won't have children,' he said.

'You might. You're still young.'

'It's not that. I . . . er, don't think I actually can.'

Miranda didn't know what to say. She felt all chewed up inside. How could he think that? Had he had mumps or chemotherapy or something since that long-ago summer?

'Why do you think so?'

'Oh, just . . . when I was married I thought Janie was on the pill. I knew she wanted children but I didn't so she agreed we'd wait. But then later she told me she hadn't taken it for a year, and nothing had happened.'

Miranda gasped. 'Jesus, Steve, what makes you think it was you?'

He laughed. 'The fact she's now down the school gates every day with her two little boys by her new husband?'

She took a deep breath. Something had to be said. 'Steve, there was something that summer. There was no point in saying anything before because it went away. It just . . . wasn't to be. Not that time.'

'What wasn't?'

'I was pregnant.' He looked at her, those grey eyes wondering, searching for answers. 'I lost the baby at about eleven weeks. And yes, it was you. There wasn't anyone else, never before and not for about two years after you. So no doubts.' She could feel her eyes filling. This was likely to be the moment where he told her what a heartless bitch she was and stormed away for ever.

'That's so sad.'

She sniffed and fished a tissue out of her bag. 'Is it? I was only sixteen, Steve. But yes, sad. I . . . er, Jess and me, we had a little funeral on the beach. I said a prayer and we went to the pub.'

She waited, feeling slightly sick. She didn't want her drink. She leaned back against the bench, feeling the rust crunch against her shoulders.

Steve was still silent. But a moment later he slid his arm round her and pulled her close against him.

'You poor kid. It must have been horrendous.'

'It wasn't fun, no,' she wept into his warm shoulder. But a little part of her was beginning to think, but maybe something could be . . . one day.

'And it seems Freddie clouted the Jules boy and shoved him off the rock into a deep pool.' Harriet was laughing. 'He's a hero!'

They were all outside in the sun by the pool, loving the warmth, and Miranda was wishing it wasn't her last day. Steve was on the lounger beside her, having brought the newspapers for them and a bottle of wine which they were now drinking. She was glad to see him and dreaded going home. But she'd be seeing him soon. Seeing him for ever, she hoped.

'And of course the poor boy hadn't known she was only just fourteen and not really up for that kind of rolling in the sand dunes. And ugh, you two,' Harriet said to Steve and Miranda, 'will you get over yourselves and stop looking so loved up?'

'You can talk,' Steve said. 'I saw you at the Pengarret, all gooey-eyed with Mr Goalkeeper.'

'And I saw you. But what I didn't see was that you were also with your mum.'

'Birthday,' he said. 'She likes a treat.'

Miranda picked up the nearest paper. 'Oh, wow, would you look at this?' She held up the front page, on which there was a photo of a couple looking even more lovingly at each other than Steve and Miranda had been. '"Reformed man: the power of love" it says here.'

Cheryl and Pablo beamed out from the front page against the background of the Pengarret hotel's famous wedding arch. 'The engagement is announced . . .' she read.

'Well, I hope they'll be very happy,' Harriet said, raising her glass. 'In fact, I hope we all will.'

Revisit the characters from

IN THE SUMMERTIME

in Judy Astley's first novel

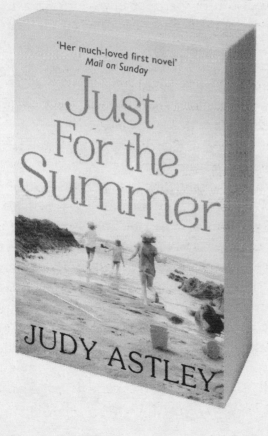

'Her much-loved first novel'
Mail on Sunday

Just
For the
Summer

JUDY ASTLEY

Just for the Summer

Judy Astley

Every July, the lucky owners of Cornish holiday homes set off for their annual break. Loading their estate cars with dogs, cats, casefuls of wine, difficult adolescents and rebellious toddlers, they close up their desirable semis in smartish London suburbs – having turned off the Aga and turned on the burglar alarm – and look forward to a carefree, restful, somehow more *fulfilling* summer.

Clare is, this year, more than usually ready for her holiday. Her teenage daughter, Miranda, has been behaving strangely; her husband, Jack, is harbouring unsettling thoughts of a change in lifestyle; her small children are being particularly tiresome; and she herself is contemplating a bit of extra-marital adventure, possibly with Eliot, the successful – although undeniably heavy-drinking and overweight – author in the adjoining holiday property. Meanwhile Andrew, the only son of elderly parents, is determined that this will be the summer when he will seduce Jessica, Eliot's nubile daughter. But Jessica spends her time in girl-talk with Miranda, while Milo, her handsome brother with whom Andrew longs to be friends, seems more interested in going sailing with the young blond son of the club commodore.

Unexpected disasters occur, revelations are made and, as the summer ends, real life will never be quite the same again.

'Oh, what a find! A lovely, funny book'
Sarah Harrison

'A sharp social comedy . . . sails along very nicely
and fulfils its early promise'
JOHN MORTIMER, *MAIL ON SUNDAY*

'Wickedly funny . . . a thoroughly entertaining romp'
VAL HENNESSY, *DAILY MAIL*

I Should Be So Lucky

Judy Astley

Viola hasn't had much luck with men. Her first husband, Marco, companion of her youth and father of her only child, left her when he realized he was gay. Her second, Rhys, ended his high-octane, fame-filled life by driving his Porsche into a wall. No wonder her family believes she needs Looking After, and her friends think she really shouldn't be allowed out on her own . . . Which is why, at the age of thirty-five, she finds herself shamefully back at home, living with Mum.

Viola knows she has to take charge; she needs to get a life, and fast. With a stroppy daughter, a demanding mother, and siblings who want to control her life for her, where is she going to turn?

'Astley is a great writer, funny and sharp . . . her prose
is a pleasure to read, her dialogue sparkles'
DAILY MAIL

The Look of Love

Judy Astley

Bella has given up on men.

Her latest boyfriend 'forgot' to tell her about his current wife, so she's single *again*.

And then her ex-husband turns up, wanting to sell the family home in which she and their two teenage children are happily living their lives.

Then Bella sees a chance to stay in the house and earn some money from it. She rents it out for a reality TV fashion makeover programme and it turns out that the house isn't the only thing that will benefit from a change . . .

'I just love Judy Astley's books'
JILL MANSELL

Other People's Husbands

Judy Astley

When Sara, as an art student, first met Conrad he seemed like the most glamorous man in the world. Already a famous painter, he was the sexiest thing she'd ever met. Her mother *told* her that she shouldn't marry him – that the twenty-five-year age gap would tell in the end – and the end is now (apparently) approaching fast. Conrad has decided that it would be good to die before he gets seriously old, and has started behaving very strangely.

Sara, meanwhile, teaching art at a local college, is not short of younger male company – other people's husbands, ones she tells Conrad all about, who are just good friends. But there's one she somehow doesn't get round to mentioning . . .

Pleasant Vices

Judy Astley

The residents of the Close were much concerned with crime –
preventing it, that is. With all those out-of-work teenagers on
the nearby council estate hanging around, stealing, joy-riding
and goodness knows what else, it was just as well that Paul
Mathieson was setting up a Neighbourhood Watch scheme.

Not that the inhabitants of the Close did not have their own
little activities, of course, but these were hardly the same
thing. If Jenny and Alan's daughter was caught travelling on
the underground without a ticket, and their son was doing a
little experimenting with certain substances, and Fiona didn't
see the need to declare her earnings from hiring out her house
to a film crew, and Jenny drove home only *just* over the legal
limit – well, these were quite different matters, not to be
compared with what went on in the Estate. And then there
was Jenny's discovery, when she advertised flute lessons, that
she could work up quite a nice little earner in a rather
unexpected way . . .

As the leafy London street resounded to the efforts of its
citizens to keep crime at bay, Jenny realized that it was her
marriage, rather than her property, that needed watching.

'This deliciously funny novel had me laughing out loud'
WOMAN AND HOME

'Light, fast and funny . . . by the time you turn the
last page, you'll never be able to look your next-door
neighbour in the eye again'
PRIMA

Laying The Ghost

Judy Astley

Have you ever wondered what your ex is up to?

When Nell was a student, she and Patrick were a serious item. Nell really thought Patrick was The One, despite their often tempestuous relationship. But then Alex came along. He seemed the safer, more restful option, and thanks to her over-controlling mother she opted for him instead.

Now nothing is going right. Alex has left her to live in New York with a younger, blonder woman. Escaping to the Caribbean for a recuperative holiday, she is mugged at Gatwick and her bag is stolen. It's crisis time – and she makes two decisions:

First – she will take lessons in self-defence.
Second – she will try and find Patrick again.

Is she trying to put the past behind her - or setting out to ruin her future?

'Warm, funny and unnervingly true to life'
KATIE FFORDE